Maturin Murray Ballou

Genius in Sunshine and Shadow

Maturin Murray Ballou

Genius in Sunshine and Shadow

ISBN/EAN: 9783744754576

Printed in Europe, USA, Canada, Australia, Japan

Cover: Foto ©Andreas Hilbeck / pixelio.de

More available books at **www.hansebooks.com**

GENIUS

IN SUNSHINE AND SHADOW

BY

MATURIN M. BALLOU

AUTHOR OF "EDGE-TOOLS OF SPEECH," ETC.

'T is in books the chief
Of all perfection to be plain and brief.
BUTLER

BOSTON

TICKNOR AND COMPANY

1887

𝔘niversity 𝔓ress :

JOHN WILSON AND SON, CAMBRIDGE.

PREFACE.

THE volume in hand might perhaps better have been entitled " Library Notes," as the pages are literally the gathered notes of the author's library-hours. The reader will kindly peruse these pages remembering that they assume only to be the gossip, as it were, of the author with himself, — notes which have grown to these proportions by casual accumulation in the course of other studies, and without consecutive purpose. That these notes thus made have been put into printed form, is owing to the publisher's chance knowledge and hearty approval of them. These few lines are by way, not of apology, — no sensible person ever made an apology, according to Mr. Emerson, — but of introduction; so that the reader may not fancy he is to encounter a labored essay upon the theme suggested by the title of the volume.

These pages may not be without a certain wholesome influence, if, fortunately, they shall incite others to analyze the character of genius as exhibited by the masters of art and literature. The facts alluded to, though familiar to many, are not so to all ; wherefore the volume may indirectly promote the knowledge of both history and biography, at the same time leading the thoughtful reader to seek further and more ample information concerning those individuals who are here so briefly introduced.

M. M. B.

GENIUS

IN SUNSHINE AND SHADOW.

———•———

CHAPTER I.

THE ever-flowing tide of time rapidly obliterates the footprints of those whom the world has delighted to honor. While it has caused heroic names, like their possessors, to lapse into oblivion, it has also shrouded many a historical page with the softened veil of distance, like ivy-grown towers, rendering what was once terrible now only picturesque. In glancing back through thousands of years, and permitting the mind to rest on the earliest recorded epochs, one is apt to forget how much human life then, in all its fundamental characteristics, was like our own daily experience. There never was a golden age; that is yet to come. The most assiduous antiquarian has only corroborated the fact that human nature is unchanged. Conventionalities, manners and customs, the fashions, may change, but human nature does not. As an example of the mutability of fame, we have only to ask ourselves what is actually known

1

to-day of Homer,[1] Aristophanes, and their renowned
contemporaries, or even of our more familiar Shakspeare?[2]   Of the existence of the first named we have
evidence in his two great epics, the Iliad and the
Odyssey; but, though deemed the most famous poet
that ever lived, we do not even know his birthplace.

> "Ten ancient towns contend for Homer dead,
>   Through which the living Homer begged his bread."

The cautious historian only tells us that he is supposed to have flourished about nine hundred years
before the time of Christ; while there are also learned
writers who contend that no such person as Homer[3]
ever lived, and who attribute the two most famous
poems of antiquity to various minstrels or ballad-
mongers, who celebrated the "tale of Troy divine"
at various periods, and whose songs and legends were
fused into unity at the time of Pisistratus.

----

[1] Goldsmith makes his Chinese philosopher recount the name
of Homer as the first poet and beggar among the ancients, — a
blind man whose mouth was more frequently filled with verses
than with bread.

[2] Shakspeare's line expired in his daughter's only daughter.
Several of the descendants of Shakspeare's sister Joan, bearing a
strong family likeness to the great poet, were, so late as 1852,
living in and about Stratford, chiefly in a state of indigence.

[3] I have no doubt whatever that Homer is a mere concrete
name for the rhapsodies of the Iliad. Of course there was *a*
Homer, and twenty besides. I will engage to compile twelve
books, with characters just as distinct and consistent as those of
the Iliad, from the metrical ballads and other chronicles of England, about Arthur and the Knights of the Round Table. —
Coleridge.

Over the personality of Aristophanes,[1] the great comic poet of Greece, who is supposed to have flourished some five or six hundred years later than Homer, there rests the same cloud of obscurity, and he is clearly identified only by eleven authentic comedies which are still extant, though he is believed to have written fifty. Of Shakspeare, born some two thousand years later (1564), how little is actually known beyond the fact of his birthplace! Even the authorship of his plays, like that of Homer's poems, is a subject of dispute. Perhaps, however, this loss of individuality but adds to the influence of the poet's divine mission. The really great men of history, benefactors of their race, are those who still live in the undying thoughts which they have left behind them.

In this familiar gossip we propose to glance briefly at such names as may suggest themselves, without observing any strict system of classification. The theme is so fruitful, the pages of history so teem with portraits which stand forth in groups to attract the eye, that one hardly knows where to begin, what matter to exclude, what to adduce; and therefore, closing the elaborate records of the past, we will trust to momentary inspiration and the ready promptings of memory.

The first thought which strikes us in this connection is, that the origin of those whom the world has

---

[1] They must needs be men of lofty stature, whose shadows lengthen out to remote posterity. — *Hazlitt.*

called great — men who have written their names
indelibly upon the pages of history — is often of the
humblest character. Such men have most frequently
risen from the ranks. In fact, genius ignores all social barriers and springs forth wherever heaven has
dropped the seed. The grandest characters known
in art, literature, and the useful inventions have
illustrated the axiom that "brave deeds are the
ancestors of brave men;" and it would almost appear that an element of hardship is necessary to
the effective development of true genius. Indeed,
when we come to the highest achievements of the
greatest minds, it seems that they were not limited
by race, condition of life, or the circumstances of
their age. "It is," says Emerson, "the nature of
poetry to spring, like the rainbow daughter of Wonder, from the Invisible, to abolish the past and refuse all history." But this of course refers only to
poetry in its loftiest and noblest conceptions and
sentiments; and then only in passages of a great
work.

Æsop, the fabulist, who flourished six hundred
years before Christ, and whose fables are as familiar
to us after the lapse of twenty-five hundred years as
household words; Publius Syrus,[1] the eminent mor-
alist, who lived in the time of Julius Cæsar, and
whose wise axioms are to be found in every library;

---

[1] The Edinburgh "Review," once the most formidable of critical journals, took its motto from Publius Syrus: —

"Judex damnatur cum nocens absolvetur."

Terence,[1] the Carthaginian poet and dramatist; Epictetus, the stoic philosopher, — all were slaves in early life,[2] but won freedom and lasting fame by force of their native genius. No man is nobler than another unless he is born with better abilities, a more amiable disposition, and a larger heart and brain. The field is open to all; for it is fixedness of purpose and perseverance that win the prizes of this world, — qualities that can be exercised by the most humble.

Protagoras, the Greek sophist and orator, was in his youth a street porter of Athens, carrying loads upon his back like a beast of burden. He was a singularly independent genius, and was expelled from his native city because he openly doubted the existence of the gods. His countryman, Cleanthes the stoic, was also "a hewer of stone and drawer of water," but rose among the Athenians to be esteemed as a rival of the great philosopher Zeno. He wrote

[1] The kindly human sympathy exhibited by Terence contributed largely to the popularity of his dramas. Whenever the often-quoted words, "I am a man; and I have an interest in everything that concerns humanity," were spoken upon the Roman stage, they were received with tumultuous applause by all classes.

[2] Crassus, a Roman triumvir, noted for his great wealth, who lived about a hundred years before the Christian Era, bought and sold slaves. These he educated, and taught the highest accomplishments of the day, sparing no labor or expense for the purpose. These educated slaves were then sold for large sums of money, so that any rich man could own his private poet and scholar. We are told by Plutarch that some of these slaves brought enormous prices into the treasury of Crassus.

many works in his day, — about three hundred years
before the Christian Era, — none of which have
been preserved except a hymn to Jupiter, which is
remarkable for purity of thought and elevation of
sentiment.

We need not confine ourselves, however, to so remote a period to illustrate that genius is independent
of circumstances. In our random treatment of the
subject there occurs to us the name of Bandoccin, one
of the most learned men of the sixteenth century, who
was the son of an itinerant shoemaker, and who was
himself brought up to the trade. Gelli, the prolific
Italian author, and president of the Florentine Academy, was a tailor by trade, and of very humble birth.
His moral dialogues entitled, *I Capricci del Bot-
tajo* ("The Whims of the Cooper"), have been pronounced by competent critics to be extraordinary for
originality and piquancy, while all his works are remarkable for purity of diction. Canova, the sculptor
of world-wide fame, was the son of a day-laborer in
the marble quarries. Opie, the distinguished English
painter, earned his bread at the carpenter's trade
until his majority, but before his death became professor of painting in the Royal Academy. Amyot,
the brilliant scholar, and professor of Greek, Hebrew,
and Latin, who is ranked among those who have contributed most towards the perfection of the French
language, learned to write upon birch-bark with
charcoal, while he lived on a loaf of bread per day.
This man rose to be grand almoner of France, and

proved that courage, perseverance, and genius need no ancestors.[1]

Akenside, the English didactic poet, wit, essayist, and physician, author of the " Pleasures of the Imagination," was a butcher's boy. His developed genius caused him to be appointed to the Queen's household. Sir Humphry Davy was an apothecary's apprentice in his youth. Matthew Prior, the English poet and diplomatist, began life as a charity scholar. Rollin, famous for his " Ancient History," was the son of a poor Parisian cutler, and began life at an iron-forge. James Barry, the eminent historical painter, was in his minority a foremast hand on board an Irish coasting-vessel. D'Alembert, the remarkable French mathematician, author, and academician, was at birth a poor foundling in the streets of Paris, though it must be added that he was the illegitimate and discarded son of Madame de Tencin, one of the wickedest, most profligate, most cynical, and ablest of the high-placed women of France. D'Alembert scorned her[2] proffered help when she, learning that he was the offspring of one of her desultory amours, attempted to assist him by her money and patronage. He lived austerely poor, and his love was lavished, not on his natural, or rather unnatural, mother, but on the

---

[1] " What can they see in the longest kingly line in Europe," asks Sir Walter Scott, " save that it runs back to a successful soldier ?"

[2] When approached by Madame de Tencin, who was finally eager to acknowledge so distinguished a son, he replied : —

" Je ne connais qu'une mère, c'est la vitrière."

indigent woman who had picked him up in the street, and who by self-denial had enabled him to obtain sustenance and education. As soon as he was old enough to realize his true situation, he said, " I have no name, but with God's help I will make one!" The time came when Catherine II. of Russia offered him one hundred thousand francs per annum to become the educator of her son, which he declined.

Béranger, the lyric poet of France, whose effectiveness and purity of style defy criticism, was at one time a barefooted orphan on the boulevards of the great city. His verses, bold, patriotic, and satirical, were in every mouth among the masses of his countrymen, contributing more than any other cause to produce the revolution of 1830.[1] He had the noble independence to refuse all official recognition under government. Rachel, it will be remembered, was in her childhood a street-ballad singer. A resident of the French capital once pointed out to the writer a spot on the Champs Élysées where at the age of twelve, so pale as to seem scarcely more than a shadow, she used to appear daily, accompanied by her brother. A rude cloth was spread on the ground, upon which she stood and recited tragic scenes from Corneille and Racine, or sang patriotic songs for pennies, accompanied upon the violin by her brother.

---

[1] I knew a very wise man that believed if a man were permitted to make all the ballads, he need not care who should make the laws of a nation. — *Andrew Fletcher of Saltoun.*

Her attitudes, gestures, and voice always captivated
a crowd of people. Rachel was a Jewish pedler's
daughter, though she was born in Switzerland; and
in these youthful days she wore a Swiss costume upon
the boulevards.[1]

Boccaccio, the most famous of Italian novelists, was
the illegitimate son of a Florentine tradesman, and
began life as a merchant's clerk. It is well known
that Shakspeare borrowed the plot of "All's Well
that Ends Well" from Boccaccio.[2] In fact, the "De-
cameron" furnished him with plots for several of

---

[1] Rachel made her début at the Théâtre Français of Paris,
in 1838. She came to this country in 1855, and performed in
our Eastern cities. Three years later she died of consumption,
near Cannes, in the South of France. When she was giving one of her readings before the Duke of Wellington, she
perceived that all her audience were ignorant of the French
language except the Duke himself. She went on, however,
at her best, consoling herself that he at least understood her.
After it was over, the Duke approached the great actress, and
said : "Mademoiselle, our guests have had a great advantage over
me ; they have had the happiness of hearing you : I am as deaf as
a post."

[2] Hazlitt, after remarking that Shakspeare's play of "All's
Well that Ends Well" is taken from Boccaccio, adds : "The
poet has dramatized the original novel with great skill and comic
spirit, and has preserved all the beauty of character and sentiment
without improving upon it, which is impossible." In the town
of Certaldo, Tuscany, the house in which Boccaccio was born is
shown to curious travellers. On the façade is an inscription
speaking of the small house and a name which filled the world.
"Before seven years of age," says Boccaccio, "when as yet I
had met with no stories, was without a master, and hardly knew
my letters, I had a natural talent for fiction, and produced some
small tales."

his plays. Chaucer derived from the same source his poem of the "Knight's Tale." We never hear shallow people reflecting upon the Bard of Avon for taking some of his plots from earlier writers, and weaving about them the golden threads of his superb genius, without recalling Dryden's remark relative to Ben Jonson's adaptations and translations from the classics, in such plays as "Catiline" and "Sejanus." "He invades authors," says Dryden, "like a monarch; and what would be theft in other writers is but victory in him." Sterne's idea upon the same subject also suggests itself. "As monarchs have a right," he says, "to call in the specie of a State and raise its value by their own impression, so are there certain prerogative geniuses who are above plagiaries, who cannot be said to steal, but from their improvement of a thought, rather to borrow it, and repay the commonwealth of letters with interest again, and may more properly be said to adopt than to kidnap a sentiment, by leaving it heir to their own fame."

Columbus, who gave a new world to the old, was a weaver's son, and in his youth he earned his bread as a cabin-boy in a coasting-vessel which sailed from Genoa. The story of the great Genoese pilot possesses a more thrilling interest than any narrative which the imagination of poet or romancer has ever conceived. His name flashes a bright ray over the mental darkness of the period in which he lived. In imagination one sees him wandering for years from court to court, begging the necessary means wherewith to prosecute his inspired purpose,[1] and finally, after successfully accomplishing his mission, languishing in chains and in prison.

How naturally Halleck's invocation to Death, in "Marco Bozarris," occurs to us here, as the hero, when his object has been attained, joyfully faces the grim monarch :

> " Thy grasp is welcome as the hand
>   Of brother in a foreign land ;
>   Thy summons welcome as the cry
>   That told the Indian isles were nigh,
>   To the world-seeking Genoese,
>   When the land wind from woods of palm
>   And orange-groves and fields of balm
>   Blew o'er the Haytian seas."

De Foe, the author of " Robinson Crusoe," and of over two hundred other books, was a hosier by trade, the son of a London butcher named James Foe. The particle *De* was added by the son without other authority than the suggestion of his own fancy. Cardinal Wolsey and Kirke White were also sons of butchers.

Claude Lorraine, the glorious colorist, whose very name has become a synonym in art, was in youth employed as a pastry-cook. Molière, the great French dramatist and actor, who presents one of the most

---

[1] The author has stood upon the Bridge of Pinos, at Granada, from whence Columbus, discouraged and nearly heart-broken, was recalled by Isabella, after having been denied and dismissed, as he supposed, for the last time. The messenger of the relenting queen overtook the great pilot at the bridge, and conducted him back to the Hall of the Ambassadors, in the Alhambra.

remarkable instances of literary success known to history, was the son of a tapestry-maker, and was himself at one time apprenticed to a tailor, and afterwards became a *valet-de-chambre*. When Molière was valet to Louis XIII., he had already appeared upon the stage, and was rather sneered at by the other members of the king's household. The generous monarch observed this, and determined to put a stop to it: "I am told you have short commons here, Molière, and some of my people decline to serve you," said Louis, as he rose from his breakfast one day. "Sit down here at my table. I warrant you are hungry." And the king cut him a portion of chicken and put it upon his plate just at the moment when a distinguished member of the royal household entered. "You see me," said the king, "giving Molière his breakfast, as some of my people do not think him good enough company for themselves." From that hour the royal valet was treated with due consideration. William Cobbett, the English author and vigorous political writer, was a poor farmer's boy and entirely self-educated. Izaak Walton, the delightful biographist and miscellaneous author, whose "Complete Angler" would make any man's name justly famous, was for years a linen-draper in London. Pope and Southey were the sons of linen-drapers.

How rapidly instances of the triumphs of genius over circumstances multiply upon us when the mind is permitted to roam at will through the long vista of the past! Cervantes, the Spanish Shakspeare, whose

" Don Quixote " is as much a classic[1] as " Hamlet," was a common foot-soldier in the army of Castile. In 1575 he was captured by an Algerine corsair and carried as a slave to Algiers, where he endured the most terrible sufferings. He was finally ransomed and returned to Spain. Alexandre Dumas's grandmother was an African slave. Hugh Miller, author, editor, poet, distinguished naturalist, whose clear, choice Saxon-English caused the Edinburgh " Review" to ask, " Where could this man have acquired his style?" was a stone-mason, and his only college was a stone-quarry.[2]

Keats, the sweetest of English poets, whose delicacy of fancy and beauty of versification are " a joy forever," was born in a stable. Oliver Cromwell, one of the most extraordinary men in English history,

---

[1] Disraeli tells us that the French ambassador to Spain, meeting Cervantes, congratulated him on the great success and reputation gained by his " Don Quixote; " whereupon the author whispered in his ear: " Had it not been for the Inquisition, I should have made my book much more entertaining." When Cervantes was a captive, and in prison at Algiers, he concerted a plan to free himself and his comrades. One of them traitorously betrayed the plot. They were all conveyed before the Dey of Algiers, who promised them their lives if they would betray the contriver of the plot. " I was that person," replied Cervantes ; " save my companions, and let me perish." The Dey, struck with his noble confession, spared his life and permitted them all to be ransomed.

[2] " The Testimony of the Rocks," a noble and monumental work, by Hugh Miller, was published in 1857. The night following its completion its author shot himself through the heart. The overworked brain had given out, and all was chaos. He had sense enough left to write a few loving lines to his wife and children, and to say farewell.

famous as a citizen, great as a general, and greatest as a ruler, was the son of a malt-brewer. Howard, the philanthropist and author, whose name stands a monument of Christian fame, was at first a grocer's boy. Rossini, one of the greatest of modern composers, was the son of an itinerant musician and a strolling actress. Andrea del Sarto was the son of a tailor, and took his name from his father's trade. Perino del Vaga was born in poverty and nearly starved in his boyhood. Perugino, whose noble painting of the "Infant Christ and the Virgin" adorns the Albani Palace at Rome, grew up in want and misery. We all remember the story of the shepherd-boy Giotto, who finally came to be so eminent a painter, and the intimate friend of Dante; like Michael Angelo, he was an architect and sculptor. Paganini, one of the greatest of instrumental performers that ever lived, was born in poverty and was illegitimate. He gained enormous sums of money by his wonderful exhibitions and musical compositions, but was spoiled by adulation, becoming reckless and dissipated. His performances in the cities of Europe created a *furore* before unparalleled in the history of music, and never since surpassed.

Wilson the unequalled ornithologist, Dr. Livingstone the heroic missionary and African traveller, and Tannahill[1] the Scottish poet, — author of that

---

[1] Falling into a state of morbid despondency and mental derangement, Tannahill committed suicide, by drowning, in his thirty-sixth year. James Hogg, the "Ettrick Shepherd," visited

familiar and favorite song, " Jessie, the Flower of
Dumblane,"—earned their living in youth as journey-
men weavers. Joost van den Vondel, the national
poet of Holland, was a hosier's apprentice. Molière,
already referred to, began his career as a journeyman
tailor, but occasionally his maternal grandfather took
him to the play, and thus were sown the seeds which
led to his greatness as a dramatic author and actor.
Samuel Woodworth, author of the " Old Oaken
Bucket," one of the sweetest lyrics in our language, was a journeyman printer. Richard Cobden,
statesman, economist, and author, was a poor Sussex
farmer's son, whose youthful occupation was that of
tending sheep. John Bright, the intimate friend and
coadjutor of Cobden, one of the greatest, most eloquent, and most successful of English reformers, was
the son of a cotton-spinner. Lord Clyde, the successful general who crushed the rebellion in India, and
who was made a peer of England, was the son of a
carpenter. The motto of his life, always inscribed
upon the fly-leaf of his pocket memorandum-book,
was: " By means of patience, common-sense, and time,
impossibilities become possible."

John Bunyan,[1] the author of " Pilgrim's Progress,"
the solace and delight of millions, and a text-book for

him a short time before his death. " Farewell," said Tannahill,
as he grasped his brother poet's hand ; " we shall never meet
again !"

[1] One of Bunyan's biographers tells us his library consisted of
two books, — the Bible and Fox's " Book of Martyrs." The latter
work, in three volumes, is preserved in the Bedford town library,

all future time, was a tinker.   His great work is said
to have obtained a larger circulation than any other
English book except the translation of the Bible.
Benjamin Franklin, statesman, philosopher, epigram-
matist, was a tallow-chandler.[1]   Nathaniel Bowditch,
the eminent mathematician, was a cooper's apprentice.
He was twenty-one years of age before he may be said
to have begun his education, but in his prime was
a Fellow of the Royal Society of London, and was
offered the chair of mathematics in Harvard College.
Hiram Powers, the first sculptor from this country to
win European fame, was brought up a ploughboy on a
Vermont farm ; his " Greek Slave " gave him high rank
among modern sculptors.   Elihu Burritt, the remarkable linguist, was a Connecticut horse-shoer.   White-
field, the eloquent English preacher and father of the

and contains Bunyan's name at the foot of the titlepages written by himself.   Bunyan's crime, for which he was imprisoned
twelve years, was teaching plain country people the knowledge
of the Scriptures and the practice of virtue.

[1] Is it generally known that among the accomplishments of his
after years was that of music and an instrumental performer ?
Leigh Hunt says that " Dr. Franklin offered to teach my mother
the guitar, but she was too bashful to become his pupil.   She
regretted this afterwards, possibly from having missed so illustrious a master.   Her first child, who died, was named after him."

In his Autobiography Franklin says : " At ten years of age I
was called home to assist my father in his occupation, which was
that of a soap-boiler and tallow-chandler, a business to which he
had served no apprenticeship, but which he embraced on his arrival in New England, because he found his own, that of a dyer,
in too little request.   I was accordingly employed in cutting the
wicks, filling the moulds," etc.

sect of Calvinistic Methodists, was in youth the stable-
boy of an English inn. Cardinal Wolsey, chief minister of Henry VIII., was brought up to follow his
father's humble calling of a butcher. Horne Tooke,
the English wit, priest, lawyer, and genius, was the
son of a poulterer.[1] Correra, afterwards president of
Guatemala, was born in poverty, and for years was
a drummer-boy in the army, where he was laughed
at for saying that the world should some day hear
from him, being reminded that his present business
was to make a noise in the world. But he meant
what he said, and acted under Lord Clyde's motto.
He rose by degrees to the highest position in the gift
of his countrymen. "To the persevering mortal the
blessed immortals are swift," says Zoroaster.

Ebenezer Elliott, the English "Corn-Law Rhymer,"[2]
was a blacksmith, but a poet by nature, and his songs

[1] His original name was John Horne, but being adopted and
educated by William Tooke, he assumed his name. His humble
birth being suspected by the proud striplings at Eton, when he
was questioned as to his father he replied, "He was a Turkey
merchant!" He was imprisoned for a year because he said that
certain Americans were "murdered" by the king's troops at Lex-
ington!

[2] Elliott, the Corn-Law Rhymer, was no pander to popular cries unless they were founded on reason. Being asked,
"What is a communist?" he answered, "One who has yearn-
ings for equal division of unequal earnings. Idler or bungler,
he is willing to fork out his penny and pocket your shilling."
Whipple says: "His poetry could hardly be written by a man
who was not physically strong. You can hear the ring of his
anvil, and see the sparks fly off from his furnace, as you read
his verses."

created a political revolution in his native land,
though unlike Béranger's, in France, it was a peaceful
revolution. He was ever a true champion of the poor
and oppressed. In the latter portion of his life he
was in easy pecuniary circumstances. William Lloyd
Garrison,[1] the beloved philanthropist, orator, and
writer, was born in poverty, and was early apprenticed to a shoemaker, but became a journeyman
printer before his majority. He suffered imprisonment for his opinions' sake, and may be said to have
been the father of Abolitionism in America, fortunately living long enough to see the grand effort of
his life crowned with success, in the emancipation of
the blacks and the abolishment of slavery throughout
the length and breadth of his native land. Kepler, the
famous German astronomer, was the son of a poor
innkeeper, and though enjoying royal patronage, often
felt the pressure of poverty. Coleridge said : " Galileo
was a great genius and so was Newton ; but it would
take two or three Galileos and Newtons to make one
Kepler." We owe our knowledge of the laws of the
planetary system to him.

Sir Richard Arkwright, inventor of the spinning-
jenny, and founder of the great cotton industries of
England, never saw the inside of a schoolhouse until
after he was twenty years of age, having long served

---

[1] While these notes are writing, the city of Boston is erecting a
bronze statue to the memory of Garrison, which is to adorn one
of its finest and largest public parks, — a fitting tribute to the
honored philanthropist.

as a barber's assistant. Justice Tenterden, and
Turner, greatest among landscape-painters, were also
brought up to the same trade. James Brindley, the
English engineer and mechanician, and Cook, the
famed navigator, were day-laborers in early life.
Romney, the artist, John Hunter, the physiologist,
Professor Lee, the Orientalist, and John Gibson,
the sculptor, were carpenters by trade. Shakspeare
was a wool-comber in his youth. These low estates,
the workshop and the mine, have often contributed
liberally to recruit the ranks of those whom the world
has recognized as men of genius.

Horace Mann declared that education is our only
political safety. He might have gone further, and
said our only moral safety also. It is not, however,
the school and the college alone that bring about this
grand object, though they are natural adjuncts. Real
education is the apprenticeship of life, and that is
always the best which we realize in our struggle to
obtain a livelihood. Genius, as a rule, owes little to
scholastic training, — within these pages there will be
found proof sufficient of this. Sir T. F. Buxton says
he owed more to his father's gamekeeper, who could
neither read nor write, than to any other source of
knowledge. He said this man was truly his " guide,
philosopher, and friend," whose memory was stored
with more varied rustic knowledge, good sense, and
mother wit, than his young master ever met with
afterwards. He adds that he was his first instructor, and that he profited far more by his remarks

and admonitions than by those of his more learned tutors.[1]

Perhaps at first thought it may seem singular that so many unschooled geniuses should have risen to be famous in their several departments, but it is because they were geniuses. They saw and understood nature and art by intuition, while those of us who can claim no such distinction have been compelled to acquire knowledge by plummet and line, so to speak. "The ambition of a man of parts," says Sydney Smith, "should be not to know books, but things; not to show other men that he has read Locke, and Montesquieu, and Beccaria, and Dumont, but to show that he knows the subjects upon which they have written." Let us pursue our examples still further, for they are both interesting and remarkable when brought thus together.

Benjamin West[2] was born in Pennsylvania, a poor farmer's boy; but the genius of art was in him, and after patient study he became an eminent painter, finally succeeding Sir Joshua Reynolds as president of

[1] Hosea Biglow's words are specially applicable here : —

"An' yit I love th' unhighschooled way
Ol' farmers hed when I wuz younger ;
Their talk wuz meatier, an' 'ould stay,
While book-froth seems to whet your hunger."

[2] His "Death on the Pale Horse," now in the Academy of Fine Arts at Philadelphia, is the most remarkable of his productions in this country. The Pennsylvania Hospital, in the same city, has also "Christ Healing the Sick," by West, — a truly noble conception, a vigorous work of art, and a generous gift from the author.

the Royal Academy in 1792. George III. was his personal friend and patron. He was so thoroughly appreciated there that he made England his home, where he died in 1820. John Britton, author of the "Beauties of England and Wales," as well as of several valuable works on architecture, was born in a mud cabin in Wiltshire, and was for years engaged as a bar-tender. He was finally turned adrift by his employer with two guineas in his pocket, but before his death his list of published books exceeded eighty volumes! Sir Francis Chantrey, the eminent sculptor, was in his minority a journeyman carver in wood. Talma, the great tragic actor of France, and favorite of the first Napoleon, was a dentist by trade. Gifford, the eminent English critic and essayist, was "graduated" from a cobbler's bench. When Cicero was asked concerning his lineage, he replied, "I commence an ancestry." Beaumarchais, the successful French dramatist, author of the "Barber of Seville" and the "Marriage of Figaro," was a watchmaker by trade, but developed such versatile genius as finally to excite the jealousy of the unscrupulous Voltaire.

Thomas Ball, the sculptor, who has done so much to ornament the parks and squares of Boston, used as a lad to sweep out the halls of the Boston Museum.[1] The author has often been within the walls

---

[1] His old employer, Moses Kimball, paid Ball twenty thousand dollars for the bronze group now standing in Park Square. It represents President Lincoln Freeing the Slaves. The purchaser presented it to the city of Boston.

of his pleasant studio in the environs of Florence, adjoining his charming domestic establishment. It is near to the spot where Powers produced his " Greek Slave," and overlooks the lovely city of Florence, divided by the Arno. Andrew Jackson, who became President of the United States, was the son of a poor Irish emigrant, and so was John C. Calhoun, the great Southern statesman and Vice-President. Abraham Lincoln and the late President Garfield were both sons of toil, the former being commonly designated as " the rail-splitter," the latter as " the canalboy." Andrew Johnson was a journeyman tailor. Henry Wilson was a cobbler at the bench until he was nearly twenty-one. So also was Andersen,[1] the Danish novelist. Jasmin, who has been called the Burns of France, was the son of a street beggar. Allan Cunningham, poet, novelist, and miscellaneous writer, began life as a stone-mason; he became the father of four sons, all of whom won distinction in literature. Among the father's novels was that of " Paul Jones," which was remarkably successful. Dr. Isaac Miller, Dean of Carlisle, began life as a weaver, and Dr. Prideaux, Bishop of Worcester, earned his living in youth as a kitchen-boy at Oxford. Watt, the great Scotch inventor, whose steam-engine has revolutionized modern industry, and Whitney,

[1] Hans Christian Andersen was one of the most gifted of modern authors. In his story entitled " Only a Fiddler," he has given many striking pictures from the experience of his own life. His best books are his fairy-tales, of which he has published several volumes.

inventor of the cotton-gin, were street gamins in childhood. Both these inventors were thought by their associates to be "beside themselves" as they grew towards maturity. "No man is quite sane," says Emerson; "each has a vein of folly in his composition, a slight determination of blood to the head, to make sure of holding him hard to some one point which nature has taken to heart."

The world's great men, according to the acceptation of the term, have not always been great scholars. General Nathaniel Greene, the successful Revolutionary commander, second only in military skill to Washington, was brought up at a blacksmith's forge. Horace Greeley, orator and journalist, was the son of a poor New Hampshire farmer and earned his living for years by setting type. William Sturgeon the able and famous electrician, Samuel Drew the English essayist, and Bloomfield the poet, all rose from the cobbler's bench; and so did Thomas Edwards, the profound naturalist. Robert Dodsley, the poet, dramatist, and friend of Pope began life as a London footman in livery. His tragedy of "Cleone" was so successful and well constructed, that Dr. Johnson said, "If Otway had written it, no other of his pieces would have been remembered," which was certainly extravagant praise.[1] Douglas Jerrold was born in a garret at Sheerness. Hobson, one of England's

---

[1] Any one who could place the tragedy of "Cleone" before that of "Venice Preserved," by Otway, in point of merit, must have been singularly prejudiced.

admirals, was a tailor's apprentice in early life. Hunt-
ington, the remarkable preacher and revivalist, was
originally a coal-heaver, and Bewick, the father of
wood-engraving, was a laborer in a coal mine for
many years.

John Gay, the English poet, was not "born with a
silver spoon in his mouth," but in youth he came up to
London, where he served as a clerk to a silk-mercer.
"How long he continued behind the counter," says
Dr. Johnson, "or with what degree of softness and
dexterity he received and accommodated the ladies,
as he probably took no delight in telling it, is not
known." He wrote comedies, fables, farces, and ballads, and wrote well, and was vastly popular. Gay
was a great gourmand, very lazy, and fond of society.[1]
The silk-mercer's clerk attained the much-coveted
honor of resting at last in Westminster Abbey.
Boffin, the great navigator, served at first before
the mast as a common sailor. Robert Dick, the
geologist and botanist, followed his trade as a baker
through his whole life.

Would it not seem, in the light of these many instances, that practical labor forms the best training
even for genius?

---

[1] Thackeray says : "He was lazy, kindly, uncommonly idle ;
rather slovenly, forever eating and saying good things. A little
French abbé of a man, sleek, soft-handed, and soft-hearted."
A Mr. Rich was the manager of the theatre in which Gay's
"Beggar's Opera" was brought out. Its unprecedented success suggested the epigram that "it made Rich gay, and Gay
rich."

Linnæus (Karl von Linné), the great Swedish botanist, the most influential naturalist of the eighteenth
century, was a shoemaker's apprentice. His works
upon his favorite study are authority with students of
science all over the world. He became physician to
the king and made his home at Stockholm, but
roamed over all Scandinavia in pursuing his special
science of botany and also that of zoölogy. He will
always be remembered as having been the first to
perfect a systematic and scientific classification of
plants and animals. He lies buried in the Upsala
Cathedral.

Thorwaldsen, the great Danish sculptor, was the
son of an humble Icelandic fisherman, but by reason
of native genius he rose to bear the name of the
greatest of modern sculptors. He left in the Copenhagen museum alone six hundred grand examples of
the art he adorned. Many of our readers will remember having seen near Lucerne, Switzerland, one of his
most remarkable pieces of sculpture, representing a
wounded and dying lion of colossal size, designed to
commemorate the heroic fidelity of the Swiss guards
who fell Aug. 10, 1792. Thorwaldsen was passion-
ately fond of children, so that the moment he entered
a house he gathered all the juveniles about him ; and
in most of his marble groups he introduces children.
He never married, but made his beautiful mistress,
the Roman Fortunata, celebrated by repeating her
face in many of his ideal groups. Thorwaldsen gave
an impulse to art in his native country which has

no like example in history; indeed, art is to-day the religion of Copenhagen, and Thorwaldsen is its prophet.

George Stephenson, the English engineer and inventor, was in his youth a stoker in a colliery, learning to read and write at a laborers' evening school. John Jacob Astor began life as a pedler in the streets of New York, where his descendants own a hundred million dollars worth of real estate.[1] The elder Vanderbilt, famous not alone for his millions but also for his vast enterprise in the development of commerce and railroads, served as a cabin-boy on a North River sloop during several years of his youth. George Peabody, the great American philanthropist and millionnaire, was born in poverty. Fisher Ames, the eminent statesman and orator, eked out a precarious living for years as a country pedagogue. Greatness lies not alone in the possession of genius, but in the right and effective use of it.

We have given examples sufficient to illustrate this branch of our subject, though they might be almost indefinitely extended. It was Daniel Webster [2] who

---

[1] Among his liberal bequests were four hundred thousand dollars for the establishment of a public library in New York, to which his son, William B. Astor, subsequently added as much more. The Astor Library is therefore one of the best endowed institutions of the kind in America.

[2] Webster, when told that there was no room for new lawyers in a profession already overcrowded, answered, with the proud consciousness of genius and character, "There is always room at the top."

said that "a man not ashamed of himself need not be ashamed of his early condition in life." Titles are vendible, but genius is the gift of Heaven.

Enthusiasm is the heritage of youth ; it plans with audacity and executes with vigor : " It is the leaping lightning," according to Emerson, " not to be measured by the horse-power of the understanding." In the accomplishment of great deeds it is undoubtedly the keenest spur, and consequently those who have become eminent in the history of the world have mostly achieved their greatness before gray hairs have woven themselves about their brows. Unless the tree has borne ample blossoms in the spring, we shall look in vain for a generous crop in the fall. Notwithstanding the abundance of axioms as to youth and rashness dwelling together, we have ample evidence that it is the period of deeds, when the senses are unworn and the whole man is in the vigor of strength and earnestness. Goethe tells us that the destiny of any nation depends upon the opinions of its young men. Let us recall a few examples, in corroboration of this view, among those who have made their mark upon the times in which they lived.

Alexander the Great reigned over the Macedonians at sixteen ; Scipio was but twenty-nine at the zenith of his military glory ; Charles XII.[1] was only nine-

---

[1] Charles XII. put his whole soul into the cause of Sweden at the time when she was threatened with extinction by her enemies. He fought all Europe, — Danes, Russians, Poles, Germans, — and gave away a kingdom before he was twenty. At his coronation at

teen when, as commander-in-chief, he won the famous
battle of Narva; Condé was twenty-two when he
gained the battle of Rocroi; Scipio the Younger conquered Carthage at thirty-six, and Cortes subdued
Mexico at the same age. At thirty Charlemagne was
master of France and Germany; at thirty-two Clive
had established the British power in India. Hannibal
won his greatest victories before he was thirty, and
Napoleon was but twenty-seven when he outgeneralled
the veteran marshals of Austria on the plains of Italy.
George Washington won his first battle as a colonel
at twenty-two; Lafayette was a major-general in our
army at the age of twenty. Nor are we to look only
for youthful greatness among those who have won laurels in war. William Pitt was prime minister of England at twenty-four; Calhoun had achieved national
greatness before he was thirty; while the names of
John Adams, Alexander Hamilton, and the elder Pitt in
England also suggest themselves in this connection.[1]

Upsala, he snatched the crown from the hands of the archbishop
and set it proudly on his head with his own hands.

[1] Whipple speaks of three characters "who seem to have been
statesmen from the nursery." These were : "Octavius Cæsar,
more successful in the arts of policy than even the great Julius,
never guilty of youthful indiscretion, or, we are sorry to say, of
youthful virtue; Maurice of Saxony, the preserver of the Reformed religion in Germany, in that memorable contest in which
his youthful sagacity proved more than a match for the veteran
craft of Charles V.; and the second William of Orange, the preserver of the liberties of Europe against the ambition of Louis
XIV., who, as a child, may be said to have prattled treaties and
lisped despatches."

Handel composed sonatas at ten years of age; Mozart was equally precocious, and died at thirty-six, at which age Shakspeare had written "Hamlet." Bellini, the composer, had produced "Il Pirata," "La Sonnambula," and "La Norma," before his thirtieth year; "I Puritani" was finished at thirty, and he died two years later. Charles Matthews the elder began to write for the press at fourteen, and Moore wrote verses for print at the same age; undoubtedly both were open to cool and judicious criticism.[1] Henry Kirke White published a volume of poems at seventeen. Bryant, the first American poet of celebrity, began to write verses at the age of ten, and his most celebrated poem, "Thanatopsis," was written before he was twenty. Fitz-Greene Halleck, author of "Marco Bozzaris," wrote verses for the magazines at fourteen. Congreve was at the height of his literary fame at four-and-twenty, — he to whom Dryden said Shakspeare had bequeathed his poetical crown, and to whom Pope dedicated his version of the Iliad. Watt invented the steam-engine before he was thirty. The reproof administered by his grandmother for his idleness in taking off and replacing the cover of the teakettle, and "playing with the steam to no purpose," will occur to the reader. Joan of Arc[2] was but eighteen when she raised the siege of Orléans

---

[1] Nothing is so beneficial to a young author as the advice of a man whose judgment stands constitutionally at the freezing point. — *Douglas Jerrold.*

[2] The life of Jeanne d'Arc is like a legend in the midst of history. — *Waller.*

and conquered city after city, until Charles VII. was crowned king at Rheims.

Guizot, the distinguished French statesman and historian, seems to have been "a child who had no childhood." At eleven years of age he was able to read in their respective languages Thucydides, Demosthenes, Dante, Schiller, Gibbon, and Shakspeare.

Robert Hall, the eloquent English clergyman, was a remarkable instance of early mental development. It is said that before he was ten years of age he perused with interest and understanding Edwards's treatises on the "Affections" and on the "Will." His sermons, essays, and writings generally were eagerly read and admired by the public; but excessive application at last brought on insanity. It was gracefully said of him that his imperial fancy laid all nature under tribute. Even in madness he did not lose his power of retort. A hypocritical condoler visited him in the madhouse, and asked in a servile tone: "Pray, what brought you here, Mr. Hall?" Hall touched his brow significantly with his finger, and replied, "What'll never bring you, sir, — too much brains!"[1]

Macaulay had already won an exalted reputation for prose and poetry before he was twenty-three, and N. P. Willis, before he left college, had achieved

[1] After a couple of years Hall was restored to the full possession of his faculties, and for twenty years thereafter maintained his high reputation as a pulpit orator. He died in 1831.

enduring fame by his sacred poems,[1] which, in fact,
he never afterwards excelled in a long and successful literary career. Schiller wrote and published in
his fourteenth year a poem on Moses. Klopstock
began his "Messiah" at seventeen, and Tasso had
produced his "Rinaldo," and completed the first three
cantos of "Jerusalem Delivered," before he was nineteen. Milton was an unremitting student at ten.
Southey began to write verses before he was eleven,
Chaucer and Cowley at twelve, and Leigh Hunt at
about the same age. Pope,[2] like so many others,
began to write poetry as a child, thus proving that
"poets are born and not made." Chatterton, the remarkable literary prodigy, died at eighteen, but not
until he had established a lasting reputation. Bulwer-
Lytton was a successful author at about the same age,
and so were Keats and Bayard Taylor. Dickens
produced the "Pickwick Papers" before he was
twenty-five, and it may safely be said that in wit,
humor, and originality he never surpassed that delicious book. These seem interesting facts to remember, though they do not establish any actual criterion,
since the thoughtful student of the past can adduce

---

[1] Fifty years after these poems were published, as we are informed by the publishers, there is a steady demand for from two
to three hundred copies annually. Of how many American books,
of a similar character, can this be said?

[2] I wrote things, I'm ashamed to say how soon. Part of an
epic poem when about twelve. The scene of it lay at Rhodes and
some of the neighboring islands; and the poem opened under
water, with a description of the Court of Neptune. — *Pope.*

many notable examples of mature development in art and literature.

Among these is that of Edmund Burke, on the whole the greatest of English philosophical statesmen. He is the most remarkable instance of a number of men of genius who seem to have grown younger as they grew older, — that is, mentally and morally. Macaulay has noticed that Bacon's writings towards the close of his career exceeded those of his youth and manhood " in eloquence, in sweetness and variety of expression, and in richness of illustration." [1]   He adds : " In this respect the history of his mind bears some resemblance to the history of the mind of Burke.   The treatises on the ' Sublime and Beautiful,' [2] though writ-

---

[1] Lord Brougham hoped to see the day when every man in the United Kingdom could read Bacon. "It would be much more to the purpose," said Cobbett, "if his lordship could use his influence to see that every man in the kingdom could *eat* bacon."

[2] On a certain occasion when Barry, the eminent painter, exhibited one of his admirable pictures, some one present doubted that it was his work, so remarkable was its excellence, and Barry at the time had not established any special fame. The artist was so affected by the remark that he burst into tears and retired. Burke, who was present, followed him to pacify his grief. The painter by chance quoted some passages of the newly published essay on the "Sublime and Beautiful." It appeared anonymously, and Burke took occasion to sneer at it, when Barry showed more feeling than he had done about his picture. He commended the essay in the most earnest language. Burke, smiling, acknowledged its authorship. "I could not afford to buy it," replied the astonished artist, "but I transcribed every line with my own hands ;" at the same time pulling the manuscript from his pocket. This was commendation so sincere and appreciative, that the great author and the great painter clasped hands in mutual friendship.

ten on a subject which the coldest metaphysician could hardly treat without being occasionally betrayed into florid writing, is the most unadorned of Burke's works. It appeared when he was twenty-five or twenty-six. When, at forty, he wrote the 'Thoughts on the Causes of the Present Discontents,' his reason and judgment had reached their full maturity, but his eloquence was in its splendid dawn. At fifty his rhetoric was as rich as good taste would admit; and when he died, at almost seventy, it had become ungracefully gorgeous. In his youth he wrote on the emotions produced by mountains and cascades, by the masterpieces of painting and sculpture, by the faces and necks of beautiful women, in the style of a Parliamentary report. In his old age he discussed treaties and tariffs in the most fervid and brilliant language of romance."

Socrates learned to play on musical instruments in his old age. Cato at eighty first studied the Greek language, and Plutarch did not apply himself to learn the Latin language until about the same age. Theophrastus [1] began his "Character of Man" on his ninetieth birthday. Peter Rusard, one of the fathers of French poetry, did not develop his poetic faculty until nearly fifty. Arnauld, the learned French theologian and philosopher, translated Josephus in his eightieth year. Lope de Vega, one of the most learned men of the sixteenth century, wrote his best at seventy years of age. Dr. Johnson applied himself

---

[1] Menander, the poet, was Theophrastus's favorite pupil.

to learn the Dutch language at seventy. At seventy-three, when quite feeble, he composed a Latin prayer to test to his own satisfaction the loss or retention of his mental faculties. Chaucer's " Canterbury Tales " were the work of the author's last years. Franklin's philosophical pursuits were but fairly begun at fifty. La Mothe le Vayer's best treatises were written after he was eighty years of age, and Izaak Walton's when he was nearly ninety. Thomas Hobbes, the remarkable English philosopher and author, published his version of the Odyssey in his eighty-seventh year, and his Iliad in his eighty-eighth. Winckelmann,[1] author of the " History of Ancient Art," lived in ignorance and obscurity until the prime of his life, when he became famous. Landor was busy with authorship until after he was eighty. The Earl of Chatham made his most remarkable oratorical effort at seventy, and our own American orator and statesman, Robert C. Winthrop, at a still later period of his life. Fontenelle continued his literary pursuits until he was ninety-nine, " blossoming in the winter of his days," as Lord Orrery wrote of him. Ménage, the celebrated French critic and scholar, wrote sonnets and epigrams at ninety. Julius Scaliger, the renowned Italian scholar and poet, dictated to his son,

---

[1] Winckelmann, one of the most distinguished writers on classic antiquities and the fine arts, was the son of a shoemaker. He contrived, by submitting to all sorts of personal deprivation, to fit himself for college, and to go through with the studies there by teaching young and less advanced fellow-students, at the same time supporting a bedridden and helpless father.

at the age of seventy, two hundred verses of his own
composition from memory.   Mr. Gladstone and John
Bright, the English statesmen, are more recent examples of oratorical, mental, and physical powers in
advanced years.   George Bancroft the American historian, in his eighty-sixth year is still engaged in authorship, and Whittier and Holmes are writing with
unabated vigor at nearly eighty years of age.   Miss
Elizabeth Peabody at eighty-four is still a vigorous
writer and active philanthropist, and the same may
be said of Mrs. Julia Ward Howe at the age of sixty-
six.   Mrs. Howe, indeed, is one of the foremost of
American women, whether we regard the ripeness of
her scholarship, the breadth of her understanding, the
richness of her imagination, or the quiet intrepidity
with which she champions great reforms.

CHAPTER II.

WHO does not enjoy recalling these silent friends, favorite authors grown dear to us by age and long association ? Some one has said that authors, like coins, grow dearer as they grow old. Indeed, Samuel Rogers, the banker and poet, declared that when friends at his famous "breakfasts" were praising a new book, he forthwith began to re-read an old one. All these writers were double-sided, so to speak ; they had their book natures and their human natures, and it is when we prefer to contemplate them in the latter aspect that we like them best. Carlyle calls them " the vanguard in the march of mind, the intellectual backwoodsmen reclaiming from the idle wilderness new territory for the thought and activity of their happier brethren." It is true that we can form but a partial judgment of authors by their books, their motives being not always as pure as we are inclined to believe.[1] A traitor like Bolingbroke is quite capable of writing a captivating book on patriotism; and it has been said if Satan were to write one, it would be upon the advantages of virtue.

[1] "People may be taken in once, who imagine that an author is greater in private life than other men," says Dr. Johnson.

It is certain he has ever shown such a hearty appreciation of virtue that he holds in highest estimation his success in corrupting it. Examples flash across the memory. There was Sir Thomas More advocating toleration, while he was himself a fierce persecutor; Sallust declaring against the licentiousness of his age, yet addicted to habitual debaucheries; Byron assuming a misanthropy which he never felt; and Cowley boasting of his mistresses, though he had not the courage even to address one. Smollett's descriptions and scenes were often indelicate, though he was himself in that respect a faultless man. "As a rule, the author who is not in genius far above his productions must be a second-rate one at best," says Bulwer-Lytton. Sometimes we detect striking likenesses between the author and his works. Goldsmith, for instance, was the same hero to low-bred women, and the same coward to ladies, that he depicts in his charming comedy. It is difficult, however, in the light of Handel's inspired music, to realize what an animal nature possessed him in his every-day mood, — what a glutton he was at table; or to reconcile the sublime strains of Mozart with his trivial personality.[1] Still, Buffon persistently declares, "Le style c'est l'homme."

[1] Such incongruities do exist : nothing is infallible ; phrenologists even find the crania of some men to exhibit contradictory evidences. When Sydney Smith with some friends submitted his head to be examined by a phrenologist who did not know him, the party were amused at the examiner declaring him to be a great naturalist, — "never happier than when arranging his birds and fishes." "Sir," said the divine, "I don't know a fish from a bird!"

Addison, recognized as the purest and most perspicuous writer of the English language, though exercising such mastership of the pen, had no oral ability, and rarely attempted to talk in social circles. He said of himself that though he had a hundred pounds in the bank, he had no small coin in his pocket.[1]

Dr. Johnson and Coleridge were famous for their colloquial facility, but both of these were rather lecturers than talkers, however delightful in this respect the latter may have been. Johnson during his life was undoubtedly more of a power as a talker than as a writer. It has been said that Scott talked more poetry and Edmund Burke more eloquence than they ever wrote. Emerson thought that " better things are said, more incisive, more wit and insight are dropped in talk and forgotten, than gets into books." E. H. Chapin and H. W. Beecher have talked sounder and more brilliant theology than they ever preached from the pulpit. Spontaneous thoughts come from our inner consciousness; sermons and essays, from the cooler action of the brain. Coleridge, on first meeting Byron, entertained the poet with one of his monologues, wherein he ascended into the seventh heaven upon wings of theology and metaphysics. Leigh Hunt described the scene to Charles Lamb, and expressed his wonder that Coleridge should have chosen so unsym-

---

[1] " Men of genius," says Longfellow, " are often dull and inert in society; as the blazing meteor, when it descends to earth, is only a stone."

pathetic an auditor. " Oh, it was only his fun," explained Lamb; "there's an immense deal of quiet
humor about Coleridge!" Wordsworth speaks of him
as the "rapt one, with the godlike forehead," the
" heaven-eyed creature." Hazlitt says that " no idea
ever entered the mind of man, but at some period or
other it had passed over his head with rustling pin-
ions." Talfourd writes of seeing " the palm-trees
wave, and the pyramids tower, in the long perspective
of his style." When Coleridge once asked Lamb,
" Charles, did you ever hear me preach ?" he received
the quiet reply, " I never heard you do anything else."
Rogers tells us : " Coleridge was a marvellous talker.
One morning, when Hookham Frere also breakfasted
with me, Coleridge talked for three hours without
intermission about poetry, and so admirably that I
wish every word he uttered had been written down."
Madame de Staël said of him that he was great in
monologue, but that he had no idea of dialogue.

Macaulay was also remarkable for his conversational powers, which were greatly aided by an excellent memory. He has been accused of talking too
much ; and Sydney Smith one said of him: " He is
certainly more agreeable since his return from India.
His enemies might perhaps have said before — though
I never did so — that he talked rather too much ; but
now he has occasional flashes of silence that make
his conversation perfectly delightful!" In a party in
which eminent men are present, the rule is said to
be that, for good conversation, the number of talkers

should never be fewer than the Graces or more than the Muses. Goldsmith, who wrote so charmingly and exhibited such a remarkable versatility with the pen, could make no figure in conversation. Fox, Bentley, Burke, Curran, and Swift were all brilliant talkers; Tasso, Dante, Gray, and Dryden [1] were all taciturn. Of Ben Jonson it is said that he was mostly without speech, sitting by the hour quite silent in society, sucking in the wine and humor of his companions.

Sheridan had the reputation of being a brilliant conversationalist; but we all know that many of his " impromptus " were laboriously prepared beforehand, and that he was wont to lie in wait silently for half an evening watching his opportunity to discharge the arrows of his polished wit. One would be glad to learn how it was with Shakspeare in society. He could hold his own in a controversy, however, as Thomas Fuller, in his " Worthies of England," says, " Many were the wet-combats between him and Ben Jonson: [2]

---

[1] Dryden said of himself : " My conversation is slow and dull, my humor saturnine and reserved. In short, I am none of these who endeavor to break jests in company, or make repartees." And yet at Will's Coffee-House, where the wits of the town met, his chair in winter was always in the warmest nook by the fire, and in summer was placed in the balcony. " To bow to him, and to hear his opinion of Racine's last tragedy or of Bossuet's treatise on epic poetry was thought a privilege. A pinch from his snuff-box was an honor sufficient to turn the head of a young enthusiast." Every one must remember how, in Scott's novel of the " Pirate," Claud Halcro is continually boasting of having obtained at least that honor from "Glorious John."

[2] Jonson was a bricklayer, like his father before him. " Let them blush not that have, but those who have not, a lawful call-

which two I behold like a Spanish great galleon
and an English man-of-war; master Jonson, like the
former, was built far higher in learning; solid, but
slow, in his performances. Shakspeare, like the English man-of-war, lesser in bulk but lighter in sailing,
could turn with all tides, tack about, and take advantage of all winds by the quickness of his wit and invention." Shakspeare himself has said, " Silence is
only commendable in a neat's tongue dried and a
maid not vendible;" but the ancient stoics thought
that by silence they heard other men's imperfections
and concealed their own.

The diplomatist Metternich said he had never known
more than ten or twelve persons with whom it was
pleasant to converse. Margaret Fuller said Carlyle's
talk was an amazement to her, though she was familiar with his writings. His conversation, she declared, was a splendor scarcely to be faced with steady
eye. He did not converse — only harangued. She
thought him " arrogant and overbearing, but it was not
the arrogance of littleness, nor self-love, but rather
the arrogance of some old Scandinavian conqueror;
it was his nature, the untamable impulse that had
given him power to crush the dragons. She was not led
to love or revere him, but liked him heartily, — liked

ing," says Thomas Fuller as he records this fact; and goes on to
say that " Jonson helped in the construction of Lincoln's Inn,
with a trowel in his hand and a book in his pocket. Some gentlemen pitying that his parts should be buried under the rubbish
of so mean a calling, did by their bounty manumise him freely to
follow his own ingenious inclinations."

to see him the powerful smith, the Siegfried, melting all the old iron in his furnace till it glows to a sunset red and burns you, if you senselessly go too near." [1]

When Dr. Johnson was asked why he was not invited out to dine as Garrick [2] was, he answered, as if it was a great triumph to him, " Because great lords and ladies don't like to have their mouths stopped ! " He indulged a furious hatred to Americans, and whenever there was an opportunity sneered at them even more bitterly than he did at Scotchmen. It will be remembered that he thought something could be made out of a Scotchman " if you caught him young ; " but he would not admit even this saving clause as regarded Americans. He said, " I am willing to love all, all mankind, except an American." He called them " robbers and pirates ; " adding, " I'd burn and destroy them ! "

These words were addressed to Miss Anna Seward, of Lichfield. It was in the grammar school of this ancient cathedral town that Addison, Dr. Johnson,

---

[1] Margaret Fuller by marriage became the Marchioness of Ossoli, and with her husband and child perished in the wreck of the brig " Elizabeth," from Leghorn, near Fire Island, in 1850. She was one of the most gifted literary women of America.

[2] Garrick was so popular that it was impossible for him to respond to half the social invitations which he received from the nobility. Even royalty itself honored him by private interviews, often listening to his readings in the domestic circle of the palace. Though he was always rewarded by the hearty approval of the king and queen, he said its effect upon him was like a " wet blanket " compared with the thunders of applause which he usually received in public.

and Garrick received their early education, and Johnson was a native of the place. Miss Seward's father
was the canon resident of Lichfield Cathedral. In
his family there was a beautiful young lady named
Honora Sneyd, a companion to his daughter. John
André, a cultured London youth, fell in love with
Honora, and was tacitly accepted. The young man
was somewhat suddenly called back to the metropolis on business, and a separation thus ensued which
seemed to wean the lady's affections from him, so that
she soon after married a Mr. Edgeworth and in the
course of time became the mother of Maria Edgeworth,
the well-known novel-writer.[1] John André remained
faithful to his first love, and came to America carrying
in his bosom a miniature of Honora suspended from
his neck. His sad fate during our Revolutionary War
is well known to all. He was the Major André whom
Washington reluctantly executed as a spy, and whose
memorial is now conspicuous in Westminster Abbey.

Peter Corneille, the great French dramatic poet,
had nothing in his exterior that indicated his genius.
As to his conversational powers, they were simply in-
sipid, and never failed to weary all listeners. Nature
had endowed him with brilliant gifts, but forgot to
grant him the ordinary accomplishments. He did
not even speak correct French, which he never failed

---

[1] Sir Walter Scott greatly admired Maria Edgeworth's novels,
complimenting " her wonderful power of vivifying all her persons
and making them live as beings in your mind." Lord Jeffrey
honored "their singular union of sober sense and inexhaustible
invention." She died in 1849, in her eighty-second year.

to write with perfection. When his friends represented to him how much more he might please by not disdaining to correct these trivial errors, he would smile and say, " I am none the less Peter Corneille!" We learn from Rogers that in the early days of his popularity Byron was quite diffident in society, or at least never ventured to take part in the conversation. If any one happened to let fall an observation which offended him, he never attempted to reply, but treasured it up for days, and would then come out with some cutting remarks, giving them as his deliberate opinion, the result of his experience of the individual's character. Southey [1] was stiff, reserved, sedate, and so wrapped up in a garb of asceticism that Charles Lamb once stutteringly told him he was " m–made for a m–m–monk, but somehow the co–co–cowl did n't fit."

Racine made this confidential confession to his son : " Do not think that I am sought after by the great on account of my dramas ; Corneille composed nobler verses than mine, but no one notices him, and he only pleases by the mouth of the actors. I never allude to my works when with men of the world, but

[1] Southey was marvellously industrious, as over one hundred published volumes testify. Few men have been students so long and consecutively. He possessed one of the largest private libraries in England. He says : " Having no library within reach, I live upon my own stores, which are, however, more ample perhaps than were ever before possessed by one whose whole estate was in his inkstand." He generously supported the family of Coleridge, who were left destitute. His first wife was a sister of Coleridge's wife.

I amuse them about matters they like to hear. My
talent with them consists not in making them feel
that I have any, but in showing them that they have."
The well-remembered saying about Goldsmith's lack
of conversational power is excellent because it was
so true ; namely, that " he wrote like an angel and
talked like poor Poll." [1] Fisher Ames and Rufus
Choate were distinguished for their conversational
powers.   Stuart, the American painter, was remarkable in this respect; and so were Washington Allston,
Edgar A. Poe, Margaret Fuller, and the late Caleb
Cushing.   The lady just named was considered to be
the best talker of her sex since Madame de Staël.
Indeed, those who knew her well said she talked even
better than she wrote, which was saying much.

Charles Sumner used to relate a talk in a company where Daniel Webster was present.   The
question under discussion was what were the best
means of culture.   Webster was silent until all
had spoken.   He then said : " Gentlemen, you have
overlooked one of the means of culture which I
consider of the first importance, and from which
I have gained the most ; that is, good conversation." [2]

---

[1] " To expect an author to talk as he writes is ridiculous," says
Hazlitt ; "even if he did, you would find fault with him as a
pedant."

[2] There is a sort of knowledge beyond the power of learning to
bestow, and this is to be had in conversation : so necessary is this
to understanding the characters of men, that none are more ignorant of them than those learned pedants whose lives have been
entirely consumed in colleges and among books. — *Fielding.*

Whipple has said in one of his essays that "real, earnest conversation is a kind of intellectual cannibalism, where strong minds feed on each other and mightily enjoy the repast."

Charles Lamb's most sportive essays, which read as though they came almost spontaneously from his pen, are known to have been the result of intense brain labor. He would spend a whole week in elaborating a single humorous letter to a friend. Lamb was so sensitive concerning proof-reading as to be the dread of the printers. It is said of the poet-laureate of England that he has been known to re-write a poem twenty times and more before he was satisfied to give it to the printer. Dickens, when writing a book, was accustomed to shut himself up for days together, and to work with fearful energy until the task was completed; after which he would come forth presenting the appearance of a person recovering from a fit of illness. The free-and-easy spirit which characterizes his pages affords no evidence of the travail through which their author passed in giving them birth. Bulwer-Lytton took matters much more philosophically. He always worked at pen-craft leisurely, never more than three or four hours a day; and yet by carefully observing a system the aggregate of his productions was very large. Balzac, after thinking over a subject, would retire to his study and write it out half a dozen times before he gave the manuscript to the printer, whom he afterwards tormented to the very verge of exasperation by his proof alterations. To come nearer to our own time, we may remark that Longfellow, whose versification seems always to have flowed with such ease and fluency from his pen, was a slow and painstaking producer, sometimes altering and amending until the original draft of an essay or poem was quite improved out of sight.

Dr. Channing nearly drove his printers crazy; after his manuscript — almost illegible by corrections and interlineations — had been returned to them with alterations, omissions, and additions on the first proof-sheets, he would ponder over, alter, and amend three or four successive proofs before he finally allowed the result to meet the public eye, — a new edition involving another series of alterations. The lyric which cost Tennyson the most trouble was " Come into the Garden, Maud." It is said to have been held back from the public after it had been a year in his hands, going through repeated processes of alteration. What time indorses, requires time to create and finish. To this determination of Tennyson to condense all his thoughts into the smallest space, and never to expand when by patient labor he can contract, we owe the few lines in which he states in the " Princess " the whole nebular theory of the universe as expounded by Kant and Laplace ; and how much reflection must have been required to condense the description of the fundamental defect of English law, on which volumes have been written, as as he has done in " Aylmer's Field : " —

> "The lawless science of our law,
>   That codeless myriad of precedent,
>   That wilderness of single instances."

When we observe good workmanship, whether it be by a stone-mason, a cabinet-maker, or a writer, we may be sure that it has cost much patient labor. His biographer tells us that Moore thought ten or fifteen lines in twenty-four hours a good day's accomplishment in poetry; and at this rate he wrote "Lalla Rookh."[1] Wordsworth wrote his verses, laid them aside for weeks, then, taking them up, frequently rewrote them a score of times before he called them finished. Buffon's "Studies of Nature" cost him fifty years of writing and re-writing before the work was published. John Foster, the profound and eloquent English essayist, often spent hours upon a single sentence. Ten years elapsed between the first sketch of Goldsmith's "Traveller" and its final completion. Rochefoucauld[2] spent fifteen years over his

---

[1] His publishers paid Moore three thousand guineas for the copyright of "Lalla Rookh," his favorite production ; and the liberal purchasers, Longman & Co., had no reason to regret their bargain. When Moore's "Lalla Rookh" first appeared, the author was terribly taken aback in company by Lady Holland, who said to him, "Mr. Moore, I don't intend to read your Larry O'Rourke ; I don't like Irish stories !"

[2] Madame de Lafayette was a warm friend of Rochefoucauld. She was intimately allied to the clever men of the time, and was respected and loved by them. The author of the " Maxims " owed much to her, while she also was under obligations to him. Their friendship was of mutual benefit. " He gave me intellect," she said, " and I reformed his heart."

little book of Maxims, altering some of them thirty times. Rogers admitted that he had more than once spent ten days upon a single verse before he turned it to suit him. Vaugelas, the great French scholar, devoted twenty years to his admirable translation of " Quintus Curtius."

Some authors have produced with such rapidity as to approach improvisation. Perhaps the most remarkable instance of this was in the case of Lope de Vega, who composed and wrote a versified drama in a single day, and is known to have done so for seven consecutive days. Contemporary with Shakspeare and Cervantes, De Vega has left behind him two thousand original dramas sparkling with vivacity of dialogue and richness of invention. Soldier, duellist, poet, sailor, and priest, his long life was one of intense activity and adventure.[1] The name of Hardy, the French dramatic author and actor, occurs to us in this connection ; though an inferior genius to De Vega, he wrote over six hundred original dramas. He was considered the first dramatic writer of the days of Henry IV. and Louis XIII., before whom Hardy often appeared upon the stage personating the heroes of his own dramas.

[1] His enemies having declared that De Vega's dramas were not judged upon their merit, but were popular because they bore his name, — to try the public taste he wrote and published a book of poems anonymously, entitled " Soliloquies on God." Their merit was undisputed, and they were vastly popular, until the carping critics threatened him with the unknown author as a rival. His triumph when he claimed them as his own was complete.

Prynne, the English antiquary, politician, and pamphlet-writer, sat down early in the morning to his composition. Every two hours his man brought him a roll and a pot of ale as refreshment; and so he continued until night, when he partook of a hearty dinner. One of his pamphlets was entitled "A Scourge for Stage-Players," which was considered so scurrilous that the Star-Chamber sentenced him to pay a heavy fine, to be exposed in the pillory, to lose his ears, and to be imprisoned for life. He was finally released from prison. While he was confined in the pillory, a pyramid of his offending pamphlets was made close at hand, to windward of his position, and set on fire, so that the author was very nearly choked to death by the smoke. He was almost as incessant and inveterate a writer as Petrarch, and considered being debarred from pen and ink an act more barbarous than the loss of his ears. However, he partially obviated his want of the usual facilities by writing a whole volume on his prison walls while confined in the Tower of London.

Byron wrote the "Corsair" in ten days, which was an average of nearly two hundred lines a day, — a fact which he acknowledged to Moore with a degree of shame. He said he would not confess it to everybody, considering it to be a humiliating fact, proving his own want of judgment in publishing, and the public in reading, "things which cannot have stamina for permanent attention." The surpassing beauty of the "Corsair," however, excuses all the author said or did in connection with it. It may nevertheless be affirmed that, as a rule, no great work has ever been performed with ease, or ever will be accomplished without encountering the throes of time and labor. Dante, we remember, saw himself " growing lean " over his " Divine Comedy." Mary Russell Mitford, the charming English authoress, dramatist, poet, and novelist, who so excelled in her sketches of country life, says of herself: " I write with extreme slowness, labor, and difficulty; and, whatever you may think, there is a great difference of facility in different minds. I am the slowest writer, I suppose, in England, and touch and retouch incessantly." Her life was one of constant labor and self-abnegation in behalf of a worthless, selfish, and imperious father. He was a robust, showy, wasteful profligate, and a gambler. A doctor by profession, he was a spendthrift and sensualist by occupation. He contracted a venal marriage with an heiress much older than himself, and after squandering her entire fortune he fell back upon his daughter as the bread-winner for the whole family. By a remarkable chance she became the possessor of a great lottery prize, from which she realized twenty thousand pounds, every penny of which her beastly father drank and gambled away. Still, the devotion and industry of the daughter never waned for a moment. Her patient struggles have placed her name on the roll of fame, while her father's has sunk into deserved oblivion.

De Tocqueville wrote to his publishers : " You must think me very slow. You would forgive me if you knew how hard it is for me to satisfy myself, and how impossible it is for me to finish things incompletely." Horace suggested that authors should keep their literary productions from the public eye for at least nine years, which certainly ought to produce " the well-ripened fruit of sage delay." After a labor of eleven years Virgil pronounced his Æneid imperfect. This recalls the Italian saying, " One need not be a stag, neither ought one to be a tortoise." Tasso's manuscript, which is still extant, is almost illegible because of the number of alterations which he made after having written it. Montaigne, " the Horace of Essayists," could not be induced, so lazy and self-indulgent was he, to even look at the proof-sheets of his writings. " I add, but I correct not," he said.

The writer of these pages has seen the original draft of Longfellow's " Excelsior," so interlined and amended to suit the author's taste as to make the manuscript rather difficult to decipher. The poet wrote a back-hand, as it is called ; that is, the letters sloped in the opposite direction from the usual custom, and as a rule his writing was remarkably legible. Coleridge was very methodical as to the time and place of his composition. He told Hazlitt that he liked to compose walking over uneven ground, or making his way through straggling branches of undergrowth in the woods ; which was a very affected and erratic notion, and might better have been " whipped

out of him." [1] Wordsworth, on the contrary, found
his favorite place for composing his verses in walking back and forth upon the smooth paths of his
garden, among flowers and creeping vines. Hazlitt,
in a critical analysis of the two poets, traces a likeness to the style of each in his choice of exercise
while maturing his thoughts, — which, it would seem
to us, is a subtile deduction altogether too fine to
signify anything.

Charles Dibdin, the famous London song-writer
and musician, whose sea-songs as published number
over a thousand, caught his ideas " on the fly." As
an example, he was at a loss for something new to
sing on a certain occasion. A friend was with him
in his lodgings and suggested several themes. Suddenly the jar of a ladder against the street lamp-post
under his window was heard. It was a hint to his
fertile imagination, and Dibdin exclaimed, " The
Lamplighter! That 's it; first-rate idea !" and step-
ping to the piano he finished both song and words in
an hour, and sang them in public with great éclat
that very night, under the title of " Jolly Dick, the
Lamplighter." Like nearly all such mercurial gen-

---

[1] Coleridge tells us how he was once cured of infidelity by his
teacher. "I told Boyer that I hated the thought of becoming a
clergyman. 'Why so?' said he. 'Because, to tell you the truth,
sir,' I said, 'I'm an infidel!' For this, without further ado,
Boyer flogged me, — wisely, as I think, soundly, as I know.
Any whining or sermonizing would have gratified my vanity, and
confirmed me in my absurdity; as it was, I was laughed at, and
got heartily ashamed of my folly."

iuses, Dibdin was generous, careless, and improvident in his habits, dying at last poor and neglected.

Dr. Johnson was so extremely short-sighted that writing, re-writing, and correcting upon paper were very inconvenient for him; he was therefore accustomed to revolve a subject very carefully in his mind, forming sentences and periods with minute care; and by means of his remarkable memory he retained them with great precision for use and final transmission to paper. When he began, therefore, with pen in hand, his production of copy was very rapid, and it required scarcely any corrections. Boswell says that posterity will be astonished when they are told that many of these discourses, which might be supposed to be labored with all the slow attention of literary leisure, were written in haste, as the moments pressed, without even being read over by Johnson before they were printed. Sir John Hawkins says that the original manuscripts of the "Rambler" passed through his hands, "and by the perusal of them I am warranted to say, as was said of Shakspeare by the players of his time, that he never blotted a line." Johnson tells us that he wrote the life of Savage in six-and-thirty hours. He also wrote his "Hermit of Teneriffe" in a single night. When we consider the amount of literary work performed by Johnson, say in the period of seven years, while "he sailed a long and painful voyage round the world of the English language," and produced his dictionary, we must give him credit for the most remarkable industry and great rapidity of production. During these seven years he found time also to complete his "Rambler," the "Vanity of Human Wishes," and his tragedy, besides several minor literary performances. No wonder he developed hypochondria. Burke was a very slow and painstaking producer; it is even said that he had all his works printed at a private press before submitting them to his publisher.

Hume was more rapid, even careless with his first edition of a work, but went on correcting each new one to the day of his death.[1] Macaulay, in his elaborate speeches, did not write them out beforehand, but *thought* them out, trusting to his memory to recall every epigrammatic statement and every felicitous epithet which he had previously forged in his mind, so that when the time came for their delivery they appeared to spring forth as the spontaneous outpouring of his feelings and sentiments, excited by the questions discussed. Wendell Phillips followed a similar method.

Thomas Paine, the political and deistical writer, was under contract to furnish a certain amount of matter for each number of the "Pennsylvania Magazine." Aitken the publisher had great difficulty in getting him to fulfil his agreement. Paine's indo-

---

[1] When Hume was in Paris receiving the homage of the philosophers, three little boys were brought before him, who complimented him after the fashion of grown persons, expressing their admiration for his beautiful history. These children afterwards succeeded to the throne as Louis XVI., his brother, Louis XVIII., and Charles X.

lence was such that he was always behindhand with
his engagements. Finally, after it had become too
late to delay longer, Aitken would go to his house,
tell him the printers were standing idle waiting for
his copy, and insist upon his accompanying him to
the office. Paine would do so, when pen, ink, and
paper would be placed before him, and he would sit
thoughtfully, but produce nothing until Aitken gave
him a large glass of brandy. Even then he would
delay. The publisher naturally feared to give him
a second glass, thinking that it would disqualify him
altogether; but, on the contrary, his brain seemed to
be illumined by it, and when he had swallowed the
third glass, — quite enough to have made Mr. Aitken
dead drunk, — he would write with rapidity, intelligence, and precision, his ideas appearing to flow faster
than he could express them on paper. The copy produced under the fierce stimulant was remarkable for
correctness, and fit for the press without revision.[1]

Charlotte Brontë was a very slow producer of literary work, and was obliged to choose her special days.
Often for a week, and sometimes longer, she could
not write at all; her brain seemed to be dormant.
Then, without any premonition or apparent inducing
cause, she would awake in the morning, go to her
writing-desk, and the ideas would come with more

[1] This was the Tom Paine on whom was written one of the
most felicitous of epitaphs : —

"Here lies Tom Paine, who wrote in Liberty's defence,
But in his 'Age of Reason' lost his 'Common Sense.'."

rapidity than she could pen them. Mrs. Gaskell the novelist, a friend of the Brontés, was exactly the opposite in her style of composition. She could sit down at any hour and lose herself in the process of the story she was composing. She was also a prolific authoress, of whom George Sand said: "She has done what neither I nor other female writers in France can accomplish; she has written novels which excite the deepest interest in men of the world, and which every girl will be the better for reading." Bacon [1] often had music played in the room adjoining his library, saying that he gathered inspiration from its strains. Warburton said music was always a necessity to him when engaged in intellectual labor. Curran, the great Irish barrister, had also his favorite mode of meditation; it was with his violin in hand. He would seem to forget himself, running voluntaries over the strings, while his imagination, collecting its tones, was kindling and invigorating all his faculties for the coming contest at the bar. Bishop Beveridge adopted Bacon's plan, and said, "When music sounds sweetest in my ears, truth commonly flows the clearest in my mind." Even

---

[1] Bacon was full of crotchets, so to speak. In spring, he would go out for a drive in an open coach while it rained, to receive "the benefit of irrigation," which, he contended, was "most wholesome because of the nitre in the air, and the universal spirit of the world." He had extraordinary notions and indulged them freely, such as dosing himself with chemicals, rhubarb, nitre, saffron, and many other medicines. At every meal his table was abundantly strewn with flowers and sweet herbs.

the cold, passionless Carlyle said music was to him a kind of inarticulate speech which led him to the edge of the infinite, and permitted him for a moment to gaze into it.

John Foster, the English essayist, declared that the special quality of genius was " the power to light its own fire;" and certainly Sir Walter Scott was a shining example of this truth. Shelley, a poet of finer but less robust fibre, decided that " the mind, in creating, is as a fading coal, which some passing influence, like an invisible wind, wakens into momentary brightness."

As already remarked, ten years transpired between the first sketch of the " Traveller," which was made in Switzerland, and its publication ; but the history of the " Vicar of Wakefield " was quite different. Goldsmith hastened the closing pages to raise money, being terribly pressed for the payment of numerous small bills, and also by his landlady for rent. He was actually under arrest for this last debt, and sent to Dr. Johnson to come to him at once. Understanding very well what was the trouble, Johnson sent him a guinea, and came in person as soon as he could. He found, on arriving, that Goldsmith had already broken the guinea and was drinking a bottle of wine purchased therewith. The Doctor put the cork into the bottle, and began to talk over the means of extricating the impecunious author from his troubles. Goldsmith told Johnson that he had just finished a small book, and wished he would look at it; perhaps it would bring in some money. He brought forth the manuscript of the "Vicar of Wakefield." Johnson hastily glanced over it, paused, read a chapter carefully, bade Goldsmith to be of good cheer, and hastened away with the new story to Newbury the publisher, who, solely on Johnson's recommendation, gave him sixty pounds for the manuscript and threw it into his desk, where it remained undisturbed for two years.[1]

A voluminous writer once explained to Goldsmith the advantage of employing an amanuensis. "How do you manage it?" asked Goldsmith. "Why, I walk about the room and dictate to a clever man, who puts down very correctly all that I tell him, so that I have nothing to do but to look it over and send it to the printers." Goldsmith was delighted with the idea, and asked his friend to send the scribe to him. The next day the penman came with his implements, ready to catch his new employer's words and to record them. Goldsmith paced the room with great thoughtfulness, just as his friend had described to him, back and forth, back and forth, several times; but after racking his brain to no purpose for half an hour, he gave it up. He handed the scribe a guinea, saying, "It won't do, my friend; I find that my head and hand must work together."

---

[1] It is curious that St. Pierre's story of Paul and Virginia, which has since proved one of the most popular tales ever written, was at first listened to by the author's friends so coldly that after it was finished he laid it by for months; but when it once got into print the public indorsed it immediately, and fresh editions followed each other in rapid succession.

Milton dictated that immortal poem, "Paradise Lost," his daughters being his amanuenses; but Milton was then blind. It is said of Julius Cæsar that while writing a despatch he could at the same time dictate seven letters to as many clerks. This seems almost miraculous; but in our own day Paul Morphy has performed quite as difficult a feat at chess, playing several games at once, blindfolded.

One of the most eminent and eloquent of American preachers and lecturers, Thomas Starr King, was accustomed to dictate to an amanuensis; but when a difficulty would occur in developing his thought, he would take the pen in his own hand, and, abstracting himself entirely from the wondering reporter by his side, would spend perhaps half an hour in deeper thinking and more exact expression than when he dictated. Those who have examined his manuscript since his death easily perceive that the portions of a sermon or a lecture which he personally wrote are better than those which he poured forth to his amanuensis as he walked the room. On one occasion a friend who was in favor of making the pen and brain work together went to hear Mr. King deliver a lecture on Pope Gregory VII. (Hildebrand), and at its conclusion told the lecturer that he could distinguish, without seeing the manuscript, the portions he wrote with his own hand from those he dictated. He succeeded so well, in the course of half an hour's conversation, as to surprise the orator by hitting on the passages in dispute, and proving his case.

To write an acceptable book, poem, or essay, is quite as much of a trade as to make a clock or shoe a horse. To produce easy-flowing sentences, as they finally appear before the reader's eye, has cost much careful thought, long and patient practice, and even with some famous authors, as we have seen, many hours of writing and re-writing. So far as it is applied to authorship, we are not surprised at Hogarth's remark : " I know no such thing as genius ; genius is nothing but labor and diligence." Buffon's definition is nearly the same ; he says, " Genius is only great patience." Authors are generally very commonplace representatives of humanity, and remarkably like the average citizen whom we meet in our daily walk. Rogers, in his " Table Talk," says : " When literature is the sole business of life, it becomes a drudgery ; when we are able to resort to it only at certain hours, it is a charming relaxation. In my early years I was a banker's clerk, obliged to be at the desk every day from ten to five o'clock, and I shall never forget the delight with which, on returning home, I used to read and write during the evening." He was a great reader, but said that " a man who attempts to read all the new publications must often do as a flea does — skip." [1]

---

[1] Poor, dear Rogers! Smith was disposed to be a little too hard on him. Some one having asked after Rogers's health in Smith's presence, he replied, " He 's not very well." " Why, what 's the matter ? " rejoined the querist. " Oh, don't you know," said Smith, " he 's produced a couplet ; " and added : " When our friend is delivered of a couplet with infinite labor and pain, he takes to

To recur to Charles Dickens, is it generally known that his favorite novel of "David Copperfield" partially relates to the history of his own boyhood? The story of David's employment, when a child, in washing and labelling blacking-bottles in a London cellar, was true of Dickens himself. If it were possible to read between the lines, we should not infrequently find the most effective narrative sketches little less than biography or autobiography. Thackeray and Dickens both wrote under the thin gauze of fiction. "Vivian Gray" is but a photograph of its dilettante author; and every character drawn by Charlotte Brontë is a true portrait, all being confined within so small a circle as to be easily recognizable. Smollett sat for his own personality in that of Roderick Random; while Scott drew many of his most strongly individualized characters, like that of Dominie Sampson, from people in his immediate circle.

Coleridge says of Milton: "In 'Paradise Lost,' indeed in every one of his poems, it is Milton himself whom you see. His Satan, his Adam, his Raphael, almost his Eve, are all John Milton; and it is a sense of this intense egotism that gives one the greatest pleasure in reading Milton's works." It is well known that many of Byron's[1] poetical plots are

his bed, has straw laid down, the knocker tied up, expects his friends to call and make inquiries, and the answer at the door invariably is, 'Mr. Rogers and his little couplet are as well as can be expected'!"

[1] That excellent and conservative critic, Epes Sargent, says of the author of "Don Juan," "He may have been overrated in his

almost literally his personal experiences. This was especially the case as to the " Giaour." A beautiful female slave was thrown into the sea for infidelity, and was terribly avenged by her lover, while Byron was in the East; being impressed with the dramatic character of the tragedy, he gave it expression in a poem. Carlyle says that Satan was Byron's grand exemplar, the hero of his poetry, and the model, apparently, of his conduct. In Bulwer-Lytton's " Disowned," one of his earliest and best stories, the hero, Clarence Linden, a youth of eighteen, while journeying as a pedestrian, makes the acquaintance of a free-and-easy person named Cole, — a gypsy king, — in whose camp he passes the night: all of which was an actual experience of Bulwer himself. Hans Christian Andersen gives us many of his personal experiences in his popular tale, " Only a Fiddler; " so is "Gilbert Gurney," a novel by Theodore Hook, a biography of himself as a practical joker. It will thus be seen that authors do not always draw entirely upon the imagination for incidents, characters, and plot, but that there is from first to last a large amount of actual truth in seeming fiction.

When Goldsmith was a lad of fifteen or there-

day; but his place in English literature must ever be in the front rank of the immortals." " Byron," said Emerson once, " had large utterance, but little to say," — a half-truth pointedly expressed ; but, alluding to Byron's poems in his later life, acknowledging their captivating energy, Emerson denied having uttered, even in conversation, so derogatory a remark of him who was, with all his limitations, a bard palpably inspired.

about, some one gave him a guinea, with which, and
a borrowed horse, he set out for a holiday trip. He
got belated when returning, and, inquiring of a
stranger if he would point out to him a house of
entertainment, was mischievously directed to the
residence of the sheriff of the county. Here he
knocked lustily at the door, and sending his horse
to the stable, ordered a good supper, inviting the
" landlord " to drink a bottle of wine with him. The
next morning, after an ample breakfast, he offered
his guinea in payment, when the squire, who knew
Goldsmith's family, overwhelmed him with confusion
by telling him the truth. Thirty years afterwards
Goldsmith availed himself of this humiliating blunder
at the time he wrote that popular comedy, " She
Stoops to Conquer." When Goldsmith was talking
to a friend of writing a fable in which little fishes
were to be introduced, Dr. Johnson, who was present,
laughed rather sneeringly. " Why do you laugh ? "
asked Goldsmith, angrily. " If you were to write a
fable of little fishes, you would make them speak like
whales ! " The justice of the reproof was perfectly
apparent to Johnson, who was conscious of Goldsmith's superior inventiveness, lightness, and grace
of composition.

Speaking of authors writing from their own personal experience recalls a name which we must not
neglect to mention. Laurence Sterne, author of
" Tristram Shandy," various volumes of sermons, the
" Sentimental Journey," etc., was a curious com-

pound in character, but possessed of real genius. He
was quite a sentimentalist in his writings, and those
who did not know him personally would accredit him
with possessing a tender heart. The fact was, however, as Horace Walpole said of him, "He had too
much sentiment to have any feeling." His mother,
who had run in debt on account of an extravagant
daughter, would have been permitted to remain indefinitely in jail, but for the kindness of the parents of
her pupils. Her son Laurence heeded her not. "A
dead ass was more important to him than a living
mother," says Walpole. Sterne also used his wife
very ill. One day he was talking to Garrick in a fine
sentimental manner in praise of conjugal love and
fidelity. "The husband," said Sterne, "who behaves
unkindly to his wife, deserves to have his house
burned over his head." Garrick's reply was only
just: "If you think so, I hope *your* house is in-
sured." He is known to have been engaged to a
Miss Fourmantel for five years, and then to have
jilted her so cruelly that she ended her days in a mad-
house. Such was the great Laurence Sterne. It was
poetical justice that he should repent at leisure of
his subsequent hasty marriage to one whom he had
known only four weeks. He twice visited the lady
whom he had deceived, in the establishment where
she was confined; and the character of Maria, whom
he so pathetically describes, is drawn from her, showing how cheaply he could coin his pretended feelings.
Contradictions in character are often ludicrous, and

5

go to show that the author and the man are seldom one. What can be more contradictory in the nature of the same individual than Sterne whining over a dead ass and neglecting to relieve a living mother; or Prior addressing the most romantic sonnets to his Chloe, and at the same time indulging a sentimental passion for a barmaid?

Goldsmith's " Deserted Village," according to Mr. Best, an Irish clergyman, relates to the scenes in which Goldsmith was himself an actor. Auburn is a poetical name for the village of Lissoy, county of Westneath. The name of the schoolmaster was Paddy Burns. " I remember him well," says Mr. Best; " he was indeed a man severe to view. A woman called Walsey Cruse kept the ale-house. I have often been within it. The hawthorn bush was remarkably large, and stood in front of the ale-house." The author of the " Deserted Village," however, made his best contemporary " hit " with his poem of the " Traveller." He always distrusted his poetic ability, and this poem was kept on hand some years after it was completed, before he published it in 1764. It passed through several editions in the first year, and proved a golden harvest to Newbury the publisher; but Goldsmith received only twenty guineas for the manuscript.

The character of Sober, in Johnson's " Idler," is a portrait of himself; and he admitted more than once that he had his own outset in life in his mind when he wrote the Eastern story of " Gelaleddin."

Is not "Tristram Shandy" a synonym for its author,
Sterne? Hazlitt and many others fuse the personality
of the author of the "Imaginary Conversations" with
this admirable work from his pen: certainly a high
compliment to Landor, if the portraiture is a likeness.
Walter Savage Landor [1] was a most erratic genius, a
man of uncontrollable passions which led him into
constant difficulties; at times he must have been partially deranged. In all his productions he exhibits
high literary culture; and being born to a fortune, he
was enabled to adapt himself to his most fastidious
tastes, though in the closing years of his life, having
lost his money, he learned the meaning of that bitter
word dependence. The severest critic must accord
him the genius of a poet; but his literar reputation
will rest upon his elaborate prose work, "Imaginary
Conversations" of literary men and statesmen, upon
which he was engaged for more than ten years. He
lived to the age of ninety, and found solace in his pen
to the last.

[1] "I had learned from his works," remarks Lady Blessington,
after meeting Landor at Florence, in May, 1825, "to form a high
opinion of the man as well as the author. But I was not prepared to find in him the courtly, polished gentleman of high
breeding, of manners, deportment, and demeanor, that one might
expect to meet with in one who had passed the greater part of his
life in courts."

CHAPTER III.

As we have already remarked, authors are very much like other people, rarely coming up to the idea formed of them by enthusiastic readers. They are pretty sure to have some idiosyncrasies more or less peculiar; and who, indeed, has not? To know the true character of these individuals, we should see them in their homes rather than in their books.

Having so lately spoken of Landor, we are reminded of another literary character who in many respects resembled him. William Beckford, the English author, utterly despised literary fame, and when he wrote he could afford to do so, for he was a millionnaire. His romance of "Vathek," as an Eastern tale, was pronounced by the critics superior to "Rasselas;" and indeed "Rasselas, Prince of Abyssinia," is hardly in any sense an Eastern tale. "Johnson," says Macaulay, "not content with turning filthy savages, ignorant of their letters and gorged with raw steaks cut from living cows, into philosophers as eloquent and enlightened as himself or his friend Burke, and into ladies as accomplished as Mrs. Lennox or Mrs. Sheridan, transferred the whole domestic system of England to Egypt." Beckford read to Rogers one of his novels in which the hero was a Frenchman who was ridiculously fond of dogs, and in which his own life was clearly depicted. Even this millionnaire author was finally reduced to such necessity as obliged him to sell his private pictures for subsistence. The last which he disposed of was Bellini's portrait of the "Doge of Venice," which was bought for and hung in the National Gallery on the very day that Beckford died, in 1844.

Certainly those authors who give us their own personal experience as a basis for their sketches are no plagiarists. The late Wendell Phillips [1] delighted, in his lecture on the "Lost Arts," to prove that there was nothing new under the sun; a not uncongenial task for this "silver-tongued orator," who was an iconoclast by nature. So early as the age of twenty-five he relinquished the practice of the law because he was unwilling to act under an oath to the Constitution of the United States. In one sense there is nothing new under the sun. Genius has not hesitated to borrow bravely from history and legend. The "Amphitrion" of Molière was adopted from Plautus, who had borrowed it from the Greeks, and they from the Indians. Any one reading a collection of the Arabian stories for the first time will be surprised at meeting so many which are familiar, and which he

---

[1] This man scornfully renounces your civil organizations, — county and city, or governor or army; is his own navy and artillery, judge and jury, legislature and executive. He has learned his lessons in a bitter school. — *Emerson.*

had thought to be of modern birth. La Fontaine borrowed from Petronius the "Ephesian Matron," which had been taken from Greek annals, having been previously transferred from the Arabic, where it appeared taken from the Chinese. There is no ignoring the fact that a large portion of our plots belonged originally to Eastern nations. The graceful, attractive, and patriotic story of William Tell was proven by the elder son of Haller, a century ago, to have been, in the main features, but the revival of a Danish story to be found in Saxo Grammaticus. The interesting legend of the apple was but a fable revived. The English story of Whittington and his Cat was common two thousand years ago in Persia.

When the writer of these pages visited the grand temples of Nikko, in the interior of Japan, he was told that the wonderfully preserved carvings beneath the eaves and on the inner walls, thousands of years old, were executed by one who was known as the "Left-Handed Artist," who was a dwarf, and had but partial use of the right hand. It seems, according to the local legend preserved for so many centuries, that while this artist was working at the ornamentation of the temples at Nikko he saw and fell in love with a beautiful Japanese girl resident in the city; for Nikko was then a city of half a million, though now but a straggling village. The girl would have nothing to do with the artist, on account of his deformity of person. All his attempts to win her affection were vain; she was inflexible. Finally the heart-broken artist returned to Tokio, his native place. Here he carved in wood a life-size figure of his beloved, so perfect and beautiful that the gods endowed it with life, and the sculptor lived with it as his wife, in the enjoyment of mutual love, all the rest of his days. Here, then, in Japan, we have the legend upon which the Greek story of Pygmalion and Galatea is undoubtedly founded.

As regards the subject of plagiarism in general, which is so often spoken of as connected with literary productions, it should be remembered, as Ruskin says, that all men who have sense and feeling are being constantly helped. They are taught by every person whom they meet, and enriched by everything that falls in their way. The greatest is he who has been oftenest aided.[1] " Literature is full of coincidences," says Holmes, "which some love to believe plagiarisms. There are thoughts always abroad in the air, which it takes more wit to avoid than to hit upon."

It has been truthfully said that no man is quite sane ; each one has a vein of folly in his composition, a view which would certainly seem to be illustrated

---

[1] " Every one of my writings," says Goethe, " has been furnished to me by a thousand different persons, by a thousand different things. The learned and the ignorant, the wise and the foolish, infancy and age, have come in turn, generally without having been the least suspicious of it, to bring me the offering of their thoughts, their faculties, their experience ; often have they sown the harvest I have reaped. My work is that of an aggregation of human beings taken from the whole of nature ; it bears the name of Goethe."

by circumstances which are easily recalled. Take, for instance, the fact that Schiller[1] could not write unless surrounded by the scent of decayed apples, with which he kept one drawer of his writing-desk well filled. Could we have a clearer instance of monomania? He also required his cup of strong coffee when he was composing, and the coffee was well "laced" with brandy. Bulwer-Lytton, in his life of Schiller, declares that when he wrote at night he drank hock wine. As an opposite and much more agreeable habit, we have that of Méhul, the French composer, and author of over forty successful operas, who could not produce a note of original music except amid the perfume of roses. His table, writing-desk, and piano were constantly covered with them; in this delicious atmosphere he produced his "Joseph in Egypt," which alone would have entitled him to undying fame.

Father Sarpi, who was Macaulay's favorite historian, best known as the author of the "History of the Council of Trent," having the idea that the atmosphere immediately about him became in a degree impregnated with the mental electricity of his brain, was accustomed to build a paper enclosure about his head and person while he was writing. "All air is

---

[1] When only eighteen years of age, in 1777, he wrote "The Robbers," a tragedy of extraordinary power, though he characterized it at a later day as "a monster for which fortunately there was no original." During a few years after its first publication it was translated into various languages and read all over Europe.

predatory," he said. Salieri, the Venetian composer,
prepared himself for writing by filling a capacious
dish at his side with candy and bonbons, which he
consumed in large quantities during the process.
Sarti, the well-known composer of sacred music, was
obliged to work in the dark, or thought that he was,
as daylight or artificial light of any sort at such
moments utterly disconcerted him. Rossini, on the
contrary, seemed to have no special ideas about his
surroundings when he was in a mood for composing.
He sat down among his friends, laughing and talking
all the while that he was creating, and framing with
marvellous rapidity strains that will live for all time.
The whole of " Tancredi," which first made his fame,
was produced in the very midst of social life and
merry companionship. He said he found inspiration
in the cheerful human voices about him. As to the
peculiarities we have noted in others, they must at
first have been mere affectations ; but such is the
force of habit, that no doubt these individuals became
confirmed in them and really believed their indulgence a necessity.

Carneades, the Greek philosopher, so famed for his
subtle and powerful eloquence, before sitting down to
write dosed himself with hellebore, — a strange resort,
as it is supposed to act directly upon the liver, and
only very slightly to stimulate the brain, besides being
a fatal poison in large doses. It is well known that
Dryden resorted to singular aids as preparatory to
literary composition ; being in the habit of first having

himself bled and then making a meal of raw meat.
The former process, he contended, rendered his brain
clear, and the latter stimulated his imagination. In
1668 he held the position now filled by Tennyson, as
poet-laureate of England. He was a notable instance
of power in poetry, satire, and indecency, whom Cowper characterized as a lewd writer but a chaste companion. Dryden's own couplet will forcibly apply to
himself : —

> "O gracious God ! how far have we
> Profaned thy heavenly gift of poesy ! "

His " Essay on Dramatic Poesy," according to Dr.
Johnson, entitled him to be considered the father of
English criticism. His dramas, such as " Mariage
à-la-Mode," " All for Love," " Don Sebastian," etc.,
were, by reason of their indecency, examples of per-
verted genius. He was sixty-six years old when he
wrote his " Alexander's Feast," by far his best literary effort. While Macaulay calls him " an illustrious
renegade," [1] Dr. Johnson says, " he found the English

---

[1] Such facts as the following lead us to draw rather disparaging
conclusions as to Dryden's character. He was short of money at
a certain time, and sent to Jacob Tonson, his publisher, asking
him to advance him some, which Tonson declined to do ; whereupon Dryden sent him these lines, adding, " Tell the dog that he
who wrote these can write more": —

> "With leering looks, bull-faced, and freckled skin,
> With two left legs, and Judas-colored hair,
> And frowzy pores, that taint the ambient air ! "

The bookseller felt the force of the description, and to avoid
trouble immediately sent the insulting poet the money.

language brick and left it marble," — a most superlative and ridiculous comment to be made by so erudite a critic.

When James Francis Stephens, the English entomologist, was about to write, he mounted a horse and arranged his thoughts and sentences while at full gallop. This was a plan that Sir Walter Scott also adopted when he wrote " Marmion," galloping up and down the shore of the Firth of Forth. But he concluded that he could do better pen-work in a more rational manner, so this practice did not become habitual with him. Scott made an interesting confession when writing the third volume of " Woodstock." He declared that he had not the slightest idea how the story was to be wound up to a catastrophe. He said he could never lay out a plan for a novel and stick to it. " I only tried to make that which I wrote diverting and interesting, leaving the rest to fate." Sir David Dalrymple (afterwards Lord Hailes) was a voluminous author on historical and antiquarian subjects. His " Annals of Scotland," published in 1792, was his most important work ; Dr. Johnson called it " a book which will always sell, it has such a stability of dates, such a certainty of facts, and such punctuality of citation." Lord Hailes's mode of writing was very domestic, so to speak, being performed by the parlor fire, and amid his family circle of wife and children. He was always ready to answer any appeal, however trifling, and to enter cheerfully into all current family affairs. This seems hardly reconcilable with the extreme nicety and absolute correctness of his work.

Cormontaigne, the French military engineer, wrote an elaborate treatise on fortification in the trenches and while under fire. The Duke of Wellington, when his army was at San Christoval awaiting battle with the French, wrote a complete essay on the purpose of establishing a bank at Lisbon after the English methods. Thomas Hood wrote at night, when the house was still and the children asleep. Ouida [1] writes with her dogs only as companions, while they lie contentedly at her feet in the bright sunny library whose windows overlook the valley of the Arno and her well-beloved Florence. In the flower-garden before the villa her favorite Newfoundland dog, not long since dead, lies buried beneath a marble monument. Her productive literary capacity is wonderfully rapid, but the demand far exceeds it, and the prices she receives are unprecedented. She has few if any intimate friends, and no confidants, leading a life of almost perfect isolation.

Notwithstanding common-sense and experience have ever taught that the brain is capable of producing its best work when in its normal condition, still a host of writers have resorted systematically to some

---

[1] The real name of this lady is Louise de la Rame. Her father was a Frenchman and her mother of English birth. The name of "Ouida" is an infantine corruption of her baptismal name Louise. Her first episode in love occurred when she was a maiden of forty years, resulting finally in a most embittering disappointment.

sort of artificial stimulant to aid them in authorship. History tells us that Æschylus, Eupolis, Cratinus, and Ennius, in the olden time, would not attempt to compose until they had become nearly intoxicated with wine. In more modern times, we know that Shadwell, De Quincey, Psalmanazar the famous literary impostor, Coleridge, Robert Hall, and Bishop Horsley stimulated themselves with fabulous doses of opium. Alfred de Musset, Burns, Edgar A. Poe, Dickens, Christopher North, and a host of others whose names will only too readily occur to the reader, were reckless as to the use of alcohol. They were both fed and consumed by stimulants. We are inclined, however, to forgive much of indiscretion in a brilliant and ardent imagination. Schiller, so lately referred to, was addicted to Rhenish wine in large quantities. Blackstone, author of "Commentaries on the Laws of England," remarkable for his clearness and purity of style, never wrote without a bottle of port by his side, which he emptied at a sitting.

It is related of Bacon that he did not drink wine when engaged in pen-craft, but he was accustomed to have sherry poured into a broad open vessel, and to inhale its fragrance with great relish. He believed that his brain thus received the stimulating influence without the narcotic effect. Sheridan could neither write nor talk until warmed by wine. If about to make a speech in the House, he would, just before rising, swallow half a tumbler of raw brandy. Burke presents a remarkable contrast; his great stimulant being *hot water.* The most impassioned passages of his speeches had no other physical inspiration; all the rest came from his glowing soul, which was powerful enough to vitalize his body for an oration of four hours' length. The food which sustained him on such occasions was *cold* mutton, the drink being *hot* water. Brandy and port, even claret and champagne, would have driven him wild, though they were the ordinary stimulants of his contemporaries. Burke was, like Burns, a man of an excitable temperament; but, unlike Burns, he was wise enough to avoid all dangerous alcoholic excitements, which increased the impulsive elements of his nature and diminished the action of his reason. It will be observed that even in the occasional violence of his invective, his passion is still reasoned passion, or reason penetrated by passion, so as to reach the will as well as to convince the understanding.

Addison, with his bottle of wine at each end of the long gallery at Holland House, where he walked back and forth perfecting his thoughts, will be sure to be recalled by the reader in this connection. Consciously or unconsciously he took a glass of the stimulant at each turn, until wrought up to the required point. Dr. Radcliffe, the eminent London physician and author, was often found in an over-stimulated condition. Summoned one evening to a lady patient, he found that he was too much inebriated to count her pulse, and so muttered, "Drunk! dead drunk!" and hastened homeward. The next morning, while experiencing intense mortification over the recollection, he received a note from the same patient, in which she said, she knew only too well her own condition when he called, and begged him to keep the matter secret, enclosing a hundred-pound note.

Burns was wont oftentimes to compose, as he tells us, " by the lee side of a bowl of punch, which had overset every mortal in the company except the haut-boy and the Muse."[1] Of course "the pernicious expedient of stimulants," as Carlyle would say, only served to use up more rapidly his already wasted physical strength. Sometimes, however, Burns would compose walking in the open fields. His first effort was to master some pleasing air, and then he easily produced appropriate words for it. One noble trait of Burns's character should not be forgotten. Though he died in abject poverty, he did not leave a farthing of debt owed to any one. Nothing could be finer than Carlyle's exordium in his review of Lockhart's " Life of Burns:" " With our readers in general, with men of right feeling anywhere, we are not required to plead for Burns. In pitying admiration he lies enshrined in all our hearts, in a far nobler mausoleum than that one of marble; neither will his works ever as they

---

[1] Burns realized his own unfortunate lack of self-control, but he gives good advice to others, as follows : —

> " Reader, attend ! Whether thy soul
> Soars fancy's flights beyond the pole,
> Or darkling grubs this earthly hole
> In low pursuit, —
> Know, prudent, cautious self-control
> Is wisdom's root."

are, pass away from the memory of men. While the Shakspeares and Miltons roll on like mighty rivers through the country of Thought, bearing fleets of traffickers and assiduous pearl-fishers on their waves, this little Valclusa Fountain will also arrest our eye; for this also is of Nature's own and most cunning workmanship, bursts from the depths of the earth, with a full gushing current, into the light of day; and often will the traveller turn aside to drink of its clear waters, and muse among its rocks and pines."

As we have seen, musical composers, like those devoted to literature, are apt to have singular fancies. Glück, who was at one time the music-teacher of Marie Antoinette, and whose operas have entitled him to a niche in the temple of fame, could compose only while under the influence of champagne, two bottles of which he would consume at a sitting. He was an eccentric individual, singing and acting the part for which he at the same time wrote the music. Handel, when he felt the inspiration of music upon him, sought the graveyard of some village church, and on the moss-grown stones laid his portfolio and wrote his notes, never trying their harmony until he had completed the entire piece. It seems strange to us, in the light of his great genius, to think what an immense glutton Handel was. We have already spoken of this, but recur to it again in this connection; for one is puzzled how to reconcile the grossness of his appetite with his æsthetic nature. He could devour more food at one dinner than any other composer in

three.[1] Never before was height and breadth of
musical genius combined with such enormous appetite for the good things of the table ; and yet his
digestion was as sound as his love and need of food
was portentous. Everything about this great composer was gigantesque, as became a giant. His for-
getive brain was recruited by the nourishment drawn
from a ravenous yet healthy stomach.

Unlike Handel's mode of composition, Mozart
played his music upon the harpsichord before he
wrote a note of it upon paper; but he had a most
exalted idea of his mission, and prepared himself
for composition, not by partaking of a hearty dinner,
but by reading favorite classic authors for hours
before beginning what was to him a sacred task.
His favorite authors on such occasions were Dante
and Petrarch. He chose the morning for his compositions ; but he would often delay writing his
scores for the musicians until it was too late to copy
them, and sometimes failed altogether to write out
the part intended to be performed by himself; yet
when the moment arrived, so perfectly had all been
arranged in his mind, he played it without hesi-
tation, instrument in hand. The Emperor Joseph,
before whom he was performing on one occasion,
observed that the music-sheet before him contained

---

[1] It is said to have been when Handel's great appetite was
being spoken of as rather at antipodes with his glorious musical
conceptions, that Sydney Smith remarked, " his own idea of
heaven was eating *foie gras* to the sound of trumpets ! "

no characters whatever, and asked, " Where is your part ? " " Here," replied Mozart, pointing with his finger to his forehead.[1] He became blind before he was forty years of age, but continued to compose. The duet and chorus in " Judas Maccabæus," and some others of his finest efforts were produced after his total deprivation of sight; nor did he cease to conduct his oratorios in public on account of his blindness.

Spontini, the Italian composer, like Sarti, could only produce his music in the dark, dictating to some one sitting in an adjoining room. Rossini, author of the " Barber of Seville," composed his music as the elder Dumas was accustomed to write ; namely, in bed. Offenbach, of opera-bouffe notoriety, almost lived on coffee while creating his dainty aerial music. The writer of these pages met this composer in Paris in 1873, when he was at the height of his popularity, and was told by him that he took no wine or spirit until *after* his work of composition was completed. Cimarosa, the Italian composer, who won national fame before he was twenty-five, derived his inspiration from the noisy crowd. Auber, the French composer, could write only among the green fields and the silence of the country. Sacchini, another Italian composer, lost the

---

[1] The overture to " Don Giovanni," generally considered to be the best portion of the opera, was written by Mozart in *two hours*, he having overslept himself. It was copied in great haste by the scribes, and actually played for the first time without rehearsal.

thread of his inspiration unless attended by his favorite cats, they sitting all about him while he worked,
some upon the table, some on the floor, and one
always perched contentedly between his shoulders on
his neck; he declared that their purring was to him a
soothing anodyne, and fitted him for composition by
making him content. Eugène Sue would not take
up his pen except in full dress and with white kids
on his hands. Thus he produced the "Mysteries of
Paris," which Dumas designated as "one-gross-of-
gloves long." Buffon would only sit down to write
after taking a bath and donning pure linen with
a full frilled bosom. Haydn[1] declared that he
could not compose unless he wore the large seal-ring
which Frederick the Great had given him. He would
sit wrapped in silence for an hour or more, after
which he would seize his pen and write rapidly without touching a musical instrument; and he rarely
altered a line. In early life, poor, freezing in a miserable garret, he studied the rudiments of his favorite art by the side of an old broken harpsichord.
For a period of six years he endured a bitter conflict with poverty, being often compelled for the sake
of warmth to lie in bed most of the day as well as
the night. Finally he was relieved from this thral-

---

[1] The poet Carpani once asked his friend Haydn how it happened that his church music was of so animating and cheerful a
character. "I cannot make it otherwise," replied the composer;
"I write according to the thoughts which I feel. When I think
of God, my heart is so full of joy that the notes dance and leap
as it were from my pen."

dom by the generosity of his patron, Prince Esterhazy, a passionate lover of music, who appointed him his chapel-master, with a salary sufficient to keep him supplied with the ordinary comforts of life.

Crébillon the elder, a celebrated lyric poet and member of the French Academy, was enamoured of solitude, and could only write effectively under such circumstances. His imagination teemed with romances, and he produced eight or ten dramas which enjoyed popularity in their day, — about 1776. One day, when he was alone and in a deep reverie, a friend entered his study hastily. " Don't disturb me," cried the author, " I am enjoying a moment of happiness: I am going to hang a villain of a minister, and banish another who is an idiot."

We have lately mentioned Dumas. Hans Christian Andersen, speaking of the various habits of authors, thus refers to the elder Dumas, with whom he was intimate : " I generally found him in bed," even long after mid-day, where he lay, with pen, ink, and paper by his side, and wrote his newest drama. On entering his apartment I found him thus one day ; he nodded kindly to me, and said : ' Sit down a minute. I have just now a visit from my Muse ; she will be going directly.' He wrote on, and after a brief silence shouted ' *Vivat*,' sprang out of bed, and said, ' The third act is finished ! ' " [1]

---

[1] Dumas was a charming story-teller in society. Being at a large party one evening, the hostess tried to draw him out to exhibit his powers in this line. At last, weary of being importuned,

Lamartine was peculiar in his mode of composition, and never saw his productions, after the first draft, until they were printed, bound, and issued to the public. He was accustomed to walk forth in his park during the after part of the day, or of a moonlit evening, with pencil and pieces of paper, and whatever ideas struck him he recorded. That was the end of the matter so far as he was concerned. These pieces of paper he threw into a special box, without a number or title upon them. His literary secretary with much patient ability assorted these papers, arranged them as he thought best, and sold them to the publishers at a royal price. We know of no similar instance where authorship and recklessness combined have produced creditable results. Certainly such indifference argued only the presence of weakness and irresponsibility, which were indeed prominent characteristics of Lamartine.

The remarkable facility with which Goethe's poems were produced is said to have resembled improvisation, an inspiration almost independent of his own purposes. "I had come," he says, "to regard the poetic talent dwelling in me entirely as nature; the rather that I was directed to look upon external nature as its proper subject. The exercise of this poetic gift might be stimulated and determined by occasion, but it

---

he said : "Every one to his trade, madam. The gentleman who entered your drawing-room just before me is a distinguished artillery officer. Let him bring a cannon here and fire it; then I will tell one of my little stories."

flowed forth more joyfully and richly, when it came
involuntarily, or even against my will." Addison,
whose style is perhaps the nearest to perfection in
ancient or modern literature, did not reach that standard without much patient labor. Pope tells us that
" he would show his verses to several friends, and
would alter nearly everything that any of them hinted
was wrong. He seemed to be distrustful of himself,
and too much concerned about his character as a poet,
or, as he expressed it, ' too solicitous for that kind of
praise which God knows is a very little matter after
all.'" Pope himself published nothing until it had
been a twelvemonth on hand, and even then the printer's proofs were full of alterations. On one occasion
this was carried so far that Dodsley, his publisher,
thought it better to have the whole recomposed than
to attempt to make the necessary alterations. Yet
Pope admits that " the things that I have written
fastest have always pleased the most. I wrote the
' Essay on Criticism ' fast, for I had digested all the
matter in prose before I began it in verse."

" I never work better," says Luther, " than when I
am inspired by anger: when I am angry, I can write,
pray, and preach well; for then my whole temperament is quickened, my understanding sharpened, and
all mundane vexations and temptations depart."
We are reminded of Burke's remark in this connection : " A vigorous mind is as necessarily accompanied with violent passions as a great fire with
great heat." Luther, however ribald he may have

been at times, had the zeal of honesty. There was not a particle of vanity or self-sufficiency in the great reformer. "Do not call yourselves Lutherans," he said to his followers; "call yourselves Christians. Who and what is Luther? Has Luther been crucified for the world?"

Churchill,[1] the English poet and satirist, was so averse to correcting and blotting his manuscript that many errors were unexpunged, and many lines which might easily have been improved were neglected. When expostulated with upon this subject by his publisher, he replied that erasures were to him like cutting away so much of his flesh; thus expressing his utter repugnance to an author's most urgent duty. Though Macaulay tells us that his vices were not so great as his virtues, still he was dissipated and licentious. Cowper was a great admirer of his poetry, and called him "the great Churchill." George Wither,[2] the English poet, satirist, and political writer, was compelled to watch and fast when he was called upon to write. He "went out of himself," as he said, at such times, and if he tasted meat or drank one glass of wine he could not produce a verse or sentence.

Rogers, who wrote purely *con amore*, took all the time to perfect his work which his fancy dictated, and

[1] Churchill was a spendthrift of fame, and enjoyed all his revenue while he lived; posterity owes him little, and pays him nothing. — *Disraeli*.

[2] Wither had a strange career. He was imprisoned for some published satire in 1613, at the age of twenty-five, but lived to his eightieth year, dying finally in misery and obscurity.

certainly over-refined many of his compositions. The
" Pleasures of Memory " occupied him seven years.
In writing, composing, re-writing, and altering his
" Columbus " and " Human Life," each required just
double that period of time before the fastidious author felt satisfied to call it finished. Besides this, the
second edition of each went through another series
of emendations. The observant reader will find that
Rogers has often weakened his first and best thoughts
by this elaboration. The expression of true genius
oftenest comes, like the lightning, in its full power
and effect at the first flash. " Every event that a man
would master," says Holmes, " must be mounted on
the run, and no man ever caught the reins of a thought
except as it galloped by him." One who has had
years of active editorial experience on the daily press
can hardly conceive of such fastidious slowness of
composition as characterizes some authors. Sir Joshua
Reynolds, in speaking of Rogers, Rochefoucauld, Cowper, and others, and their dilatory habits of composition, says, that although men of ordinary talents
may be highly satisfied with their productions, men of
genius never are, — an assumption which is not borne
out by facts, as we shall have occasion to show in
these chapters. Modesty is not always the characteristic of genius ; and very few popular writers are without a due share of vanity in their natures.

Voltaire somewhere says that an author should
write with the rapidity which genius inspires, but
should correct with care and deliberation ; which

doubtless expresses the process adopted by this unscrupulous but versatile writer, of whom Carlyle said :
" With the single exception of Luther, there is perhaps, in these modern ages, no other man of a merely
intellectual character, whose influence and reputation
have become so entirely European as that of Voltaire."
Sydney Smith was so rapid a producer that he had
not patience even to read over his compositions when
finished. He would throw down his manuscript and
say : " There, it is done ; now, Kate, do look it over,
and put dots to the *i's* and strokes to the *t's*." He
was once advised by a fashionable publisher to attempt
a three-volume novel. " Well," said he, after some
seeming consideration, " if I do so, I must have an
archdeacon for my hero, to fall in love with the pew-
opener, with the clerk for a confidant ; tyrannical
interference of the church-wardens ; clandestine cor-
respondence concealed under the hassock ; appeal
to the parishioners," etc. He was overflowing with
humor to the very close of life. He wrote to Lady
Carlisle during his last illness, saying, " If you hear of
sixteen or eighteen pounds of human flesh, they be-
long to *me*. I look as if a curate had been taken out
of me."

Buffon caused his " Époques de la Nature " to be
copied eighteen times, so many corrections and changes
were made. As he was then (1778) over seventy
years of age, one would think this an evidence that his
mind was failing him. Pope covered with memoranda
every scrap of clear paper which came in his way.

Some of his most elaborate literary work was begun and finished on the backs of old letters and bits of yellow wrappers. We do not wonder that such fragmentary manuscript always suggested the idea of revision and correction. It is difficult to understand why Pope should have assumed this small virtue of economy and yet often have been lavish in other directions; indeed, it may be questioned whether it was intended to be an act of economy. Such petty parsimony is inexplicable, but certainly it grew into a fixed habit with him. We believe it was Swift who first called him " paper-saving Pope; " but Swift was nearly as eccentric a paper-saver as Pope. He wrote to Dr. Sheridan: " Keep very regular accounts, in large books and a fair hand; not like me, who, to save paper, confuse everything! " Miss Mitford had the same habit of writing upon waste scraps of paper, fly-leaves of books, envelopes, and odd rejected bits, all in so small a hand as to be nearly illegible. William Hazlitt was also remarkable for the same practice, and we are told that he even made the first outline of some of his essays on the walls of his chamber, much to the annoyance of his landlady.

Some idea of the rapidity with which Byron wrote may be inferred from the fact that the " Prisoner of Chillon " was written in two days and sent away complete to the printer. The traveller in Switzerland does not fail to visit the house — once a wayside inn, at Morges, on the Lake of Geneva — where Byron wrote this poem while detained by a rainstorm, in 1816. On the heights close at hand is the Castle of Wuffens, dating back to the tenth century. Morges is a couple of leagues from Lausanne, and the spot where Gibbon finished his "Rise and Fall of the Roman Empire," in 1787. Colton, the philosophical but erratic author of "Lacon," wrote that entire volume upon covers of letters and such small scraps of paper as happened to be at hand when a happy thought inspired him. Having completed a sentence, and rounded it to suit his fancy, he threw it into a pile with hundreds of others, which were finally turned over to the printer in a cloth bag. No classification or system of arrangement was observed. Colton exhibited all the singularities that only too often characterize genius, especially as regards improvidence and recklessness of habit. He lived unattended, in a single room in Princes Street, Soho, London, in a neglected apartment containing scarcely any furniture. He wrote very illegibly upon a rough deal table with a stumpy pen. He was finally so pressed with debts that he absconded to avoid his London creditors, though he held the very comfortable vicarage of Kew, in Surrey.

Montaigne, the French philosopher and essayist, whose writings have been translated into every modern tongue, like the musician Sacchini was marvellously fond of cats, and would not sit down to write without his favorite by his side. Thomas Moore required complete isolation when he did literary work, and shut himself up, as did Charles Dickens. He was a very slow and painstaking producer. Some friend having congratulated him upon the seeming facility and appropriateness with which a certain line was introduced into a poem he had just published, Moore replied, "Facility! that line cost me hours of patient labor to achieve." His verses, which read so smoothly, and which appear to have glided so easily from his pen, were the result of infinite labor and patience. His manuscript, like Tennyson's, was written, amended, rewritten, and written again, until it was finally satisfactory to his critical ear and fancy. "Easy writing," said Sheridan, "is commonly damned hard reading."

Bishop Warburton tells us that he could "only write in a hand-to-mouth style" unless he had all his books about him; and that the blowing of an east wind, or a fit of the spleen, incapacitated him for literary work; and still another English bishop could write only when in full canonicals, a fact which he frankly admitted. Milton would not attempt to compose except between the vernal and autumnal equinoxes, at which season his poetry came as if by inspiration, and with scarcely a mental effort.[1] Thomson, Collins, and Gray entertained very similar ideas, which when expressed so incensed Dr. Johnson that he publicly ridiculed them. Crabbe fancied that there

[1] Dr. Johnson was not particularly inclined to "smash images;" but when he looked for the first time upon Callcott's picture of "Milton and his Daughters," one of whom holds a pen as if about to write from his dictation, the doctor coolly remarked, "The daughters were never taught to write!"

was something in the effect of a sudden fall of snow that in an extraordinary manner stimulated him to poetic composition ; while Lord Orrery found no stimulant equal to a fit of the gout! — all of which fancies are but mild forms of monomania. James Hogg (the Ettrick Shepherd) was only too glad to write without any of these accessories, when he could get any material to write upon. He used to employ a bit of slate, for want of the necessary paper and ink. The son of an humble Scottish farmer, he experienced all sorts of misfortunes in his endeavors to pursue literature as a calling. He was both a prose and poetic writer of considerable native genius, and formed one of the well-drawn characters of Christopher North's " Noctes Ambrosianæ." N. P. Willis in the latter years of his life was accustomed to ride on horseback before he sat down to write. He believed there was a certain nervo-vital influence imparted from the robust health and strength of the animal to the rider, as he once told the writer of these pages ; and, so far as one could judge, the influence upon himself certainly favored such a conclusion.

Some authors frankly acknowledge that they have not the necessary degree of patience to apply themselves to the correction of their manuscripts. Ovid, the popular Roman poet, admitted this. Such people may compose with pleasure, but there is the end ; neither a sense of responsibility nor a desire for correctness can overcome their constitutional laziness. Pope, Dryden, Moore, Coleridge, Swift, — in short, nine tenths of the popular authors of the past and the present, all change, correct, amplify, or contract, and interline more or less every page of manuscript which they produce, and often to such a degree as greatly to confuse the compositors. Richard Savage, the unfortunate English poet, could not, or would not, bring himself to correct his faulty sentences, being greatly indebted to the intelligence of the proof-reader for the presentable form in which his writings finally appeared. Julius Scaliger, a celebrated scholar and critic, was, on the other hand, an example of remarkable correctness, so that his manuscript and the printer's pages corresponded exactly, page for page and line for line. Hume,[1] the historian, was never done with his manifold corrections ; his sense of responsibility was unlimited, and his appreciation of his calling was grand. Fénelon and Gibbon were absolutely correct in their first efforts ; and so was Adam Smith, though he dictated to an amanuensis.

We are by no means without sympathy for those writers who dread and avoid the reperusal and correction of their manuscripts. Only those who are familiar with the detail of book-making can possibly realize its trying minutiæ. When one has finished the composition and writing of a chapter, his work

---

[1] Such a superiority do the pursuits of literature possess over other occupation, that even he who attains but a mediocrity merits pre-eminence above those that excel the most in the common and vulgar professions. — *Hume.*

is only begun ; it must be read and re-read with
care, to be sure of absolute correctness. When once
in type, it must be again carefully read for the correction of printer's errors, and again revised by second proof; and finally a third proof is necessary, to
make sure that all errors previously marked have
been corrected. By this time, however satisfactory
in composition, the text becomes " more tedious than
a twice-told tale." Any author must be singularly
conceited who can, after such experience, take up a
chapter or book of his own production and read it
with any great degree of satisfaction. Godeau, Bishop
of Venice, used to say that " to compose is an author's
heaven ; to correct, an author's purgatory ; but to
revise the press, an author's hell!"

Guido Reni, whose superb paintings are among
the gems of the Vatican, in the height of his fame
would not touch pencil or brush except in full
dress. He ruined himself by gambling and dissolute habits, and became lost as to all ambition for
that art which had been so grand a mistress to him in
the beginning. He finally arrived at that stage where
he lost at the gaming-table and in riotous living what
he earned by contract under one who managed his
affairs, giving him a stipulated sum for just so much
daily work in his studio. Such was the famous
author of that splendid example of art, the " Martyrdom of Saint Peter," in the Vatican. Parmigiano,
the eminent painter, was full of the wildness of genius.
He became mad after the philosopher's stone, jilting

art as a mistress, though his eager creditors forced him to set once more to work, though to little effect.

Great painters, like great writers, have had their peculiar modes of producing their effects. Thus Domenichino was accustomed to assume and enact before the canvas the passion and character he intended to depict with the brush. While engaged upon the " Martyrdom of Saint Andrew," Caracci, a brother painter, came into his studio and found him in a violent passion. When this fit of abstraction had passed, Caracci embraced him, admitting that Domenichino had proved himself his master, and that he had learned from him the true manner of expressing sentiment or passion upon the canvas.

Richard Wilson, the eminent English landscape-painter, strove in vain, he said, to paint the motes dancing in the sunshine. A friend coming into his studio found the artist sitting dejected on the floor, looking at his last work. The new-comer examined the canvas and remarked critically that it looked like a broad landscape just after a shower. Wilson started to his feet in delight, saying, " That is the effect I intended to represent, but thought I had failed." Poor Wilson possessed undoubted genius, but neglected his art for brandy, and was himself neglected in turn. He was one of the original members of the Royal Academy.

Undoubtedly, genius is at times nonplussed and at fault, like plain humanity, and is helped out of a temporary dilemma by accident, — as when Poussin the painter, having lost all patience in his fruitless attempts to produce a certain result with the brush, impatiently dashed his sponge against the canvas and brought out thereby the precise effect desired ; namely, the foam on a horse's mouth.

Washington Allston [1] is recalled to us in this connection, one of the most eminent of our American painters, and a poet of no ordinary pretensions. "The Sylphs of the Seasons and other Poems" was published in 1813. He was remarkable for his graphic and animated conversational powers, and was the warm personal friend of Coleridge and Washington Irving. Irving says, "His memory I hold in reverence and affection as one of the purest, noblest, and most intellectual beings that ever honored me with his friendship." While living in London he was elected associate of the Royal Academy. Bostonians are familiar with Allston's half-finished picture of "Belshazzar's Feast," upon which he was engaged when death snatched him from his work.

[1] Allston's death was peculiar. It occurred in 1843, after a cheerful evening passed in the midst of his friends. He had just laid his hand on the head of a favorite young friend, and after begging her to live as near perfection as she could, he blessed her with fervent solemnity, and with that blessing on his lips, died.

CHAPTER IV.

It has been said that the first three men in the world were a gardener, a ploughman, and a grazier; while all political economists admit that the real wealth and stamina of a nation must be looked for among the cultivators of the soil. Was it not Swift who declared that the man who could make two ears of corn or two blades of grass grow upon a spot of ground where only one grew before, deserved better of mankind than the whole race of politicians? Bacon, Cowley, Sir William Temple, Buffon, and Addison were all attached to horticulture, and more or less time was devoted by them to the cultivation of trees and plants of various sorts; nor did they fail to record the refined delight and the profit they derived therefrom. Daniel Webster was an enthusiastic agriculturist; so were Washington, Adams, Jefferson, Walter Scott, Horace Greeley, Gladstone, Evarts,[1] Wilder, Loring, Poore, and a host of other contemporaneous and noted men. "They who labor in

---

[1] The farm of William M. Evarts is situated in Vermont. He once, in eulogizing that State, declared that no criminal was allowed to enter its prisons unless he furnished evidence of good moral character before he committed his crime!

the earth," said Jefferson, "are the chosen people
of God."

But the habits and mode of composition adopted by
literary men still crowd upon the memory. Hobbes,
the famous English philosopher, author of a "Treatise on Human Nature," a political work entitled the
"Leviathan," etc., was accustomed to compose in the
open air. The top of his walking-stick was supplied
with pen and inkhorn, and he would pause anywhere
to record his thoughts in the note-book always carried
in his pocket. Virgil rose early in the morning and
wrote at a furious rate innumerable verses, which he
afterwards pruned and altered and polished, as he said,
after the manner of a bear licking her cubs into shape.
The Earl of Roscommon, in his "Essay on Translated
Verse," declared this to be the duty of the poet, —

> "To write with fury and correct with phlegm."

Dr. Darwin, the ingenious English poet, wrote his
works, like some others of whom we have spoken, on
scraps of paper with a pencil while travelling. His
old-fashioned sulky was so full of books as to give
barely room for him to sit and to carry a well-stored
hamper of fruits and sweetmeats, of which he was
immoderately fond.

Rousseau tells us that he composed in bed at night,
or else out of doors while walking, carefully recording
his ideas in his brain, arranging and turning them
many times until they satisfied him, and then he
committed them to paper perfected. He said it was

in vain for him to attempt to compose at a table surrounded by books and all the usual accessories of an author. Irving wrote most of the " Stout Gentleman " mounted on a stile at Stratford-on-Avon, while his friend Leslie, the painter, was engaged in taking sketches of the interesting locality. Jane Taylor, the English poetess and prose writer, began to produce creditable work at a very early age, and used at first to compose tales and dramas while whipping a top, committing them to paper at the close of that somewhat trivial exercise. As she grew older she said that she could find mental inspiration only from outdoor exercise.

Petavius, the learned Jesuit, when composing his " Theologica Dogmata " and other works, would leave his table and pen at the end of every other hour to twirl his chair, first with one hand, then with the other, for ten minutes, by way of exercise. Cardinal Richelieu resorted to jumping in his garden, and in bad weather leaped over the chairs and tables indoors, — an exercise which seemed to have a special charm for him. Samuel Clark, the English philosopher and mathematician, adopted Richelieu's plan of exercise when tired of continuous writing. Pope says, with regard to exercise, " I, like a poor squirrel, am continually in motion, indeed, but it is only a cage of three feet : my little excursions are like those of a shopkeeper, who walks every day a mile or two before his own door, but minds his business all the while."

We are told that Douglas Jerrold, when engaged in preparing literary matter, used to walk back and forth before his desk, talking wildly to himself, occasionally stopping to note down his thoughts. Sometimes he would burst forth in boisterous laughter when he hit upon a droll idea. He was always extremely restless, would pass out of the house into the garden and stroll about, carelessly picking leaves from the trees and chewing them; then suddenly hastening back to his desk, he recorded any thoughts or sentences which had formed themselves in his mind. Jerrold wrote so fine a hand, forming his letters so minutely, that his manuscript was hardly legible to those not accustomed to it. He was very fastidious about his writing-desk, permitting nothing upon it except pen, ink, and paper. Like most persons who habitually resort to stimulants, he could not be content with a single glass of spirits or wine, but consumed many, until he was only too often unfitted for mental labor. Jerrold's wit was of a coarser texture than that of Sheridan, but, unlike his, it came with spontaneous force; it was always ready, though it had not the polish which premeditation is able to impart. Oftentimes his wit was severely sarcastic, but as a rule it was only genial and mirth-provoking.

It was asked in Jerrold's club, on a certain occasion, what was the best definition of dogmatism. "There is but one," he instantly replied, — "the maturity of puppyism." A member remarked one day that the business of a mutual acquaintance was going

to the devil. " All right," said Jerrold; " then he's
sure to get it back again." Another member who
was not very popular with the club, hearing a certain
melody spoken of, said, " That always carries me
away when I hear it." " Cannot some one whistle it?"
asked Jerrold. Another member, who was rather
given to boasting, said : " Very singular ! I dined at
the Marchioness of So-and-so's last week, and we
actually had no fish." " Easily explained," said
Jerrold; " no doubt they had eaten it all upstairs."
When Heraud, a somewhat bombastic versifier, asked
him if he had read his " Descent into Hell," Jerrold
instantly replied, " No ; I had rather see it." Being
asked what was the idea of Harriet Martineau's
rather atheistical book, he answered that it was plain
enough, — " There is no God, and Harriet is his
Prophet." This is even better than the remark of
another wit who, when asked what was the outcome
of a meeting before which three of the ablest and
most dogmatic Positivists in England made speeches,
replied that the result arrived at was this : that there
were three persons and no God. Jerrold could not
confine himself to any regular system of work, but
drove the quill at such times and only to such purpose as his erratic mood indicated, jumping from one
subject to another like one crossing a brook upon
stepping-stones. This, however, was a habit by no
means peculiar to Douglas Jerrold. There are some
ludicrous stories told of him ; like that of his being
pursued by a printer's boy about the town, from house

to club, from club to the theatre, and so on, and finally of his being overtaken, getting into a corner and writing an admirable article with pencil and paper on the top of his hat.

Agassiz,[1] the great Swiss naturalist, who became an adopted and honored son of this country, was singularly unmethodical in his habits of professional labor. If he was suddenly seized with an interest in some scientific inquiry, he would pursue it at once, putting by all present work, though it might be that he had just got fairly started in another direction. " I always like to take advantage," he would say, " of my productive moods." The rule that we must finish one thing before we begin another, had no force with him. An individual connected with the lyceum of a neighboring city called upon Agassiz to induce him to lecture on a certain occasion, but was courteously informed by the scientist that he could not comply with the request. " It will be a great disappointment to our citizens," suggested the caller. " I am sorry for that," replied Agassiz. " We will cheerfully give you double the usual price," added the agent, " if you will accommodate us." " Ah, my dear sir," replied the scientist, with that earnest but genial expression so natural to his manly fea-

[1] E. P. Whipple said of Agassiz in 1866 : "He is not merely a scientific thinker, he is a scientific force ; and no small portion of the immense influence he exerts is due to the energy, intensity, and geniality which distinguish the nature of the man. In personal intercourse he inspires as well as informs ; communicates not only knowledge, but the love of knowledge."

tures, "I cannot afford to waste time in making money."

A very similar habit of composition or study possessed Goldsmith, Coleridge, Wordsworth, Pope, and some others of the poets, who not infrequently laid by a half-constructed composition for two or three years, then finally took up the neglected theme, finished and published it. This unmethodical style of doing things is but one of the many eccentricities of genius. Scott said he never knew a man of much ability who could be perfectly regular in his habits, while he had known many a blockhead who could. Southey and Coleridge were at complete antipodes in regard to regularity of habits and punctuality: the former did everything by rule, the latter nothing. Charles Lamb said of Coleridge, "He left forty thousand treatises on metaphysics and divinity, not one of them complete." Neither Agassiz, Coleridge, nor any of similar irregularity in work, is to be imitated in those respects. Had it not been for Agassiz's far-seeing and vigorous powers, — in short, for his great genius, he could never have accomplished his remarkable mission. The deduction which we naturally draw is, that method is a good servant but a bad master. If genius were to be trammelled by system and order, it would suffocate. Perhaps Montaigne was nearly right when he thought that individuals ought sometimes to cross the line of fixed rules, in order to awaken their vigor and keep them from growing musty.

Coleridge was much addicted to the habit of marginal writing; which, though sadly wasteful on his own part, was very enriching to those friends who loaned him from their libraries.[1] Charles Lamb, who was not inclined to spare book-borrowers as a tribe, had no reflections to cast upon Coleridge for this habit. The depth, weight, and originality of his comments as hastily and carelessly penned on the margins of books were wonderful, and if collected and classified would form several volumes, not only of captivating interest, but of rare critical value, as the few which have been brought together abundantly prove. In one volume which he returned to Lamb is this memorandum: "I shall die soon, my dear Charles Lamb, and then you will not be vexed that I have bescribbled your book. S. T. C., May 2d, 1811." "Elia" valued these marginal notes beyond price, and said that to lose a volume to Coleridge carried some sense and meaning with it. These critical notes often nearly equalled in quantity of matter the original text. In his article upon the subject, Lamb says, "I counsel thee, shut not thy heart nor thy library against S. T. C." As we have already said, while this erratic expenditure of Coleridge's rare literary taste and judgment enriched others, it in a degree impoverished

---

[1] On the fly-leaf of a volume of Anderson's "British Poets" he wrote the following lines : —

> "Ye autograph-secreting thieves,
>   Keep scissors from these precious leaves,
>   And likewise thumbs, profane and greasy,
>   From pages hallowed by S. T. C."

himself; for had the same time and thought been expended upon consecutive literary work, it would have produced volumes of inestimable value to the world at large, and have proved monumental to their author.

Byron was addicted to marginalizing; and though he could not equal Coleridge in the profundity of his criticisms, or impart such charming interest to them, still he was quite original and often piquant. Burns contented himself with trifling criticisms of approval or disapproval pencilled in the margin of books, especially poetical ones, which were nearly all he was in the habit of reading.

Many famous authors and public men have been extravagantly fond of the rod and line, disciples of that patient and poetical angler, Izaak Walton. George Herbert, the English poet; Henry Wotton, diplomatist and author; Dr. Paley, Archdeacon of Carlisle; John Dryden, poet and dramatist; Sydney Smith, the witty divine; Sir Humphry Davy, the eminent chemist, — all were devoted anglers.[1] This brief list might be largely increased. Bulwer-Lytton says: "Though no participator in the joys of more vehement sport, I have a pleasure that I cannot reconcile to my abstract notions of the tenderness due to dumb creatures, in the tranquil cruelty of angling. I can only palliate the wanton destructiveness of my

[1] The pleasant'st angling is to see the fish
Cut with her golden oars the silver stream,
And greedily devour the treacherous bait. — *Shakspeare.*

amusement by trying to assure myself that my pleasure does not spring from the success of the treachery I practise towards a poor little fish, but rather from that innocent revelry in the luxuriance of summer life which only anglers enjoy to the utmost." Walton puts himself on record in these words : " We may say of angling, as Dr. Boteler said of strawberries : 'Doubtless God could have made a better berry, but doubtless God never did ; ' and so, if I might be judge, God never did make a more calm, quiet, innocent recreation than angling." Sydney Smith declared it to be an occupation fit for a bishop, and that it need in no way interfere with sermon-making.

Perhaps the best thing said or done in angling is an unpublished anecdote of the great preacher to the seamen, — the late Father Taylor, of Boston. He was once lured to try his hand at the rod, and soon brought up a very little fish that had been tempted by his bait. He took the small creature carefully from the hook, gazed at it a moment, and then cast it back into the water, with this advice : " My little friend, go and tell your mother that you have seen a ghost ! "

Dr. Parr, the profound English scholar, was a most inveterate smoker; so was Charles Lamb,[1] who one day said to his doctor, " I have acquired this habit by toiling over it, as some men toil after virtue."

---

[1] When Lamb was once asked by a friend why he did not leave off smoking, he humorously replied that he could find no equivalent *vice*.

Robert Hall, the popular English divine, was very much addicted to tobacco and other stimulants. A friend who found him in his study blowing forth clouds of smoke from his lips, said, "There you are, at your old idol!" "Yes," replied the divine, "burning it." Napoleon could never abide smoking tobacco; yet observing how much other men seemed to enjoy it, he tried to acquire the habit, but finally gave it up in disgust. He, however, took snuff to excess. Sir Walter Scott was very fond of smoking. Thackeray, like Burns, loved to get away by himself and enjoy the flavor of a rank tobacco-pipe. Carlyle, like Tennyson, did not care for a cigar, but kept a pipe in his mouth most of his waking hours. Bulwer-Lytton was a ceaseless smoker; and there are few if any notable Germans who have not been addicted to the same indulgence. The nicotine produced from tobacco is one of the most deadly of all poisons, as has been proven by some startling experiments in the Paris hospitals.[1] Thackeray said there was good eating in Scott's novels. Extending the remark, it might be added that there was good drinking in those of Dickens, and good smoking in those of Thackeray.

Dean Swift relieved his sombre moods by harnessing his servants with cords and driving them, school-

---

[1] A patient who had been an inveterate smoker of tobacco for years, on entering the hospital was placed in a hot water bath, and here he remained for half an hour. A frog and other aqueous animals placed in the same water after it had become cool, died instantly; showing that the patient had exuded by the pores of the skin sufficient nicotine to impregnate the water.

boy fashion, up and down the stairs and through the garden of the deanery of St. Patrick's Cathedral, Dublin. Dickens was controlled by a nervous activity which made him crave physical exercise of some sort, and he daily found relief in an eight or ten mile walk. Thackeray once told the author of these pages that he preferred to take his exercise driving upon very easy roads. When Dickens was in this country he was frequently accompanied in his long walks by the late James T. Fields, who was ever ready to sacrifice himself to the pleasure of others. Mr. Fields was not partial to extreme pedestrian exercise, and the author of the "Pickwick Papers" tested his good-nature to the verge of exhaustion in this respect. Dumas, when not otherwise engaged, was accustomed to go down into his kitchen, and, deposing the servants, cook his own dinner; and an excellent cook he must have been, if one half the stories rife about him be true. Besides, did he not write an original cook-book, which still stands for good authority in the cafés of the boulevards?

Dr. Warton, the English critic and author, as represented by contemporary authority, was noted for a love of vulgar society, which he daily sought in low tap-rooms and gin-shops, where he joked away the evening hours. Turner the painter had similar tastes and habits, though he was of a reserved and unsociable character, and noted for his parsimony. Shelley, Goldsmith, and Macaulay delighted in the company of young children. "They are so near to

God," said Shelley. " Intercourse with them freshens and rejuvenates one's soul," wrote Macaulay. " I love these little people; and it is not a small thing when they, who are so fresh from God, love us," said Dickens. Children always had a most tender and humanizing effect upon Douglas Jerrold, no matter what was his mood. He writes : " A creature undefiled by the taint of the world, unvexed by its injustice, unwearied by its hollow pleasures ; a being fresh from the source of light, with something of its universal lustre in it. If childhood be this, how holy the duty to see that in its onward growth it shall be no other! "

History tells us that Henry of Navarre, who was every inch a king, was often seen upon his palace floor with two of his children upon his back, playing elephant and rider. What a peep into the king's heart we get by this little picture of his domestic life ! Where was all the monarch's pride of State, his kingly dignity ? " How hard it is to hide the sparks of nature ! " It is related of Epictetus that he would steal away from his philosophical associates to pass an hour romping with a group of children, — " to prattle, to creep, and to play with them." Charles Robert Maturin, the poet, author of the tragedy of " Bertram," and other successful dramas, could not endure to have children near him during his hours of literary composition. At such times he was particularly sensitive, and pasted a wafer on his forehead as a token to the members of his family that he was not to be interrupted. He said if he lost the thread of his ideas even for a moment, they were gone from him altogether. Sir Walter Scott, on the contrary, was ever ready to lay down his pen at any moment, to exchange pleasant words with child or adult, friend or stranger; and it was notorious that children could always interrupt him with impunity. He declared that their childish accents made his heart dance with glee. He could not check their confidence and simplicity, though pressed upon him when his thoughts were soaring in poetic flights or describing vivid scenes of warfare and carnage. Scott preserved considerable system, nevertheless, in his composition and labor. He lay awake, he tells us, for a brief period in the quiet of the early morning, and arranged carefully in his mind the work of the coming day. He laid out systematically the subject upon which he was writing, and resolved in what manner he would treat it. Thus it was that he could lay down his pen at any moment without deranging the purpose of the work. He had one axiom to which he tenaciously adhered, and was often heard to repeat it to his dependants and friends: "Do whatever is to be done, at once; take the hours of reflection or recreation after business, and never before it."

Schiller said that children made him half glad and half sorry, — always inclined to moralize. "Happy child," he exclaims, "the cradle is still to thee a vast space: become a man, and the boundless world will be too small for thee." Goethe was ever watchful, loving, and tender with the young. "Children," he says, " like dogs, have so sharp and fine a scent, that they detect and hunt out everything." He thought their innocent delusions should be held sacred. Elihu Burritt, the " Learned Blacksmith," says that he once congratulated an humble farmer upon having a fine group of sons. " Yes, they are good boys," was the father's answer. " I talk to them often, but I do not beat my children, — the world will beat them by and by, if they live." A fine thought, rudely expressed.

Shelley's interest in children was connected with his half belief in the Platonic doctrine of pre-existence. As he was passing over one of the great London bridges, meditating on the mystery, he saw a poor working-woman with a child a few months old in her arms. Here was an opportunity to bring the theory to a decisive test: and in his impulsive way he took the infant from its astonished mother, and in his shrill voice began to ask it questions as to the world from which it had so recently come. The child screamed, the indignant parent called for the police to rescue her baby from the philosophical kidnapper ; and as Shelley reluctantly delivered the infant to its mother's arms, he muttered, as he passed on, " How strange it is that these little creatures should be so provokingly reticent !" Shelley was a child himself in many respects ; in illustration of which the reader has only to recall the poet's singular amusement of sailing paper boats whenever he found himself conveniently near a pond. So long

as the paper which he chanced to have about him
lasted, he remained riveted to the spot. First he
would use the cover of letters, next letters of little
value; but he could not resist the temptation, finally,
of employing for the purpose the letters of his most
valued correspondents. He always carried a book in
his pocket, but the fly-leaves were all consumed in
forming these paper boats and setting them adrift
to constitute a miniature fleet. Once he found himself on the banks of the Serpentine River without
paper of any sort except a ten-pound note. He re-
frained for a while; but presently it was rapidly
twisted into a boat by his skilful fingers, and devoted to his boat-sailing purpose without further
delay. Its progress being watched, it was finally
picked up on the opposite shore of the river and returned to the owner for more legitimate use.

Charles Lamb in his quaint way says : " I know that
sweet children are the sweetest things in nature, not
even excepting the delicate creatures which bear them;
but the prettier the kind of a thing is, the more de-
sirable it is that it should be pretty of its kind. One
daisy differs not much from another in glory; but a
violet should look and smell the daintiest." [1]

Good and substantial food is quite as necessary to
authors and public men, as to those who gain their

---

[1] At another time, having been greatly annoyed by the per-
sistent crying and screaming of some infant children, Lamb tried
to bear it patiently; but finally he quietly ejaculated, " B-b-blessed
b-be the m-memory of g-good King Herod ! "

livelihood by laborious physical employment. Authors are, however, as a rule, rather inclined to free indulgence at table. There is as much intemperance in eating as in drinking. Tom Moore, who was the best diner-out of his day, said, by way of excusing this habit, "In grief, I have always found eating a wonderful relief." N. P. Willis was quite a gourmand. "There are," he once wrote, "so few invalids untemptable by those deadly domestic enemies, sweetmeats, pastry, and gravies, that the usual civilities at a meal are very like being politely assisted to the grave." It is certainly better to punish our appetites than to be punished by them. Dickens and Thackeray were both inclined to free indulgence at the table, the former being struck with death at a public banquet. Dean Swift often gave better advice than he was himself inclined to follow. He says: "Temperance," meaning both in eating and drinking, "is a necessary virtue to great men, since it is the parent of the mind, which philosophy allows to be one of the greatest felicities in life." Macready, the famous English tragedian, would not touch food of any kind for some hours before making one of his grand dramatic efforts, but drank freely of strong tea before appearing in public, — a subtle stimulant in which the late Rufus Choate freely indulged, particularly before addressing a jury.

Abstinence in diet was a special virtue with Milton. Shelley utterly despised the pleasures of the table. Walter Scott was an abstemious eater. Pope was a great epicure, and so was the poet Gay. Speaking of appetite, Coleridge tells us of a man he once saw at a dinner-table, who struck him as remarkable for his dignity and wise face. The awful charm of his manner was not broken until the muffins appeared, and then the wise one exclaimed, " Them's the jockeys for me ! " Dignity is sometimes very rudely unmasked, and an imposing air is nearly always the cloak of a fool. Newton lived on the simplest food. " If Aristotle could diet on acorns," he said, " so can I ; " and before sitting down to study he exercised freely and abstained from food. Dr. George Fordyce, the eminent Scotch physician, ate but one meal a day, saying that if one meal in twenty-four hours was enough for a lion, it was sufficient for a man ; but in order not to be like the lion, he drank a bottle of port, half a pint of brandy, and a pitcher of ale with his one meal. Lamartine used to pass one day in ten fasting, as he said, to clear both stomach and brain. Aristo, the stoic philosopher, used to fast for days on acorns. Thomas Byron, a well-known author, never ate flesh of any sort. Dryden's favorite dish was a chine of bacon. Charles Lamb was enamoured of roast pig. He said, " You can no more improve sucking pig than you can refine a violet! " Keats was a very fastidious eater, but was fond of the table, especially where there was good wine,[1] and yet he was

---

[1] Hayden, the painter, says of Keats, that at dinner he would swallow some grains of red pepper in order that he might enjoy the more the " delicious coolness of claret."

not addicted to its intemperate use. Dr. Johnson
was greedy over boiled mutton; and Dr. Rhondelet,
the famous writer on fishes, was so fond of figs that
he died from having at one time eaten immoderately
of them. Barrow, one of the greatest of English theo-
logians and mathematicians, is said to have died of
a surfeit of pears, — a fruit of which he was extravagantly fond.

Gastronomic appetite and reason have been compared to two buckets in a well; when one is at the top
the other is at the bottom. Byron nearly starved
himself to prevent growing gross and uninteresting in
physical aspect. Addison was addicted to port and
claret, and was accustomed, as already spoken of,
while meditating a moral or political essay, to pace
up and down the long gallery of Holland House.[1]
When a humorous suggestion occurred to his fertile
fancy, he solaced himself with claret; or fortified himself with a glass of port when a moral sentiment
required to be enforced by an impressive close to a
beautifully constructed sentence.[2]   This was after
his frigid marriage to the Dowager Countess of War-
wick.   On his death-bed he is reported to have said

---

[1] It was at Holland House, of which he became possessed by
marriage, that Addison

> "Taught us how to live; and (oh! too high
> A price for knowledge) taught us how to die."

[2] Those were days when people drank freely.   "How I should
like," said Grattan one day to Rogers, "to spend my whole life in a
small neat cottage!   I could be content with very little; I should
need only cold meat, and bread, and beer, and *plenty of claret.*"

to her graceless son, " See how a Christian can die ! " Probably the profligate youth, spying his father-in-law as he walked in the gallery, might have irreverently remarked : " See how a Christian can drink ! "   But the truth is that Addison, judged by the habits of his time, should be considered a moderate drinker. Poe's nerves were so shattered that a slight amount of wine would intoxicate him into a frenzy of dissipation ; the same amount swallowed by a regular toper would hardly disturb his brain at all.   While Pitt was quite a young man, he was so weakly that his physician ordered him to drink freely of port wine, and he thus contracted the habit of depending upon stimulants, and could not do without them.   Lord Greville tells us he has seen him swallow a bottle of port wine by tumblerfuls before going to the House. This, together with the habit of late suppers, helped materially to shorten his life.[1]

Goldsmith had a queer fancy for sassafras tea, from which he imagined he derived an excellent tonic effect. Such a relish had certainly one element to recommend it, — and that was its harmlessness.   Dr. Shaw, the English naturalist, nearly killed himself by drinking green tea to excess.   Haydn partook immoderately of strong coffee, and kept it brewing by his side while he composed.   Burns lived on whiskey for weeks together, supplemented by tobacco, which caused Byron to say that he was " a strange compound of dirt and deity."

---

[1] The blemishes of great men are not the less blemishes ; but they are, unfortunately, the easiest part for imitation. — *Disraeli.*

Aristippus of old lived up to his own motto; namely, "Good cheer is no hindrance to a good life." Few men reason about their appetites, but they give way to them until disease reminds them they are made of mortal stuff. Even Plutarch used to indulge at times in riotous living, saying, "You cannot reason with the belly; it has no ears." Addison has pithily recorded his own ideas of this matter. "When I behold a fashionable table set out in all its magnificence," he says, "I fancy that I see gouts and dropsies, fevers and lethargies, with other innumerable distempers, lying in ambuscade among the dishes. Nature delights in the most plain and simple diet. Every animal but man keeps to one dish. Herbs are the food of this species, fish of that, and flesh of a third. Man falls upon everything that comes in his way; not the smallest fruit or excrescence of the earth, scarce a berry or a mushroom, can escape him." It is among the easiest of all things to outsit both our health and our pleasure at the table. "The pleasures of the palate," said shrewd old Seneca, "deal with us like Egyptian thieves, who strangle those whom they embrace."

Thackeray said towards the close of his life, that his physicians warned him habitually not to do what he habitually did. "They tell me that I should not drink wine, and somehow I drink wine; that I should not eat this or that, and, guided by my appetite for this or that, I disregard the warning."

Eminent men are not unlike the rest of humanity in a desire for some sort of recreation, and each one finds it after his own natural bent or fancy. Literature is capable of affording the most rational and lasting enjoyment to cultured minds, but physical exercise has also its reasonable demands. The late Victor Emmanuel found recreation only in hunting, having a number of lodges devoted to this purpose in different parts of Italy. McMahon, late President of France, was also an ardent sportsman. William the Conqueror passed all his leisure in the hunting-field; and President Cleveland hastens with rod and gun to pass his vacation in the Adirondack region. Henry V. occupied a whole day at a time upon his one game, — tennis. Cardinal Mazarin, while virtual ruler of France, used to shut himself up in his library and pass an hour daily in jumping over the chairs. Louis XVI. had a passion for constructing intricate locks and keys, many curious specimens of which are still extant in the Cluny Museum. Charles II. in his leisure hours enjoyed practical chemistry. John Milton wiled away the long hours of his blindness, when not engaged in composing and dictating, by playing upon a cabinet organ; and Chief Justice Saunders was given to the same recreation. The Duke of Burgundy had a singular fancy for constructing mechanical traps and surprises in his house and grounds, so that visitors were liable to encounter practical jokes at every turn.

We might cover pages in enumerating the resorts of notable people in their instinctive search after necessary recreation from sterner duties. Man must be doing something in order to be happy; action being quite as necessary to the health of body and brain as thought. Schiller declared that he found the greatest happiness of life to consist in the regular discharge of some mechanical duty. " Cheerfulness," says the shrewd and practical Dr. Horne, is " the daughter of employment; and I have known a man come home from a funeral in high spirits, merely because he had the management of it." It is in our unoccupied moments that discontent creeps into the mind; busy people have no time to be very miserable. Amusements are not without a double purpose, and it is only a mistaken zeal which argues against those that are innocent. " Let the world," says that wise old philosopher Robert Burton, "have their May-games, wakes, whatsunales, their dancings and concerts ; their puppet-shows, hobby horses, tabors, bagpipes, balls, barley-breaks, and whatever sports and recreations please them best, provided they be followed with discretion."

Sir George Cornewall Lewis, a scholar as well as a statesman, found delight in a variety of intellectual work. He shirked as well as he could all invitations to parties, balls, and dinners, and once despairingly exclaimed, when he was called from his studies to enter into some form of amusement, " that life was tolerable were it not for its pleasures."

CHAPTER V.

LEONARDO DA VINCI, the inspired painter of the "Last Supper" upon the walls of the time-worn Milan convent,[1] is said to have had a strange inclination for dirt. One biographer tells us he grovelled in it. Da Vinci was a great engineer and scientist, as well as artist. The face of Judas in the group seated at the table carries with it a legend. The artist entertained a bitter enmity towards a priest of the Cathedral who had worked him some vital injury, either real or imaginary. His revenge was clear to him; his enemy's hated features were impressed upon his mind, and so, a little modified to suit the supposed treacherous character of the disciple, were made to constitute those of Judas at the moment when he contemplates the betrayal of his Master. The likeness was too plain not to be recognized by

[1] Occupied, the last time the author visited Milan, as barracks for a cavalry regiment. Time and exposure are fast obliterating the original work of Da Vinci. In 1520 Leonardo da Vinci visited France at the urgent solicitation of Francis I. His health was feeble, and the king often came to Fontainebleau to see him. One day when the king entered, Leonardo rose up in bed to receive him, but in the effort fainted. Francis hastened to support him; but the eyes of the artist closed forever, and he lay encircled in the arms of the monarch.

those who knew of the ill feeling existing between the artist and priest. The result was that the latter was virtually banished from the city, as he asked to be, and was transferred to Rome.

Raphael thought he could paint best under the inspiration of wine, and therefore used it freely. Some modern critics pretend to discover the vinous influence in certain exaggerations of style peculiar to his best pictures. Notwithstanding the number and grandeur of the works which he left behind him, he died prematurely at the age of thirty-seven. A book might easily be written upon the peculiarities and habits of artists ; but we continue our desultory gossip.

How often we see the lives and fortunes of individuals contingent upon seeming chance! Cromwell and Hampden, who were cousins, both took passage in a vessel that lay in the Thames, bound for this country, in 1637. They were actually on board, when an order of council prohibited the vessel from sailing. We recall two other instances of a similar character in the career of Goethe and Robert Burns, each of whom was once on the eve of sailing for America to seek a foreign home. Locke was banished from England by force of public opinion, in company with his friend Lord Ashley, and wrote his well-known "Essay on the Human Understanding"[1] in a Dutch

---

[1] The original copy of this work is still preserved, dated 1671, though it was not published until 1690, — an evidence of the author's great caution in offering his views to the public. Three of his works were not published until after his death.

garret. He finally lived down all detraction, and was himself a practical example of that self-teaching which he so strongly advocates in his writings. He possessed a wonderful memory ; so also did Thomas Fuller, who could repeat five hundred unconnected words after twice hearing them. Coleridge esteemed Fuller, not only for his wit, originality, and liberality, but as being the most sensible great man of an age that boasted a galaxy of great men.

Jeremy Taylor, whose birth is shrouded in mystery, though he is said to be the son of a barber, was a singular compound, in character, of simplicity and erudition. He was always a child among children, and it is said that a child could at any time attract his attention. He encountered many of the sterner vicissitudes of life, being more than once cast into prison. In the civil war he was a decided adherent of Charles I., and some have supposed him to have been a natural son of that monarch. Emerson calls him the Shakspeare of divines. Gibbon, the distinguished historian, composed while walking back and forth in his room, completely arranging his ideas in his brain before taking his pen in hand, which in a degree accounts for the correctness of his manuscript.[1] Mon-

---

[1] Rogers says that Gibbon took very little exercise. He had been staying some time with Lord Sheffield in the country ; and when he was about to go away, the servants could not find his hat. " Bless me," said Gibbon, " I certainly left it in the hall on my arrival here." He had not stirred out of the house during the whole of the visit.

taigne and Châteaubriand,[1] when disposed to composition, sought the open fields and unfrequented paths, where, somewhat like Gibbon, they arranged their matter with great precision before sitting down to write. Bacon always wrote in a small room, because, as he believed, it enabled him to concentrate his thoughts. Franklin wrote and studied with a plate of bread and cheese by his side to repair mental waste, as he said, and also to economize time. Is there not a ceaseless interest hanging over the domestic and professional habits of these famous men of the past?

Congreve, to whom Pope dedicated his Iliad and Dryden submitted his poems for criticism before giving them to the public, was extremely popular, witty, and original as a dramatist. Congreve was a slow writer, and was the father, as it were, of that style of writing which died with Sheridan. He wrote only a few dramas, but those were incomparable for the brilliancy of the dialogue; yet the brilliancy was obtained by the hardest intellectual *work*. According to Macaulay, no English author except Byron had at so early an age stood so high in the estimation of his contemporaries. But the licentiousness and general

---

[1] Châteaubriand was the most famous French author of the First Empire. It will be remembered that he visited this country in 1791. He wrote, relative to dining with Washington at Philadelphia : "There is a virtue in the look of a great man. I felt myself warmed and refreshed by it during the rest of my life." His career was full of remarkable vicissitudes. He was once left for dead on the battlefield, suffered banishment, and was for a time imprisoned in the Bastile.

immorality of the works of Congreve are without
excuse.[1] He had not even the paltry plea of necessity, which might lead him to pander to a vitiated
taste in seeking a market for his wares, as was
evidently the case with Fielding. He was very de-
sirous to pass for a man of fashion, and affectedly
sneered at his own literary productions, declaring
them to be produced simply to while away his idle
hours. Vanity seems to have completely overshadowed any spirit of ambition which may have originally inspired him. Flattery and royal patronage
were the ruin of Congreve so far as his after fame
is concerned. Had he known the wholesome spur of
necessity, his grand powers would have shone with
surpassing lustre. He had the genius, but not the
incentive, wherewith to make a great name. Pope is
said, on a certain occasion, to have hinted as much
to Congreve, whom he really reverenced for his ability, and to have incurred his partial enmity thereby.
"Oh that men's ears should be to counsel deaf," says
Shakspeare, "but not to flattery." The broad incon-
sistency of Congreve's dramas is the fact that all his
characters are equally endowed with wit, culture, and
genius. Collier, in his review of the profaneness of the
English stage, administered to Congreve a merited
castigation, to which the dramatist attempted to reply, but without success.

[1] Thackeray says of Congreve : "He loved, conquered, and
jilted the beautiful Bracegirdle, the heroine of all his plays, the
favorite of all the town of her day."

The remarkable vicissitudes which have waited upon the career of men of genius, and especially of authors, are very noticeable. The earliest authentic history shows us the same fatality besetting the paths of such characters as has pursued them to the present day. The student of the past will recall as examples Seneca and his friend Lucan, who were honored and famous in the days of Nero. Both of these renowned authors, when condemned to death, lanced their veins and sung a dying requiem while the tide of their lives ebbed slowly away. So Socrates drank of the fatal hemlock, like Sappho and Lucretius, voluntarily seeking death. "That which is a necessity to him that struggles, is little more than a choice to him who is willing," says Seneca. Sophocles, the Greek tragic poet and rival of Æschylus, was brought to trial by his own children as a lunatic. He composed more than a hundred tragedies, of which seven are still extant. He also excelled as a musician. Plautus, poet and dramatist, was at one time a baker's assistant, earning his bread by grinding corn in a hand-mill. Tasso, Italy's favorite epic poet, became broken-hearted from unrequited love, and was confined in a mad-house for years, and, illustrative of the mutability of fortune, was afterwards brought to Rome to be crowned, like Petrarch, with laurels, but died before the day of coronation. Euripides, one of the three tragic poets of Greece, was torn to pieces by dogs ; and Hesiod, a still more ancient poet, fell by the assassin's dagger. In later times there looms up the name of Galileo, the discoverer and natural philosopher, imprisoned by the Inquisition for teaching men that the world moved.[1] " Poor Galileo," said a modern wit, " was too honest; he should have treated these inquisitors to a champagne supper, and they would have risen from it with the conviction that the world surely *did* turn round." Galileo's greatest affliction, however, was that of becoming totally blind. Milton, who visited him in prison, tells us he was poor and old. In a letter which he dictated to a correspondent, Galileo says: " Alas! your dear friend has become irreparably blind. The heavens, the earth, this universe, which by wonderful observation I have enlarged a thousand times past the belief of former ages, are henceforth shrunk into the narrow space which I myself occupy." Handel also passed the last of his life in the gloom of blindness; and Beethoven was afflicted with incurable deafness, which nearly drove him to suicide.[2] It was perhaps the most trying misfortune possible to one with his special endowments. Have not these historic characters tested the familiar axiom that calamity is man's true touchstone?

[1] Galileo was remarkable, even in his youth, for mechanical genius, and also for his accomplishments in painting, poetry, music, and song. In early childhood, it is said of him, "while other boys were whipping their tops, he was scientifically considering the cause of the motion."

[2] " I was nigh taking my life with my own hands," he wrote, "but art held me back. I could not leave the world until I had revealed what was within me." In view of his great misfortune, his dying words are very touching: " I shall be able to hear in heaven !"

Dante, the greatest poet between the Augustan and Elizabethan ages, was expatriated and exiled from wife and children, becoming a poverty-stricken wanderer. Thus broken in heart and fortune he was hurried by persecution to his grave. Spenser, who endowed English verse with the soul of harmony while eking out a life of misery, finally died in abject poverty. Milton sold "Paradise Lost"[1] for ten pounds. "When Milton composed that grand poem," says Carlyle, "he was not only poor but impoverished; he was in darkness, and with dangers compassed round, he sang his immortal song, and found fit audience, though few." At one time Milton borrowed fifty pounds of Jonathan Hartop, of Aldborough, who lived to the remarkable age of one hundred and thirty-eight years, dying in 1791. He returned the loan at the time agreed upon, but Mr. Hartop, knowing his straitened circumstances, refused to take the money; the pride of the poet, however, was equal to his genius, and he sent the money back a second time with an angry letter, which was found years afterwards among the papers of the remarkable old man. Corneille,

[1] When "Paradise Lost" was first published, in 1667, Edmund Waller, himself a poet, politician, and critic, said : "The old blind schoolmaster, John Milton, has published a tedious poem on the fall of man ; if its length be not considered a merit, it has no other." The second edition was not brought out until seven years later, 1674, the year in which Milton died. This edition was prefaced by two short poems, the first by Andrew Marvell in English, and the second by Samuel Barrow in Latin, in which Milton's poem is placed "above all Greek, above all Roman fame."

the French dramatist; Vaugelas, a noted author of the same nationality; Crabbe, the English poet; Chatterton, the precocious and versatile genius; Holzmann, the profound Oriental scholar; Cervantes; Camoens,[1] the pride of Portugal; and Erasmus, the Dutch scholar, who rose to the leadership of the literature of his day, — all lived more or less continuously on the verge of starvation. Camoens had a black servant who had grown old with him. This man, a native of Java, is said to have saved his master's life in the shipwreck whereby he lost all his fortune except his poems. In after years, when Camoens became so much reduced as to be able no longer to support his servant, the faithful retainer begged in the streets of Lisbon for bread to sustain the one great poet of Portugal. Le Sage, author of " Gil Blas," was endowed with exquisite literary taste, but the victim of extreme poverty. De Quincey, the eminent English author, tells us that he passed much time in London in the most abject want, living upon precarious charity. Nowhere else can so vivid a picture of misused genius be found as in the " Confessions of an English Opium-Eater." De Quincey was noted for his rare conversational powers, supplemented by a vast and varied stock of information. He was finally successful in a

---

[1] When a friend complained to Camoens that he had not furnished some promised verses for him, the disheartened poet replied : " When I wrote verses I was young, had sufficient food, was a lover, and beloved by many friends, and by the ladies ; then I felt poetical ardor ; now I have no spirits to write, no peace of mind or of body."

9

business point of view, and was possessed of a noble
generosity, as he relieved at a critical moment the
necessities of Coleridge at a cost of five hundred
pounds.   This was at a comparatively early period of
De Quincey's life.   Afterwards he was himself often
in want of a tenth part of the sum.   He was a voluminous writer, though not always publishing under his
own name; his collection of works as issued in this
country, edited by J. T. Fields, forms some twenty volumes.   Let us not forget to mention Sydenham, the
English scholar who gave us, among other profound
works, the best version of Plato, and who breathed
his last in a London sponging-house.   " Genius,"
says Whipple, " may almost be defined as the faculty
of acquiring poverty."

Some writers have contended, and not without
reason, that such adversity was often providential;
that without the spur of necessity genius would rarely
accomplish its best, and that distress has often elicited
talents which would otherwise have remained dormant.
In speaking of Burns, Carlyle says: " We question
whether for his culture as a poet, poverty and much
suffering were not absolutely advantageous.   Great
men in looking back over their lives have testified to
that effect.   ' I would not for much,' says Jean Paul,
' that I had been born rich.'   And yet Jean Paul's
birth was poor enough, for in another place he adds:
' The prisoner's allowance is bread and water, and I
have often only the latter.'   But the gold that is refined in the hottest furnace comes out the purest; or,

as he has himself expressed it, 'the canary-bird sings sweetest the longer it has been trained in a darkened cage.'" Horace emphatically declares, that adversity has the effect of developing talents which prosperous circumstances would not have elicited. The hardships endured by many historic persons crowd upon the mind in this connection. We remember John Bunyan in Bedford jail,[1] writing that immortal work, "Pilgrim's Progress;" Ben Jonson,[2] the comrade of Shakspeare; John Seldon, the profound scholar and author; and Jeremy Taylor, whose "Holy Living and Dying" is only second to "Pilgrim's Progress," — all of whom endured the suffering of imprisonment.[3] Nor must we forget Sir Walter Raleigh, who during his thirteen years of prison-life produced his incomparable "History of the World."[4] Lydiat, the subtle scholar to

[1] The county jail in which Bunyan spent the twelve years of his life from 1660 to 1672 was taken down in 1801. It stood on what is now the vacant piece of land at the corner of the High Street and Silver Street, used as a market-place, in Bedford. Silver Street was so named because it was the quarter where the Jews in early times trafficked in the precious metals.

[2] Ben Jonson tried his fortune as an actor, but did not succeed. A duel with a brother actor, whom unhappily he killed, caused him to be imprisoned by the sentence of the court. He was ten years younger than Shakspeare, and survived him twenty-one years, dying in 1637.

[3] Imprisonment could not deprive Boëthius of the consolation of philosophy, nor Raleigh of his eloquence, nor Davenant of his grace, nor Chaucer of his mirth : nor five years of slavery at Algiers deaden the wit of Cervantes. — *Willmott.*

[4] Urged by the King of Spain to punish Raleigh for his attack on the town of St. Thomas, James I. basely resolved to carry into

whom Dr. Johnson refers, wrote his "Annotations on the Parian Chronicles," while confined for debt in the King's Bench; and Wicquefort's curious work on Ambassadors is dated from the prison to which he was condemned for life. Voltaire wrote his "Henriad" while confined in the Bastile; De Foe produced his best works within the walls of Newgate; and Cervantes gave the world "Don Quixote" from a prison.[1]

Some of the sweetest love-lyrics extant were written by Charles, Duke of Orleans, during his captivity of twenty-five years. Baron Trenck wrote his wonderful book of personal experience during a ten years' captivity in a subterranean dungeon at Magdeburg, — a book which has been translated into every modern language. He was released from prison, but died by the guillotine at Paris in 1794. Silvio Pellico, the Italian poet and dramatist, who wrote the well-known story of his prison life, was ten years confined in the fortress of Spielberg, in Moravia. Ponce de Leon,

execution a sentence sixteen years old, which had been followed by an imprisonment of thirteen years, and then a release. So Raleigh was brought up before the Court of King's Bench to receive sentence, and was beheaded the next morning.

[1] Philip III., King of Spain, saw a student one day at a distance on the banks of the river Manzanares, reading a book, and from time to time breaking off to roar with laughter and show other signs of delight. "That person is either mad or is reading 'Don Quixote,'" said the king, — a volume of panegyric in a few words. Cervantes did not have to wait the verdict of posterity as to his incomparable history of the famous Knight La Mancha; it sprung at once into unbounded popularity, while "it laughed Spain's chivalry away."

among the foremost of Spanish poets, as well as the poet Alonzo de Ercilla, were victims of long and severe incarceration because they dared to translate the Biblical Songs of Solomon into Spanish. James Howell, the English author, wrote his "Familiar Letters" in the Fleet Prison. So popular were they, that he had the pleasure of seeing ten editions of them published in rapid succession; this was about the year 1646. William Penn and Roger Williams, both founders of States in this country, suffered imprisonment. The former wrote his well-known "No Cross, No Crown" in the Tower of London. Oakley, the great Oriental scholar, whose remarkable Asiatic researches have rendered his name famous, wrote his work on the Saracens in jail. Cobbett, the political satirist, was no stranger to the inside of a prison; and we all remember Cooper, the English chartist, who made himself famous by his "Prison Rhymes," written behind the frowning bars. Montgomery suffered the same chilling influences for daring to make a public plea for freedom of speech. Theodore Hook, the novelist, delightful miscellaneous writer, and unrivalled wit, was for a long period imprisoned.[1]

Richard Lovelace, the English poet, was a gallant

---

[1] During Theodore Hook's confinement in a sponging-house in London he was visited by an old friend. Astonished at the comparative spaciousness of the apartment, the latter observed by way of consolation, "Really, Hook, you are not so badly lodged, after all. This is a cheerful room enough." "Oh, yes," replied Theodore, pointing significantly to the iron defences outside; "remarkably so — barring the windows."

soldier who spilled his blood for his king in the civil war and impoverished himself in the same cause, was imprisoned for political reasons, and died poor and neglected at the age of forty. He wrote to " Lucasta," [1] when going to the wars, that fine and often-quoted couplet : —

> " I could not love thee, dear, so much,
>   Loved I not honor more."

Lucasta (*Lux casta*, " pure light "), to whom his verses were dedicated, was Lady Sacheverell, whom he devotedly loved, but who married another after having been deceived by the false report that Lovelace had been killed. He was liberated from prison under Cromwell, but lived a wretched life thereafter. Leigh Hunt, the most genial of essayists, was imprisoned for two years, when he was visited by Lamb, Byron, and Moore. His offence was a libel on the Prince Regent, afterwards George the Fourth. Madame Guyon wrote the most of her beautiful poems — so greatly admired by Cowper — while a captive for four

[1] " Tell me not, sweet, I am unkind,
    That from the nunnery
Of thy chaste breast and quiet mind
    To war and arms I fly.

" True, a new mistress now I chase,
    The first foe in the field ;
And with a stronger faith embrace
    A sword, a horse, a shield.

" Yet this inconstancy is such
    As you too shall adore ;
I could not love thee, dear, so much,
    Loved I not honor more."

years in the Bastile. The great public library of
Paris contains forty octavo volumes of her writings.
Why does not some popular author give us a book
upon this theme, and entitle it " Behind the Prison
Bars " ? The suggestion is freely offered, and is perhaps worth considering. Disraeli tells us : " The
gate of the prison has sometimes been the porch of
fame."

The reference to Lovelace reminds us that sometimes the female favorites of poets are selected from
rather questionable positions, and certainly with very
questionable taste. Prior poured out his admiration
in verses addressed to Chloe, a fat barmaid ; and
Bousard addressed poems to Cassandra, who followed
the same refining occupation. Colletet, a French
bard, addressed his lines to his servant-girl, whom
he afterwards married. No doubt that oftenest the
poet's mistress has no actual existence, but, like the
sculptor's ideal, is the combined result drawn from
several choice models.

Gilbert Wakefield, the erudite scholar, theologian,
and author, suffered two years' imprisonment for publishing his " Enquiry into the Expediency of Public
and Social Worship." " The sentence passed upon
him was most infamous," says Rogers, who, in company with his sister, visited the prisoner in Dorchester
jail. While incarcerated here, Wakefield wrote his
" Noctes Carcerariæ " (" Prison Nights "). Matthew
Prior, the poet, diplomatist, courtier, and versatile
author, was the son of a joiner, though it is not known

exactly where he was born. Chancing to interest
the Earl of Dorset, he was educated at the cost of
that liberal nobleman. He [1] was one of those, as
Dr. Johnson said, "that have burst out from an
obscure original to great eminence." Thackeray says
of him, "He loved, he drank, he sang; and he was
certainly deemed one of the brightest lights of Queen
Anne's reign." His contempt for pedigree was very
natural, and was wittily expressed in the epitaph
which he wrote for himself: —

> "Nobles and heralds, by your leave,
> Here lies what once was Matthew Prior;
> The son of Adam and of Eve :
> Can Bourbon or Nassau claim higher?"

Schumann, the German musical composer, author
of " Paradise and the Peri," in a fit of mental depres-
sion threw himself into the Rhine, but was rescued.
Goethe, Alfieri, Raphael, and George Sand all strug-
gled against a nearly fatal temptation to end their
earthly careers. The last named declared that at
the sight of a body of water or a precipice she could
hardly restrain herself from committing suicide!
" Genius bears within itself a principle of destruction,
of death, and of madness," says Lamartine. De
Quincey, who was never quite sane, was given to queer
habits in connection with his literary work. He was

---

[1] Swift and Prior were very intimate, and he is frequently
mentioned in the "Journal to Stella." "Mr. Prior," says Swift,
"walks to make himself fat, and I to keep myself lean. We
often walk round the Park together."

wont to keep his manuscripts stored in his bath-tub, and carried his money in his hat.[1] Cowper, after a fruitless attempt to hang himself, became a religious monomaniac, "hovering in the twilight of reason and the dawn of insanity."[2] Moore, the gay, vivacious, witty, diner-out, sank finally into childish imbecility. John Clare, the English peasant poet, was born in poverty; his early productions accidentally attracted attention and gained him patrons, but after a brief, irregular, unhappy career he died in an insane asylum. So also died Charles Fenno Hoffman, our own popular poet, editor, and novelist, who wrote "Sparkling and Bright." Cruden, the industrious author and compiler of the Biblical Concordance, suffered from long fits of insanity; and so did Jeremy Bentham,[3] though he lived to extreme old age, and died so late

[1] De Quincey was often very happily delivered of witty ideas. He said on one occasion, "If once a man indulges himself in murder, very soon he comes to think little of robbing; and from robbing he comes next to drinking and Sabbath-breaking, and from that to incivility and procrastination. Once being upon this downward path, you never know where you are to stop. Many a man has dated his ruin from some murder or other that perhaps he thought little of at the time."

[2] "I cannot bear much thinking," said Cowper. "The meshes of the brain are composed of such mere spinner's threads in me, that when a long thought finds its way into them, it buzzes and twangs and bustles about at such a rate as seems to threaten the whole contexture."

[3] Macaulay spoke with great admiration of Bentham, and placed him in the same rank with Galileo and Locke, designating him as "the man who found jurisprudence a gibberish, and left it a science."

as 1832. Congreve said it was the prerogative of great souls to be wretched; and Jean Paul, that great souls attract sorrows as lofty mountains do storms. Lenau, the Hungarian lyric poet, died in a mad-house; in the height of his fame he refused, when invited, to visit an asylum, saying, " I shall be there soon enough as it is." It would seem but charitable to attribute fits of insanity to Carlyle, who pronounced most of his contemporaries " fools and lunatics." His wife confessed that she felt as if she were keeping a mad-house. Vaugelas died in such poverty that he bequeathed his body to the surgeons at Paris for a given sum with which to pay his last board-bill. In his will he wrote: "As there may still remain creditors unpaid after all that I have shall be disposed of, it is my last wish that my body should be sold to the surgeons to the best advantage, and that the purchase-money should go to discharge those debts which I owe to society, so that if I could not while living, at least when dead I may be useful." Vauglas was called the owl, because he ventured forth only at night, through fear of his creditors.

Next to the " Newgate Calendar," it has been said, the biography of authors is the most sickening chapter in the history of man. " Woe be to the youthful poet who sets out upon his pilgrimage to the temple of fame with nothing but hope for his viaticum ! " wrote Southey, in 1813, to a young man who had consulted him. " There is the Slough of Despond, and the Hill of Difficulty, and the Valley of

the Shadow of Death upon the way." Coleridge's
exhortation to youthful literati may be summed up in
one sentence : "Never pursue literature as a trade."
Béranger's advice was by no means to be despised.
He spoke as one having authority, and he certainly
had experience.[1] "Write if you will," he says,
"versify if you must, sing away if the singing mood
is an imperative mood, but on no account give up
your other occupation; let your authorship be a pas-
time, not a trade; let it be your avocation, not your
vocation." Even the successful Washington Irving
speaks of "the seductive but treacherous paths of
literature." He adds : "There is no life more precarious in its profits and more fallacious in its enjoy-
ments than that of an author." But these lines were
addressed to his nephew, and must be taken *cum grano
salis.* He had genius, his nephew had not; he never
could have acquired so much money had he, like
Halleck, become a clerk,—even the clerk of Mr. Astor.
The truth is, most writers have failed in authorship
because they have not had talent enough to write books
that an intelligent public would buy and read, and
because their vagabond habits deterred them from
being employed by merchants and tradesmen as sales-
men and clerks. Real genius now obtains a remuner-

---

[1] Béranger's first collection of songs was published in 1815
and received with great favor by the people ; but the bold, patriotic, and often satirical tone of these songs gave offence to the
Government ; and as the author did not abate the freedom of his
criticism in future poems, he was condemned to imprisonment
and to pay a heavy fine.

ation always higher than that of clerks and tradesmen.
It is mediocre writers who mourn in our days; but
they should never have taken as a profession a rôle
they were incompetent to fill.   They are like doctors
who cannot obtain patients, and lawyers who cannot
attract clients.

But we were considering the past, not the present.
Robert Heron, author, scholar, teacher, who wrote
much that will live in literature, died in hopeless
poverty.   His " History of Scotland " and his " Universal Geography " are still among our best books of
reference.   He says of himself in a paper written just
before he died : " The tenor of my life has been temperate, laborious, humble, and quiet, and, to the utmost
of my power, beneficent.   For these last three months
I have been brought to the very extremity of bodily
and pecuniary distress, and I shudder at the thought
of perishing in jail."   Yet such was his fate; he died
in Newgate.   Thomas Decker, the English author, and
collaborator with Ford and Rowley in the production
of popular dramas, died in a debtor's prison.   Christopher Smart, the personal friend of Dr. Johnson,
produced his principal poem while confined in a mad-
house.   Richard Savage, the English poet, experienced
a life which reads like fiction.[1]   The natural son of
an English earl and countess, he was abandoned by his

---

[1] " In a cellar, or the meanest haunt of the casual wanderer,
was to be found," as Dr. Johnson says, " the man whose knowledge of life might have aided the statesman, whose eloquence
might have influenced senates, and whose conversation might
have polished courts."

mother to the care of a nurse who brought him up in ignorance of his parentage. Before he was thirty years of age he was tried and condemned for murder; and, though finally pardoned, he died in jail. During a considerable portion of the time that Savage was engaged upon his tragedy of "Sir Thomas Overbury," he was without lodgings and often without meat; nor had he any other convenience for study and composition than the open fields or the public streets. Having formed his sentences and speeches in his mind, he would step into a shop, ask for pen and ink, and write down what he had composed upon such scraps of paper as he had picked up by chance, often from the street gutters.

Thomas Hood, the famous English humorist, began at first as a clerk in a store, then became apprentice to an engraver; but his genius soon led him to seek literary occupation as a regular means of support. He was endowed with an unlimited fund of wit and comic power. His "Song of the Shirt" showed that he had also great tenderness and pathos in his nature. He edited various magazines and weekly papers, and published two or three humorous books; but his career was far from a success in any light. His life was occupied in incessant brain-work, aggravated by ill-health and the many uncertainties of authorship. He finally died poor in his forty-seventh year, leaving a dependent family.

William Thom was an English poet of genius, but very humbly born. He was at first a weaver and afterwards a strolling pedler, often only too glad to obtain a lodging in a country barn. The poor fellow said, " There 's much good sleeping to be had in a hay-loft." In one of these deplorable shelters his only child, who followed him, perished from hunger and exposure. Thom published so late as 1844 a col-lection of his poems entitled, "Rhymes and Recol-lections of a Hand-Weaver." The volume was well received, and the author was given a dinner by his London admirers. He died at the age of fifty-nine in extreme poverty. We find two admirable poems by him in Sargent's " British and American Poets."

The reader who has perused these pages thus far will doubtless have come to the conclusion that even talent is not developed as a rule in calm and sunshine, but that it must encounter the tempest in some form before the fruit can ripen. Byron, in the third canto of " Childe Harold," thus gloomily declares the penal-ties of becoming famous : —

> " He who ascends to mountain-tops shall find
> The loftiest peaks most wrapt in clouds and snow ;
> He who surpasses or subdues mankind
> Must look down on the hate of those below.
> Though high *above* the sun of glory glow,
> And far *beneath* the earth and ocean spread,
> *Round* him are icy rocks, and loudly blow
> Contending tempests on his naked head,
> And thus reward the toils which to those summits led."

Longfellow's idea is true and forcible : " Time has a doomsday book, in which he is continually recording illustrious names. But as soon as a new name is written there, an old one disappears. Only a few stand in illumined characters never to be effaced."

Thackeray's tender and beautiful thoughts upon this subject occur to us here: "To be rich, to be famous? do these profit a year hence, when other names sound louder than yours, when you lie hidden away under ground, along with the idle titles engraven on your coffin? Only true love lives after you, follows your memory with secret blessings, or pervades you and intercedes for you. *Non omnis moriar*, if, dying, I yet live in a tender heart or two; nor am lost and hopeless, living, if a sainted departed soul still loves and prays for me."

CHAPTER VI.

Our familiar gossip thus far concerning those whose lives by universal consent, " rising above the deluge of years," bear the impress of genius, has led us to speak of the hardships and vicissitudes to which they have so often been subjected. At this sad yet interesting aspect of genius we will continue to glance, observing, as hitherto, no chronological order, but discussing the personalities of each character as they are unrolled before us on the panorama of memory.

Handel, most original of composers, after losing his entire fortune in a legitimate effort to further the interests of the art he loved so well, passed the last of his life in the gloom of blindness. His glorious oratorios were most of them produced under the stress of keen adversity, loss of fortune, and failing health, quite sufficient to have discouraged any one not truly inspired.[1] Mozart also labored under the ban of poverty. He was glad to accept even the position of chapel-master. It is well known that during the

---

[1] Mozart said of him that he struck you, whenever he pleased, with a thunderbolt. Leigh Hunt also said he was the Jupiter of music ; nor is the title the less warranted from his including in his genius the most affecting tenderness as well as the most overpowering grandeur.

composition of some of his masterpieces he and his family suffered for bread. The great composer was so absorbed in music that he was but a child in matters of business.[1] Whatever may be the true definition of genius, perseverance and application form no inconsiderable part of it. " It is a very great error," said Mozart, " to suppose that my art has been easily acquired. I assure you that there is scarcely any one that has so worked at the study of composition as I have. You could hardly mention any famous composer whose writings I have not diligently and repeatedly studied throughout." A boy came to Mozart wishing to compose something, and inquiring the way to begin. Mozart told him to wait. " You composed much earlier," said the youth. " But asked nothing about it," replied the musician.[2] Willmott says very truly that genius finds its own road and carries its own lamp.

[1] His biographer tells us that the King of Prussia offered him three thousand crowns a year, to attract him to Berlin ; but he declined to quit the service of the Emperor Joseph, who paid him only eight hundred florins ; and that he was often reduced to painful distress for want of money while he lived in Vienna.

[2] We see that which we bring eyes to see, and appreciation presupposes a degree of the same genius in ourselves. Mozart's wife said of him that he was a better dancer than musician. Leigh Hunt tells us that when Mozart became a great musician, a man in distress accosted him in the street, and as the composer had no money to give him, he bade him wait a little, while he went into a coffee-house, where he wrote a beautiful minuet extempore, and, sending the poor man to the nearest music-dealer's, made him a present of the handsome sum gladly paid by the publisher.

We have seen that Goldsmith produced some of his finest literary work under stress of circumstances. "Oh, gods! gods!" he exclaimed to his friend Bryanton, "here in a garret, writing for bread and expecting to be dunned for a milk-score!" Like so many other children of genius, he was careless, extravagant, irregular, always in debt and difficulty, all which hurried him to his grave. He died at the age of forty-five. When, on his death-bed, the physician asked him if his mind was at ease, he answered, "No, it is not!" and these were his last words. In that exquisite story, the "Vicar of Wakefield,"[1] we have the explanation of how he supported himself while on his travels. "I had some knowledge of music," he says, "and now turned what was once my amusement into a present means of subsistence. Whenever I approached a peasant's house towards nightfall, I played one of my most merry tunes; and that procured me not only a lodging, but subsistence for the next day." Goldsmith's many faults were all on the amiable side, though he was perhaps a little inclined to find fault with his ill-fortune in good set phrases. Sometimes we are forced to remember that the misery which can so readily find relief in words of complaint is not dis-

---

[1] This book, which none of us fail to read and read again with delight, was at first very coldly received, and severely attacked by the reviewers; until Lord Holland, being ill, sent to his bookseller for some amusing book to read, and received the "Vicar of Wakefield." He read it, and was so much pleased with it that he mentioned it wherever he visited. The consequence was, the first edition was rapidly exhausted, and the fame of the book established.

similar to that love which Thackeray thought quite a bearable malady when finding an outlet in rhyme and prose. Real suffering and profound sorrow are nearly always silent in proportion to their depth. It is evanescent afflictions which most readily find tongue. " To write well," says Madame de Staël, " we should feel truly ; but not, as Corinne did, heartbreakingly." If Goldsmith did grumble, he had bitter cause. At one time having pawned everything that would bring money, he resorted to writing ballads at five shillings apiece, going out secretly in the evening to hear them sung in the streets. His five shillings were often shared with some importunate beggar. One day he gave away his bed-clothes to a poor woman who had none ; and then, feeling cold at night, he ripped open his bed and was found lying up to his chin in the feathers ! The very name of Goldsmith seems to us to ring with a generous tone of unselfishness and human sympathy. The story is true of his leaving the card-table to relieve a poor woman whose voice as she sang some ditty in passing on the street came to his sensitive ear indicating distress. Not a line can be found in all his productions where he has written severely against any one, though he was himself the subject of bitter criticism and literary abuse. He was not a very thorough reader of books, but owed his ability as a writer more to the keenness of his observation. Nature and life were the books he studied ; which was simply going to the fountain-head for his information.

Machiavelli, the renowned Italian statesman, philosopher, and dramatist, whose picturesque history of Florence alone would have entitled him to fame, was entirely misconstrued by the times in which he lived, suffering imprisonment, torture, and banishment in the cause of public liberty. Macaulay says of him: "The name of a man whose genius has illumined all the dark places of policy, and to whose patriotic wisdom an oppressed people owed their last chance of emancipation, passed into a proverb of infamy." The victim of one age often becomes the idol of the next. Dante,[1] expatriated, and exiled from wife and children, is not forgotten. The greatest genius between the Augustan and Elizabethan ages, an accomplished musician, a painter of no mean repute, and a brilliant scholar, he yet enjoyed no contemporary fame. "The inventor of the spinning-jenny is pretty sure of his reward in his own day," says Carlyle; "but the writer of a true poem, like the apostle of a true religion, is nearly as sure of the contrary." Dante poured out the deep devotion of his youthful heart at the feet of that Beatrice whose name he has rendered classic by the genius of his pen, though she did not live to bless him. His later marriage was ill-assorted and unhappy. The sublime and unique

---

[1] Perhaps the cause of Dante's struggle through life lay in that reckless sarcasm which prompted his answer to the Prince of Verona, who asked him how he could account for the fact, that in the household of princes the court fool was in greater favor than the philosopher. "Similarity of mind," said the fierce genius, "is all over the world the source of friendship."

" Divine Comedy " was not even published until after
its author's death. Now the pilgrim bends with reverence over the grave whither he was hurried by persecution. How absurd are the transitions of which human
appreciation is capable! Even the cool, philosophical
Carlyle was struck with admiration of the poet's devotion. He says : " I know not in the world an affection
equal to that of Dante. It is a tenderness, a trembling,
longing, pitying love, like the wail of Æolian harps, —
soft, soft, like a child's young heart; one likens it to
the song of angels ; it is among the purest utterances
of affection, perhaps the very purest that ever came
out of a human soul."

Hard indeed seems to have been the fate of the
Italian dramatist and poet, Bentivoglio, who, after
impoverishing himself in acts of charity, literally selling all and giving the proceeds to the poor, when old
and miserable was refused admission into a hospital
which he had himself founded in his days of prosperity.
Kotzebue, the German author and dramatist, who
wrote that remarkable play " The Stranger," was a
man beset with morbid melancholy, causing him to
pray for death, which came at last by a murderous
hand.[1] Philip Massinger, the creator of " Sir Giles
Overreach," a dramatic conception almost worthy of
Shakspeare, despite his rare and wondrous powers,

---

[1] Kotzebue was fifty-eight years of age when he was assassi-
nated at Mannheim, in 1819, by Karl Ludwig Sand, who was
actuated by a fanatical zeal against one whom he considered a
traitor to liberty. Kotzebue was a prolific writer, and has left
several dramas.

was the child of adversity. Massinger wrote in conjunction with Beaumont and Fletcher, they getting whatever of credit was earned by the three. In those days, an established writer for the stage would frequently utilize the brains of others of less note, calling them to aid in productions which bore only the employer's name. There seemed to be no sunshine in Massinger's life; it was all in shadow.[1] Could anything be more pathetic than this brief entry in the death chronicle of a London parish, under date of March 20, 1639 : " Buried — Philip Massinger — a stranger."

Erasmus, the Dutch scholar and philosopher, defrauded of his patrimony while an orphan of tender years, devoted himself to learning, and cheerfully submitted to every deprivation to secure it. While pursuing his studies in Paris he was clothed in rags, and his form was cadaverous from want of food. It was at this time that he wrote to a friend, " As soon as I get any money, I will buy first Greek books and then clothes." Thus nurtured in the school of adversity, he rose to a proud distinction ; and to him, more than to any other writer, was attributed the success of

---

[1] The sad lines in his last poem, entitled " Waiting for Death," will long be remembered : —

> " Deformed and wrinkled ; all that I can crave
> Is quiet in my grave.
> Such as live happy hold long life a jewel ;
> But to me thou art cruel
> If thou end not my tedious misery,
> And I soon cease to be.
> Strike, and strike home then ; pity unto me,
> In one short hour's delay, is tyranny ! "

the Reformation, — it being expressively remarked that
he laid the egg which Luther hatched. If it be true
that an atmosphere of hardship is necessary to the
nurture of genius, then certainly Erasmus encountered the requisite discipline; but as Dr. Johnson
says in his epigrammatic way, "there is a frightful
interval between the seed and the timber." Death
is the dropping of the flower that the fruit may ripen.
Thus fame may follow, but seldom is contemporary;
nor does true genius fail to recognize this. Milton's
ambition, to use his own words, was, "to leave something, so written, to after ages that they should not
willingly let it die;" and Cato said he had rather
posterity should inquire why no statues were erected
to him, than why they were. Motherwell calls fame
" a flower upon a dead man's heart." Were it otherwise, were fame contemporary, it would be but the
breath of popular applause, the shallowest phase of
reputation. " I always distrust the accounts of eminent men by their contemporaries," says Samuel
Rogers. " None of us has any reason to slander
Homer or Julius Cæsar; but we find it difficult to
divest ourselves of prejudices when we are writing
about persons with whom we have been acquainted."

It is tears which wash the eyes of poor humanity,
and enable it to see the previously invisible land of
beauty; it is threshing which separates the wheat
from the chaff; every ripened genius has passed its
Gethsemane hours. " The eternal stars shine out
as soon as it is dark enough!" says Carlyle. Izaak

Walton, the delightful biographer and charming miscellaneous writer, was an humble hosier in London
in early life. It was sorrow caused by the death of
his wife and children in the stived quarters of a
poor city tradesman, which led him finally to turn
his back upon the great metropolis and seek a home
in the country. What seemed to him to be "dim fu-
nereal tapers," proved to be "heaven's distant lamps."
Influenced by the inspiring surroundings of Nature, he
produced his "Complete Angler;" of which Charles
Lamb said, "It might sweeten a man's temper at any
time to read it," and which modern criticism has pronounced one of the best pastorals in the English language. Spenser, author of the "Faerie Queene," of
whose birth little is known, died in great destitution,
though he was buried near Chaucer in Westminster
Abbey. Of his poetry Campbell says: "He threw
the soul of harmony into our verse, and made it more
warmly, tenderly, and magnificently descriptive than
it ever was before, or, with a few exceptions, it has
ever been since." The best critics agree that the
originality and richness of his allegorical personages
vie with the splendor of ancient mythology.

Let us not forget to speak of Schiller in his early
indigence and distress, wanting friends and wanting
bread, but yet bravely fighting the battle of life. The
humble cottage is still extant, near Leipsic, where he
wrote the "Song of Joy" in those trying days.[1] We

[1] "Schiller," says Coleridge, "has the material sublime to produce an effect; he sets a whole town on fire, and throws infants

recall Crabbe, stern poet of life's strivings and hard-ships, reduced to the verge of starvation, and only relieved by the noble charity of Edmund Burke; and Otway, one of the most admirable of English dra-matists, author of "Venice Preserved," choked to death by the crust of bread he eagerly swallowed when weakened by famine. Butler, the author of "Hudibras,"[1] died in poverty in a London garret. Santara, the famous French painter, died neglected and penniless in a pauper hospital. Andrea del Sarto labored hard and patiently at a tailor's bench to procure the means of pursuing art; and Benvenuto Cellini[2] languished in the dungeons of San Angelo.

We have spoken of De Foe in prison, he who pro-duced two hundred volumes, yet died insolvent. Dr. Johnson said there was never anything written by man that was wished longer by its readers, except "Don Quixote," "Robinson Crusoe," and "Pilgrim's Progress." The author of "Robinson Crusoe" says of himself: "I have gone through a life of wonders,

with their mothers into the flames, or locks up a father in an old tower. But Shakspeare drops a handkerchief, and the same or greater effect follows."

[1] "'Hudibras,'" says Hallam, "was incomparably more popular than 'Paradise Lost.' No poem in our language rose at once to so great reputation; nor can this remarkable popularity be called ephemeral, for it is looked upon to-day as a classic." Butler died in 1680.

[2] "Benvenuto Cellini, the jeweller, engraver, poet, musician, soldier, sculptor, and lover: and in all so truly admirable!" His autobiography remained in dusty oblivion for the period of two hundred years after his death before it met the public eye.

and am the subject of a great variety of providences.
I have been fed more by miracles than Elijah when
the ravens were his purveyors. In the school of
affliction I have learned more philosophy than at the
academy, and more divinity than from the pulpit.
In prison I have learned that liberty does not consist in open doors and the egress and regress of loco-
motion. I have seen the rough side of the world as
well as the smooth, and have in less than half a year
tasted the difference between the closet of a king
and the dungeon of Newgate." "Talent is often to
be envied," says Holmes, "and genius very commonly
to be pitied; it stands twice the chance of the other
of dying in a hospital, in jail, in debt, in bad repute."

The example of Robert Greene's life carries with it
an impressive moral. He was well educated, taking
his degree at Cambridge, England, and was a successful playwright and poet; but he was also improvident
and reckless in his life, exhibiting more than the usual
eccentricities of genius. He squandered his patrimony
in dissipation, and died in great poverty. His last
book, "The Groatsworth of Wit bought with a Million
of Repentance," is a book both curious and rare.[1]

---

[1] We quote a verse from his "Death-Bed Lament," contained
in this volume : —

> "Deceiving world, that with alluring toys
> Hast made my life the subject of thy scorn,
> And scornest now to lend thy failing joys,
> To out-length my life, whom friends have left forlorn; —
> How well are they that die ere they are born,
> And never see thy slights, which few men shun,
> Till unawares they helpless are undone !"

With all his dissipated proclivities, Henry Fielding had much more genius than Robert Greene. He too was constantly poor through his own recklessness. Lady Montagu, who was a kinswoman of his, said: " He was always wanting money, and would have wanted it had his hereditary lands been as extensive as his imagination." And yet he was a marvel of industry, ever slaving with the pen, writing often under excruciating pain, and producing his most famous work, " Tom Jones," as has been said, with an ache and a pain to every sentence. He was, as usual, very short of money when this work was finished, and tried to sell it to a second-class publisher for twenty-five pounds. Thomson the poet heard of this from Fielding, and told him to come to Miller the book-publisher. This individual gave it to his wife to read, and she bade him to secure it by all means; so the publisher offered the impecunious author two hundred guineas for it, and the bargain was closed, to the entire satisfaction of both parties.[1] Critics have remarked upon the similarity between Steele and Fielding, though attributing the greater genius and learning to the latter. They were certainly alike in one respect; namely, as regarded a chronic state of impecuniosity.

---

[1] Before Miller died, he had cleared over eighteen thousand pounds by the publication of " Tom Jones." The number of editions that has been published is almost fabulous. The popularity of Fielding may be judged of from what Dr. Johnson says of his "Amelia": "It was, perhaps, the only book, of which, being printed off betimes one morning, a new edition was called for before night."

Fielding said of himself that he had no choice but to be a hackney writer or a hackney coachman for a living. His genius deserved a better fate. Owing to his poverty he was forced to throw upon the market many productions which he had much better have thrown into the fire. Fortunately, in literature it is the rule that the unworthy perishes, and only the good remains. Many of Fielding's works have a just and lasting fame, and no library is complete without them. In spite of his many imperfections, which made brusque Dr. Johnson refuse to sit at table with him, there was much that was fine and lovable in Harry Fielding, — truthful, generous to a fault, and with wit and wisdom marvellously combined. Gibbon, speaking of his own genealogy, refers to the fact of Fielding being of the same family as the Earl of Denbigh, who, in common with the imperial family of Austria, is descended from the celebrated Rodolph of Hapsburg. "While one branch," he says, "have contented themselves with being sheriffs of Leicestershire and justices of the peace, the other has furnished emperors of Germany and kings of Spain; but the magnificent romance of 'Tom Jones' will be read with pleasure when the palace of the Escurial is in ruins and the imperial eagle of Austria is rolling in the dust."

Justice, like the sword of Damocles, is ever suspended. Nemesis is not dead, but sleepeth. Sometimes old age seizes upon an ill-spent life, and gives us a striking example of the vicissitudes of genius. Dean Swift, the great master of biting satire and

felicitous analogy, possessing the rarest qualities of
wit, humor, and eloquence, was yet so paradoxical
and inconsistent withal, as to lie under the suspicion
of madness half of his life. Ambitious, talented, ever
seeking preferment, never satisfied, now a busy Whig
and now a noisy Tory, he was a perfect brigand in
politics, and his motto was, " Stand and deliver."
Swift's bitterness, scorn, and subsequent misanthropy were the sequence of disappointment. " All
my endeavors to distinguish myself," he wrote to
Bolingbroke, " were only for want of a great title
and fortune, that I might be used like a lord by those
who have an opinion of my parts; whether right or
wrong is no great matter." Coarse, sceptical, and
irreligious,[1] he was arrogant where he dared to be,
and cautious with his money, though having a reputation for charity. " If you were in a strait," asks
Thackeray, " would you like such a benefactor? I
think I would rather have had a potato and a friendly
word from Goldsmith, than be beholden to the Dean
for a guinea and a dinner." Heartlessly vibrating
between Stella and Vanessa, to the misery and mortification of both, he finally married the former, only
to separate from her at the church door. We are

---

[1] Swift has had many biographers ; his life has been told by the
kindest and most good-natured of men, Scott, who admired but
could not bring himself to love him ; and by stout old Johnson, who, forced to admit him into the company of poets, receives
the famous Irishman, and takes off his hat to him with a bow of
surly recognition, scans him from head to foot, and passes over to
the other side of the street. — *Thackeray.*

fain to abhor the man while we freely acknowledge
the lustre of his genius, and to see only providential
justice in his fate, when in the later years of his life,
grown morose, misanthropic, and solitary, watched
at all times by a keeper, his memory and other faculties failed him, and the great Dean became a picture
of death in life. He made many enemies, and was
bitterly criticised by his contemporaries, often not
without ample justice. He has been stigmatized as
"the apostate politician, the perjured lover, and the
ribald priest, — a heart burning with hatred against
the whole human race, a mind richly laden with
images from the gutter and the lazar-house." [1]

At complete antipodes to this portrait is that of
Richard Steele, the popular dramatist, essayist, and
editor; the friend of Addison, and one of the wittiest
and most popular men of his day. His also was an
erratic career, alternating between vice and virtue; or,
as he says of himself, always sinning and repenting,
until he finally outlived his relish for society, his income, and his health. " He was the best-natured
creature in the world," says Young; "even in his
worst state of health he seemed to desire nothing but
to please and be pleased." Worn out and forgotten
by his contemporaries, Steele retired into the country

---

[1] Swift at one time in his subtle way declared with elaborate
reasons, that on the whole it would be impolitic to abolish the
Christian religion in England. We have yet to discover a finer
piece of irony. His exquisitely ridiculous proposition to utilize
for *food* the babies born in Ireland, so as to prevent their becoming a burden to the country, will also be remembered.

and left posterity to appreciate his genius. With a warm heart overflowing with love of wife and children, his checkered life was yet full of faults and careless blunders, many of which were directly traceable to strong drink. Little learned in books, but with a large knowledge of men and the world, he wrote with captivating simplicity and in the most colloquial style. Social and kindly in the extreme, his whole character is in strong contrast with the harshness of Swift and the dignified loneliness of Addison.[1] Somehow we forget about the sword of Damocles, and ignore Nemesis altogether in connection with the name of Steele; and while we do not forget his weaknesses, we recollect more readily his loving nature, his appreciation of beauty and goodness, and his warm sympathy and kindness of heart. It was Steele who said of a noble lady of his time, that to love her was a liberal education.

Dr. Johnson spent much of his early life in penury, wandering in the streets, sometimes all night, without the means to pay for a lodging. A garret was a luxury to him in those days.[2] Alas! what a satire upon

---

[1] It is in the nature of such lords of intellect to be solitary; they are in the world, but not of it; and our minor struggles, brawls, successes, pass over them. —*Thackeray.*

[2] "In London," says Dawson, "Johnson suffered a great deal from poverty, and made use of many little artifices to eke out his scanty means. All the great kindly acts which his large manly heart prompted him to do cost him much self-denial. When he said that a man could live very well in a garret for one-and-six-pence a week, the statement was not a speculative but an experimental one."

learning and authorship! Notwithstanding his powerful intellect, he was subject to such a singular and
even superstitious dread of death, that he could hardly
be persuaded to execute his will in later years. When
Garrick showed Johnson his fine house and grounds
at Hampton Court, the mind of the great lexicogra-
pher reverted to his special weakness, saying, "Ah!
David, David, these are the things which make a
death-bed terrible." When he and Garrick both became famous, they used to chaff each other about who
came to London with two shillings, and who had two-
and-sixpence. Johnson was a confirmed hypochon-
driac; hence the gloom and morbid irritability of his
disposition. His disorder entailed upon him perpetual
fretfulness and mental despondency. Had it not been
for the wonderful vigor of his mind, — as in the case
of Cowper, who was similarly affected, — he would
have been the inmate of a mad-house. Macaulay says
of Johnson grown old: "In the fulness of his fame,
and in the enjoyment of a competent fortune, he is
better known to us than any other man in history.
Everything about him, his coat, his wig, his figure, his
face, his scrofula, his St. Vitus's dance, his rolling
walk, his blinking eye, the outward signs which too
clearly marked his approbation of his dinner, his in-
satiable appetite for fish-sauce and veal-pie with plums,
his inextinguishable thirst for tea, his trick of touching the posts as he walked, his mysterious practice
of treasuring up scraps of orange-peel, his morning
slumbers, his midnight disputations, his contortions,

his mutterings, his gruntings, his puffings, his vigorous, acute, and ready eloquence, his sarcastic wit, his vehemence, his indolence, his fits of tempestuous rage, his queer inmates, old Mr. Levitt and blind Mrs. Williams, the cat Hodge and the negro Frank, — are all as familiar to us as the objects by which we have been surrounded from childhood."

The greatest talents are usually coupled with the most acute sensibility. Rousseau imagined a phantom ever by his side; Luther had his demon, who frequented his study at all hours. So realistic was the great reformer's imagination, that he was accustomed to throw at the intruder any article nearest at hand. The confusion thus caused may easily be conceived when on one such occasion he cast his inkstand, with its contents, at the supposed demon. Cowper's weird and fatal messenger will also be remembered. Tasso's spirits glided in the air,[1] and Mozart's "man in black" induced him to write his own requiem. But Johnson saw omens in the most trifling circumstances. If he chanced, in passing out of the house, to place his left foot foremost, he would return and start with the right, as promising immunity from accident and a safe return. Strange as it may seem, this eminent and profound man put faith in a long list of equally ridiculous omens in every-day life. He was a most

---

[1] Tasso was often obliged to borrow a crown from a friend to pay for his month's lodging. He has left us a pretty sonnet to his cat, in which he begs the light of her eyes to write by, being too poor to purchase a candle.

voluminous and versatile writer, and excelled in de-
lineating female characters ; though Burke did say " all
the ladies of his dramatis personæ were Johnsons in
petticoats." Few persons with means so limited as
his ever spent more for charitable purposes ; and if
his disposition was irritable, his heart was kind.
" He loved the poor," says Mrs. Thrale, " as I never
yet saw any one else love them. He nursed whole
nests of people in his house, where the lame, the blind,
the sick, and the sorrowful found a sure retreat."
Now and then, throughout Johnson's life, we get a
glimpse that shows us the man, not as the world at
large knew him, but as his unmasked heart appeared.
Does the reader recall the incident of his kneeling by
the dying bed of an aged woman, and giving her a
pious kiss, afterwards recording, " We parted firmly,
hoping to meet again " ?

Melancholy has been the very demon of genius, the
skeleton in the closet of poets and philosophers.
Burton composed his " Anatomy of Melancholy " to
divert his own depressed spirits.[1] Cowper is another
example. He says of himself, " I was struck with
such a dejection of spirits as none but they who
have felt the same can have the least conception
of." He was tenderly attached, it will be remem-

---

[1] Burton is said to have been, in the intervals of his vapors,
the most facetious companion in the university where he was
educated. So great was the demand for his " Anatomy of Melancholy," when published, that his publisher is said to have acquired
an estate by the sale of it.

bered, to his cousin Theodora, who returned his
love; but disappointment was the lot of both, as
her parents, doubtless for good reasons, forbade the
union. While the vastly humorous and popular ballad of "John Gilpin" was delighting the Londoners,
and was being read to crowded audiences at high
prices, the poor unhappy author was confined as a
lunatic, and, to use his own words, was " encompassed
by the midnight of absolute despair." [1]   The poet, like
the clown in the ring, when he appears before the
public must be all smiles and jests, though concealing
perhaps an agony of physical or mental suffering.
We know little of the real aspect which the face of
Harlequin presents beneath his mask. Be sure he
has his sorrows, deep and dark, in spite of the grin-
ning features which he wears. Who does not recall
the words which Thackeray makes his old and faithful gold pen utter : —

> " I 've help'd him to pen many a line for bread;
>   To joke, with sorrow aching in his head ;
>   And make your laughter when his own heart bled."

Was there ever pleasanter or more genial reading
than " Cowper's Familiar Letters," full to the brim
with sparkling humor? Yet these were coined from

---

[1] How appropriate are the lines by Mrs. Browning, dedicated
to Cowper's grave : —

> " O poets ! from a maniac's tongue was poured the deathless singing !
>   O Christians! at your cross of hope a hopeless hand was clinging!
>   O men ! this man in brotherhood your weary paths beguiling,
>   Groaned inly while he taught you peace, and died while we were smiling ! "

his brain while in a state of hopeless dejection. "I wonder," he writes to Mr. Newton, "that a sportive thought should ever knock at the door of my intellect, and still more that it should gain admittance. It is as if Harlequin should introduce himself into the gloomy chamber where a corpse is deposited in state." He was one of the most amiable and gifted, but also one of the unhappiest, of the children of genius.

Christopher Smart, poet, scholar, and prose writer, was an eccentric individual, but of such undoubted ability as to challenge the admiration and win the friendship of Dr. Johnson, who wrote his biography. His habits finally became very bad, so that, delirium setting in, it was found necessary to confine him in an asylum. While there he wrote a very remarkable religious poem entitled the "Song of David," produced in his rational moments, which exhibited sublimity and power, and is still considered one of the curiosities of English literature. Smart improved in health and was discharged with his full reason restored, but was soon after committed to the King's Bench prison for debt; and there he died, poverty-stricken and neglected, in 1770. Samuel Boyle was a contemporary of Smart, and was possessed of equal genius whether with the pen or the bottle. Poor fellow! he got an indifferent living as a fag author, though he was capable of fine literary work. His poem entitled the "Deity" fully proved this. Ogle, the London publisher, used to employ Boyle to translate some of Chaucer's tales into modern English, which he did with much excellence and spirit, and for which he received threepence per printed line. The poor genius sank lower and lower, lived in a miserable garret, wearing a blanket about his shoulders, having no vest or coat, and was at last found famished to death with a pen in his hand. "Hunger and naked-ness," says Carlyle, "perils and revilings, the prison, the cross, the poison-chalice, have in most times and countries been the market price the world has offered for wisdom, the welcome with which it has greeted those who have come to enlighten and purify it. Homer and Socrates and the Christian apostles be-long to old days; but the world's Martyrology was not completed with them."

Richard Payne Knight, the Greek scholar and an-tiquary, was a remarkable genius in his way. His gift of ancient coins, bronzes, and works of art pre-sented to the British Museum was valued at fifty thousand pounds. He was a poet of more than ordi-nary ability, and wrote, among other prose works, "An Analytical Enquiry into the Principles of Taste." He was for a number of consecutive years a member of Parliament. He had singular attacks of melan-choly, and finally developed such a loathing of life that he destroyed himself with poison.

Poverty has nearly always been the patrimony of the Muses. "An author who attempts to live on the manufacture of his imagination," says Whipple, "is constantly coquetting with starvation." A glance at the brief life of Chatterton is evidence enough of the truth of this remark. He began to write poems of extraordinary merit at an immature age, and when a mere boy came up to London to seek for literary employment as a means of support. He wrote sermons, poems, essays, and political articles with an ability far beyond his years. He was indeed a prodigy of genius, and probably would have stood in the front rank of English poets had he lived to maturer years. No one ever equalled him at the same age, and Tasso alone, says Campbell, can be compared to him as a youthful prodigy. His life in the metropolis was one of great hardship and deprivation, as he often suffered for want of the simplest necessities of life, and grew so emaciated in appearance from the lack of food that strangers, sometimes meeting him in the street, forced him to accept a dinner which he was too proud to ask for. All this while, with much more consideration for the feelings of the family at home than thought for himself, he wrote cheerful letters to his mother, and even sent small and acceptable presents to his sister, in order to content them for his absence. Seeking only expression for the divine afflatus within him, he had no thought of self, no care for the morrow. By degrees, young as he was, he sank into utter despondency, and was reduced to actual starvation. He was found at last upon his bed of straw, having taken his own life in a fit of desperation. At the time he swallowed the fatal poison he was not quite nineteen years of age.

George Combe, the English author, encountered a

full share of the vicissitudes of genius. He was capable of much theoretical goodness, but was not practical in that respect. He wrote in his old age, "Few men have enjoyed more of the pleasures and brilliance of life than myself;" yet he died in the King's Bench, where he had taken refuge from his creditors, not leaving enough to pay the expenses of his funeral.

Many a child of genius has been compelled to prostitute godlike powers to repel the gnawings of hunger; as for instance Holzman, the sagacious Oriental scholar and professor of Greek, who sold his notes on Dion Cassius for a dinner. The record of this learned man's struggles with dire want form a pathetic chapter in literary history. He tells us himself that at the age of eighteen he studied to acquire glory, but at twenty-five he studied to get bread.

While these pages are preparing for the press, Dr. Moshlech, a scientist, and the master of ten languages, has died in the county almshouse of Erie, Pennsylvania. He was a Prussian by birth, and graduated with high honors from the University of Bonn; made medicine a specialty, and practised the profession for several years in Paris, but finally turned his attention to science, and afterwards to the languages. He numbered among his friends many illustrious men, chief of whom were Darwin and Victor Hugo. At the beginning of our late war he visited this country, and accepted a position as Professor of Greek and Hebrew in Bethany College, West Virginia, which he held but

a short time, owing to the war excitement. He subsequently practised medicine in Ohio and Pennsylvania, and wrote for scientific publications. He was
so much interested in his work that he neglected to
make provision for his old age; and when he could
no longer pursue his profession, this man, who had
associated with the most learned men of Europe, was
compelled to apply to a poorhouse for shelter and
bread. Even after he entered the almshouse he prepared a number of young men for college, and lectured
occasionally before the Erie Historical Society.

Few authors are so calm of spirit, or so assured of
their position, as not to shrink from well-expressed
criticism, and especially when it comes in the form of
ridicule, — forgetting that although an ass may bray
at a classic statue, an ass cannot create one.[1] So sensitive was even Newton to critical attacks, that Whiston,
another English philosopher, and a personal friend of
Sir Isaac, said he was quite unmanned when any dec-
laration of his was called in question by the reviewers;
and further, that he (Whiston) lost Newton's favor,
which he had enjoyed for twenty years, by contradict-
ing him on some point of his printed works; "for," he
adds, "no man was of a more fearful temper." Some
critics use the pen as the surgeon does the scalpel:

---

[1] According to Disraeli, Dr. Hawksworth, who was employed
by the English Government to write an account of Captain Cook's
first voyage, and who was the intimate friend of Dr. Johnson,
absolutely died from the effects of severe criticism. He was an
extremely graceful, effective, and ready writer.

they do not analyze, but they dissect. The flowers of
the imagination, like the life of the body, vanish if
too closely pressed. "Criticism," says Richter, "often
takes from the tree caterpillar and blossoms together." [1]
Thus was the heart of poor Keats crushed and broken
by the malignant severity of Gifford in the "Quarterly
Review." One would have thought that this captious
critic, who by his own talent alone had worked his
way from the cobbler's bench to the editorial chair of
the "Quarterly," would have been more considerate
towards a man [2] who, like himself, rose from humble
associations. It only proved that the man who had
successfully cast the slough of vulgar life, had still
the heart of a clown. Gifford was indignant and
sensitive beyond measure at a published criticism on
his translation of Juvenal, which appeared in the
"Critical Review;" and he put forth a sharp, angry
answer, in the form of a large quarto pamphlet. No
poet ever exhibited a more vivid perception of the
beautiful, or greater powers of fancy, than Keats; but
the bitterness of the criticism referred to was too
much for his delicate health and sensitive nature,

---

[1] Racine encountered much harsh criticism, which rendered
him very unhappy. He told his son in after years that he suffered
far more pain from the fault found with his productions than he
ever experienced pleasure from their success.

[2] Richter's remark that "some souls fall from heaven like
flowers, but ere the pure fresh buds have had time to open, they
are trodden in the dust of the earth, and lie soiled and crushed
beneath the foul tread of some brutal hoof," has been aptly
applied to Keats.

hastening, if it did not actually develop, the seeds of consumption, of which he died. Keats's father was a livery-stable keeper, and it is said that the future poet was born in the most humble quarters; but the irresistible fire of genius lighted his path, and had he lived past the noon of life, he would have carved his way to the highest fame. He finally went to Rome, in the hope of recuperating his failing health; but that was not to be. In the last day of his illness a companion who had called in, asked him how he was. "Better, my friend," he answered in a low voice. "I feel the daisies growing over me!" He died at Rome in his twenty-sixth year, Feb. 23, 1821. His body lies in the English burial-ground outside the gates of the ancient city, by the Appian Way, and near to the pyramid of Cestius. The simple slab that marks the spot interests one quite as much as many of the grand historical monuments of the Via Appia.[1] We all remember the touching epitaph from his own pen : —

"Here lies one whose name was writ in water."

As to the effect of criticism in general, we are told that Pope was observed to writhe in his chair on hearing the letter of Cibber mentioned, with other severe criticism on the product of his hand and brain. The

---

[1] Keats modestly admitted the shortcomings of his early compositions. He said, "I have written independently, without judgment; I may write independently and with judgment hereafter. The genius of poetry must work out its own salvation in a man."

strictures, deserved and undeserved, which were publicly made on Montesquieu are said to have hastened
his death. Ritson's extreme sensitiveness to criticism ended in lunacy, and Racine is thought by many
to have died from the same cause.

Surely disappointment tracks the path of genius.
Thus Collins, the eminent lyric poet, whose "Ode to
the Passions" has made his name famous and familiar
in our day, did not live to enjoy his literary success ;
indeed, his death is known to have been hastened by
long neglect. The last half of his brief life was darkened by melancholy,[1] and his home was a lunatic
asylum. The money received from his publishers as
copyright on his poems he voluntarily refunded, also
paying the entire expense of the edition, after which
he made a bonfire of the sheets. As we have seen in
so many other instances, it was left for posterity to
do Collins justice. In the course of a single generation, without any adventitious aid to bring them into
notice, his poems have come to rank among the best
of their kind in the language. Poor Collins ! unfortunate in love, threatened with blindness, and harassed
by bailiffs half his life, his career was one of unrest,

---

[1] Collins was deeply attached to a young lady, who did not
return his passion, and there is little doubt that the consequent
disappointment preyed upon his mind to such an extent as finally
to dethrone his reason. Dr. Johnson says nothing of this, but
tells us how "he loved fairies, genii, giants, and monsters," and
how "he delighted to rove through the meanders of enchantment,
to gaze on the magnificence of golden palaces, and to repose by
waterfalls of Elysian gardens."

unhappiness, and despair; death, the comforter of him whom time cannot console, gave the poet an early grave.[1]

Small was the portion of happiness that fell to the share of these men of genius; the lonely places they occupied were too lofty for companionship. "The wild summits of the mountains are inaccessible," says Madame Necker; "only eagles and reptiles can get there." We have seen how hard appears the fate of genius as a rule, and that its possession is often at the cost of great deprivation and unhappiness. Is it not difficult to recall an instance where a pronounced genius has also enjoyed the quiet beauty of domestic life? Wordsworth's remark, however, is applicable: namely, that men do not make their homes unhappy because they have genius, but because they have not enough genius. The conclusion would seem to be that we may envy talent, but must oftenest pity genius.

About half a century since, the well-known indiscretions of Shelley caused his name to be tabooed in London society, though in moral attributes he stood immeasurably above his friend Byron. Still, he was amenable enough to censure. His poetry is strikingly

---

[1] Johnson met Collins one day with a book under his arm, at which the former looked inquiringly. "I have but one book," said the melancholy poet; "it is the Bible." After his death, which occurred in his thirty-sixth year, there was found among his papers an ode on the "Superstitions of the Highlands." In his last days he committed many manuscript poems to the flames.

brilliant; each line is a complete thought, and the whole sparkles like sunlight upon the sea. After being expelled from college he made a " Gretna Green " marriage with Harriet Westbrook, but eventually abandoned her with his two children, — the woman who had given up all for him, and who in her dark hour of sorrow and despair drowned herself.[1] We can describe Shelley's character no better than by comparing it to his longest poem, the " Revolt of Islam," which abounds in passages of surpassing beauty, but which as a whole is deficient in connection and human interest. It is as erratic as his own life.[2] There is so much of bad in the best, and of good in the worst, that few of us are willing to sit in judgment upon poor humanity. Time has softened the asperity of our feelings, and the productions of Shelley's genius are now justly admired. When, after his fatal accident, his body was washed on shore, a copy of Keats's poems was found in his pocket. His ashes now rest near those of his brother poet outside the gates of Rome. As a striking example of his remarkable sensibility, we may mention the effect upon him when

[1] Shelley's favorite amusement had been boating and sailing. While returning one day — July 8, 1822 — from Leghorn, whither he had been to welcome Leigh Hunt to Italy, his boat was struck by a squall and he was drowned. Thus he met the same fate as his deserted wife.

[2] As to Shelley's mode of composition, he said : " When my brain gets heated with thought, it soon boils and throws off images and words faster than I can skim them off. In the morning, when cooled down, out of that rude sketch, as you justly call it, I shall attempt a drawing."

he first listened to the reading of Coleridge's " Chris-
tabel "[1] in a small social circle. Says one who was
present, " Shelley was so affected that he fainted
dead away." He was consistent, and lived up to his
convictions. While listening to the organ in an
Italian cathedral, he sighed that charity instead of
faith was not regarded as the substance of religion.
The maintenance of his opinion cost him a fine estate, so constant and profuse were his charities
towards impoverished men of letters and the poor
generally.

The author of an " Elegy Written in a Country
Church-Yard "[2] was absolutely a slave to diffidence
and painful shyness, — a characteristic which led to
bitter persecution while he was a young student; nor
could he ever quite divest himself of this nervous
timidity. Hazlitt says of Gray that " he was terrified out of his wits at the bare idea of having his
portrait prefixed to his works, and probably died
from nervous agitation at the publicity into which
his name had been forced by his learning, taste, and
genius." On the death of Cibber, the vacant laureate-

---

[1] This production was circulated in manuscript only for the
first three or four years after it was completed. Lockhart says
that it was hearing it read from manuscript that led Scott to produce the " Lay of the Last Minstrel."

[2] " Genius is rarely conscious of its power," says Hazlitt ; " our
own idea is that if Gray had had an eye to his posthumous fame,
had cast a sidelong glance to the approbation of posterity, he
would have failed in producing a work of lasting texture like
this."

ship was offered to Gray, but his sensitiveness led
him to decline it.[1]

[1] It is not many years since the auctioneer in a public sales-
room in London, in the course of his advertised list of objects to
be disposed of, held up two small half sheets of paper, all written
over, torn, and mutilated. He called these scraps most interesting, but apologized for their condition. There was present a
highly intelligent company of amateurs in autographs, attracted by
the sale. The first offer for these scraps of paper was ten pounds.
The bids rose rapidly until sixty-five was reached, when they were
knocked off; but as there proved to be two bidders at that price,
it was necessary to put them up again. They were finally closed
at one hundred pounds. These scraps of paper, which were
almost a hundred years old to a day, were the original copy of
" Gray's Elegy."

CHAPTER VII

In these desultory chapters we have more than once seen that fame appeals to posterity; but in the instance of Byron it was contemporary, for he tells us he " awoke one morning and found himself famous." No man's errors were ever more closely observed and recorded than his ; and we are still too near the period of his life to forget his foibles and remember only the productions of his genius. Byron, like Pope, was a sufferer from physical deformity, and much of the morbid sensibility of both arose from their common misfortune. Macaulay, speaking of Byron, says : " He had naturally a generous and feeling heart, but his temper was wayward and irritable. He had a head which statuaries loved to copy, and a foot the deformity of which the beggar in the street mimicked. Distinguished at once by the strength and by the weakness of his intellect, affectionate yet perverse, a poor lord and a handsome cripple, he required, if ever man required, the finest and most judicious training. But capriciously as Nature had dealt with him, the parent to whom the office of forming his character was intrusted was more capricious still. She passed from paroxysms of rage to paroxysms of tenderness.

At one time she stifled him with her caresses ; at
another time she insulted his deformity. He came into
the world ; and the world treated him as his mother
had treated him, — sometimes with fondness, sometimes with cruelty, never with justice. It indulged
him without discrimination, and punished him without
discrimination. He was truly a spoiled child, — the
spoiled child of fortune, the spoiled child of fame, the
spoiled child of society." The author of " Don Juan "
was actuated at times by a strange recklessness, and
a desire to seem worse than he really was. He aped
the misanthrope, assumed unfelt remorse, and affected
singularity, in order to court notoriety. However
capricious may have been his temper, he came rightly
enough by it, since his mother was noted for the
frenzied violence of her passion, being wholly without
judgment or self-control, and in nearly every respect
disqualified for performing a parent's duty.[1] Byron
was also a victim of hypochondria only in a less degree than Johnson and Cowley ; and this is his one
genuine excuse for the excesses into which he sometimes rushed headlong. No matter in what light we

---

[1] Speaking of Byron's mother, Dawson, the brilliant English
lecturer, says : "She was a shrieking, howling, red-faced, passionate, self-indulgent person ; now spoiling him by ridiculous indulgence, now subjecting him to her extravagant wrath. A ridiculous
person, an absurd person, short and fat. What a sight it was to
see her in a rage, running round the room after the lame boy, and
he mocking, and dodging, and hopping about ! Although that
may be droll to hear, it was tragical to suffer from; and there is
much mercy to be bestowed upon a man whose father was a black-
guard and whose mother was a fool ! "

consider him, all must concede the fervor of his passionate genius; and therein lay his remarkable power,
for man is at his greatest when stimulated by the
passions. Enthusiasm is contagious, and infuses a
spirit of emulation; while reason, calm and forcible,
only wins us by the slow process of conviction.

The truest grandeur of our nature is often born of
sorrow. Those who have suffered most have developed the profoundest sympathies and have sung for
us the sweetest notes. It is the heart which is seamed
with scars that compels other hearts. Charles Lamb,
at one time himself confined in an insane asylum,
lived to the end of his days with, and in charge of, an
unfortunate sister, who in a fit of madness murdered
her mother, — an experience sufficient to cast, as it
did, an awful blight over his whole life; but it was
the occasion in him of an instance of holy human
love and pure self-denial seldom equalled. Poor Mary
Lamb [1] knew when these mental attacks were coming
on, and then her brother and herself, hand in hand,
sought the asylum, to the matron of which he would
say, "I have brought Mary again;" and presently,

---

[1] We quote from one of his sister's letters to a confidential
friend : "Charles is very busy at the office; he will be kept there
to-day until seven or eight o'clock. He came home very smoky
and drinky last night, so that I am afraid a hard day's work will
not agree very well with him. I have been eating a mutton-chop
all alone, and I have just been looking into the pint porter-pot,
which I find quite empty, and yet I am still very dry; if you
were with me, we would have a glass of brandy and water, but it
is quite impossible to drink brandy and water by one's self." Is
not this a quiet peep behind the curtain ?

when the attack had passed, he was at the door of the asylum to receive her once more and take her kindly home. The domestic tragedy and his sister's condition caused Lamb to give up all idea of marriage, though at the time of the sad occurrence he was sincerely attached to a lovely woman. The court, after Mary's trial, consigned her to her brother's care. He wrote to his friend Coleridge, " I am wedded to the fortunes of my sister and my poor old father." The father died not long subsequent, but Mary survived Charles thirteen years, dying in 1847. With considerable ability as a versifier, Lamb will not be remembered as a poet ; his fame will rest on his essays and his sagacious criticisms. The " Essays of Elia " are inimitable, full of the author's personality, exquisitely delicate, poetical, whimsical, witty, and odd. The only fault to be reasonably found with them is their brevity. We wish there were a dozen volumes in place of one. They are the pedestal upon which the fame of this gentle, charitable, and quaint genius will ever rest. Lamb's character was amiably eccentric, but always full of loving-kindness. The pseudonym of " Elia " has become famous, and was first assumed in the author's contributions to the " London Magazine." While his lovable disposition and pensive cast of thought tinge all his productions, there is ever a playfulness lurking just below the surface which is sure to captivate the most casual reader. During his life Lamb was looked upon by the world as possessing more oddity than genius ; but now all join

in admitting him to be one of the fixed stars of literature.[1] What a significant fact it is that Lamb was so
tenderly regarded by the galaxy of notable men with
whom he associated! He was a schoolmate of Coleridge and intimate with him for fifty years. Southey,
Hazlitt, Wordsworth, Godwin, De Quincey, Edward
Irving, Thomas Hood, Leigh Hunt, and other men of
literary fame were the warm and loving friends of
Charles Lamb.

With all his æsthetic proclivities, " Elia" was of
a sensuous nature. Besides roast pig, he had other
favored dishes, not rare and luxurious, but special,
nevertheless. He was particularly fond of brawn, and
considered tripe to be superlatively appetizing when
suitably prepared. He was also a connoisseur in all
sorts of drinks; not that he was extravagant,—on the
contrary, he was to a degree self-denying, and even
with all his little generosities and his care of his sister

---

[1] It was singular that with his acute sensibility and tenderness
of nature Lamb never cared for music. But this was the case
with Dr. Johnson, Fox, Pitt, and Sir James Mackintosh. Johnson was observed by a friend to be extremely inattentive at a
concert, while a celebrated solo player was running up the divisions
and subdivisions of notes upon the violin. The friend desiring to
induce the Doctor to give his attention, remarked how difficult the
performance was. "Difficult, do you call it, sir?" replied Johnson. "I wish it were impossible." It will also be remembered
that Goethe was not particularly fond of music. Once at a court
concert in Weimar, when a pianist was in the middle of a very
long sonata, the poet suddenly rose up, and, to the horror of the
assembled ladies and gentlemen, exclaimed, "If this lasts three
minutes longer, I shall confess everything!"

Mary he managed to leave two thousand pounds, saved out of his always moderate income, to make that sister comfortable. He wrote to Wordsworth: " God help me! I am a Christian, an Englishman, a Londoner, a Templar. When I put off these snug relations and go to the world to come, I shall be like a crow on the sand." Lamb said that oftentimes absurd images forced themselves with irresistible power upon his mind, — such, for instance, as an elephant in a coach office gravely waiting to have his trunk booked; or a mermaid over a fish-kettle cooking her own tail ![1]

Wordsworth — to whom we have already alluded more than once — was at times distressingly poor, and in such straitened circumstances that he and his family denied themselves meat for days together. Had it not been for the admirable influence of his sister Dorothy, who cheered his spirits and counteracted his morbid tendencies, his mind might have drifted into something like insanity. His disappointment was great at the comparative failure of his literary work, which brought him little in the way of pecuniary return during his life. A fortunate legacy and comparatively sinecure office, however, finally afforded him humble independence.

It seems gratuitous to refer to the natural weakness

---

[1] Leigh Hunt tells us that Lamb was under the middle size, and of fragile make, but with a head as fine as if it had been carved on purpose. He had a very weak stomach. Three glasses of wine would put him in as lively a condition as can be wrought in some men only by as many bottles.

of so pure and good a man as Wordsworth, but we
have tried to be impartial in these pages. Grand
and simple as our poet was, he had the element of
vanity snugly stowed away among his attributes, yet
ready to betray itself on occasion. It is related that
sometimes when he met a little child he would stop
and ask him to observe his face carefully, so that in
after years the child might be able to say he had seen
the great Wordsworth. " Wordsworth," says Charles
Lamb, "one day told me that he considered Shakspeare greatly overrated. 'There is,' said he, ' an
immensity of trick in all Shakspeare wrote, and
people are taken by it. Now, if I had a mind, I
could write exactly like Shakspeare!' So you see,"
added Lamb, " it was only the mind that was wanting!" The late James T. Fields, who was a hearty
admirer and personal friend of the poet, said, " Yes,
Wordsworth was vain; but think for a moment what
he has produced, and how much he had in him to be
self-conscious of!"

Colton, better known by his *nom de plume* of
" Lacon," is a vivid illustration of the eccentricities
of genius. Though he was a man whose personal
character is entirely unworthy of our respect, yet no
one can deny that he was endowed with marked and
original powers. He comes before us in our day
simply as the author of his remarkable Laconics,
full of spontaneous thoughts happily expressed, and
which will compare favorably with the apothegms of
Bacon or the terse brevities of Rochefoucauld. The

eccentricities and irregularities of Colton are almost
too extravagant for belief, and certainly will not bear
rehearsal. At one and the same time a clergyman of
fair repute and the secret companion of sporting-men
and gamblers, he was always playing a double part.
He was the author of several important pamphlets
and some excellent poetry, and, when abroad, the
well-paid correspondent of the London press. Notwithstanding the wit and consummate wisdom of the
volume which made him famous, it must be admitted
that he was incapable of appreciating what was grand
and noble in principle. Deeply in debt, he fled to
Paris to escape the importunities of his creditors,
where he became a confirmed and undisguised gambler. Here at one time he realized such an extraordinary run of luck as to break a famous bank, becoming
the possessor of nearly thirty thousand pounds. His
experience was like that of nearly every one who becomes suddenly rich in a similar manner. He lost
every penny of his winnings within a few weeks, and
retired to Fontainebleau, where he ended his life by
suicide.[1] In future generations, when his personal
career is forgotten, his one remarkable literary monument will still remain, like the column of Luxor,
imperishable.

---

[1] In his volume of wise sayings, which has passed through
many editions, we find this paragraph : "The gamester, if he
dies a martyr to his profession, is doubly ruined. He adds his
soul to every other loss, and by the act of suicide renounces
earth to forfeit heaven!"

It is known to every mathematician that the regular gambler must lose in the end, even though he may "break the bank" now and then. Even if the bank is honestly conducted, all the chances are against him. The theory of probabilities has become almost an exact science. Arago, — the famous French astronomer and natural philosopher, — when consulted by a gentleman who was infatuated with the terrible vice of gambling, told him, within a few francs, how much he had lost the preceding year. "But I must play," was the answer. "It is true that I find my fortune diminishing every year, as you have stated; but can you not tell me how, on a capital of five million francs, I may save enough to give me a decent burial in the end?" Arago, after learning the gambler's method of playing, and the sum he risked, told him that he must reduce the amount of his daily ventures to a certain small number of francs, and that, according to the law of chances, however cool and calm his playing, he would lose his five million francs in about fifteen years. Every body of stockholders in a faro bank can calculate on twenty per cent of their investment being returned to them yearly.

Could genius enjoy the advantage of being judged by its peers, it would stand a better chance for contemporary fame; but overshadowed, as it so often is, by foibles, waywardness, and those passions alike common to the humble and the exalted, it must pass through the crucible of time to fit it for sincere homage. Robert Burns, whose struggle with fate began almost beside the cradle, and whose youth was one ceaseless buffeting with misfortune, is an illustration in point. His productions are not of a character to set aside altogether the remembrance of his follies, though we are all inclined to treat the memory of the Scottish bard with indulgence and half reverence, while we hasten to acknowledge his great and unquestioned genius. Burns was sadly addicted to whiskey and tobacco, which led Byron, as we have already said, to call him "a strange compound of dirt and deity." The author of "Childe Harold" forgot the proverb about those who live in glass houses. Burns, from early youth, was subject to extraordinary fits of dejection, which amounted to a species of hypochondria, long before convivial society had inoculated him with the then popular vice of intemperance. He became finally an incongruous mixture of mirth and melancholy, while poverty with its attendant ills was seldom from his door. He writes to a friend : "I have been for some time pining under secret wretchedness ; the pang of disappointment, the sting of pride, and some wandering stabs of remorse settle on my vitals like vultures when my attention is not called away by the claims of society or the vagaries of the Muse." Poor, ill-fated genius ![1] By his follies and indulgences he as surely committed suicide in his thirty-seventh year

---

[1] When the last scene came, those who had neglected him in life, at least paid their respects to his remains ; twelve thousand people followed the body of Robert Burns to its resting-place in the grave.

as did the starving, half-delirious Chatterton on his bed of straw.

Mrs. Dunlop, an early patroness of Burns, had in her family an old and favored housekeeper, who did not exactly relish her mistress's attention to a man of such low estate. In order to overcome her prejudice, her mistress induced the domestic to read one of Burns's poems, the "Cotter's Saturday Night." When Mrs. Dunlop inquired her opinion of the poem, the housekeeper replied with quaint indifference, "Aweel, madam, that's vera weel." "Is that all you have to say in its favor?" asked the mistress. "'Deed, madam," she replied, "the like o' you quality may see a vast in 't; but I was aye used the like o' all that the poet has written about in my ain father's house, and atweel I dinna ken how he could hae described it any other gate." When Burns heard of the old woman's criticism, he remarked that it was one of the highest compliments he had ever received.

The name of Thoreau suggests itself in this connection. He lived in a cabin erected by himself on the borders of Walden Pond, a voluntary hermit, frugal and self-denying, that he might enjoy a studious retirement. The intimate friend of Emerson and Hawthorne must have had fine original qualities to commend him. Known at the outset only as an oddity, he grew finally to be respected and admired for his quaint genius. He experienced a disappointment in love, which doubtless had much to do with his social pecu-

liarities.[1] In business and the affairs of every-day
life he was utterly impracticable. He supported himself during his college course at Cambridge by teaching school, doing carpentering, and other work. The
restrictions of society were intolerable to him; he
never attended church, never paid a tax, and never
voted. He ate no flesh, drank no wine, never used
tobacco, and though a naturalist, used neither trap
nor gun. When asked at dinner what dish he preferred, he answered, "The nearest." "So many nega-
tive superiorities smack somewhat of the prig," says
one of his reviewers. "Time," says Thoreau, in his
fanciful way, "is but a stream I go fishing in. I
drink at it, but while I drink I see the sandy bottom
and detect how shallow it is. Its thin current slides
away, but eternity remains. I would drink deeper —
fish in the sky, whose bottom is pebbly with stars."
He worshipped Nature in all her forms, and depicted
with a loving and exuberant fancy hills and water,
with the myriad life which peopled them. He wrote
several books which are read to-day with more of
interest than when the author was alive.

Genius and inspiration are so nearly allied as to
leave no dividing line, and the sublimity of martyrdom
is often added to the column of fame. Joan of Arc,

---

[1] We find these two verses in Thoreau's published journal :

I.	II.

Canst thou love with thy mind,
   And reason with thy heart?
Canst thou be kind,
   And from thy darling part?
	Canst thou range earth, sea, and air,
	   And so meet me everywhere?
	Through all events I will pursue thee,
	Through all persons I will woo thee.

the most illustrious heroine of history, was born a poor peasant girl of Lorraine; but at the age of eighteen, impelled by an exalted enthusiasm, she commanded an army of devoted followers, and raising the siege of Orleans gave to Charles VII. a crown. At the age of thirteen she said she received commands from Heaven to go and liberate France; and with a confidence of Divine support she pursued her mission. No romancer would dare to imagine or portray so glorious a heroine; fiction could not equal the actual deeds that this pure and lowly girl accomplished.[1] That she was the agent of Divine Providence to bring about a great political object goes without saying; yet this maid of Domremy was burned at the stake.

Rachel, the child of poverty, the itinerant of the Parisian boulevards, infused with genius, suddenly became the idol of courts and of princes, being as devoutly worshipped by the lovers of art on the banks of the Neva and the Thames as on the shores of her beautiful Seine. How strange were the vicissitudes of this wonderful artist, this frail child of genius! An actress of transcendent dramatic power, she leaves us the souvenir of a splendid star of histrionic art extinguished when it burned the brightest. One day, when Rachel was thus singing and reciting on the public

---

[1] In battle, the maiden displayed a spirit of almost reckless bravery, leading her followers into the thickest of the fight. "She was benign," says Michelet, "in the fiercest conflict, good among the bad, gentle even in war. She wept after the victories, and relieved with her own hands the necessities of the wounded."

street, a benevolent-looking man, with pitying eyes, was attracted, in passing, by the child's intelligent look, and put a five-franc piece in her hand. She took the silver with a grateful courtesy and watched him until he passed out of sight. A citizen who had seen the generous act said, " That was Victor Hugo ; " and the child-actress remembered the name ever after. But little did the great poet anticipate what the pale-faced child was destined to become in that world of art of which he was so distinguished a disciple.

Edwin Forrest, our own famous tragedian, was in Paris in 1836, and was invited by the manager to see an actress who was to make her début at one of the theatres on a certain evening. The manager asked him, in the course of the performance, what he thought of the débutante. Forrest replied that he feared she would never rise above mediocrity, and added, " But that Jewish-looking girl, that little bag of bones, with the marble face and the flaming eyes, — there is demoniacal power in her. If she lives and does not burn out too soon, she will make a great actress." He referred to Rachel, then in her fifteenth year. We all know how that genius developed. Parsimony was a fixed trait of her character; she could not help it. " Is it any wonder," she once said to a friend, " that I should be fond of money, considering the suffering I went through in my youth to earn a few sous ? "

It appears as if Nature scattered her seeds of genius to the wind, so many take root and blossom in sterile places, and also that she delights to add vigor and glory to her chance productions. Thus Adelina Patti, the greatest prima donna of her day, was once a barefooted child in the streets of New York. Kings and queens, spellbound by her glorious voice, have delighted to honor her; but her domestic life was wrecked at the moment of her greatest professional triumph. Complete success is granted to none. Some bitterness is sure to tincture our cup of bliss, for, after all, it is of earth and not of heaven. Perfection may exist with angels above, but not among mortals. The life of genius is beset with extraordinary temptations; the stimulating spur of praise, flattery, and high homage should be, but rarely is, counterbalanced by the curb of reason. We have already seen that great genius and true domestic happiness are seldom found under the same roof. The extraordinary development of certain faculties argues diminution in others; and where there are extremes, it is ever difficult to harmonize the various parts.

Miss Landon, the youthful and tender poetess and novelist, known to the world by her familiar signature "L. E. L.," coined the treasures of her brain to support those who were dependent upon her. In one of her letters she says, "My life, since the age of fifteen years, has been one incessant struggle with adversity." Her productions can hardly be said to bear the stamp of high genius, but they enjoyed a certain popularity and procured the much-needed money. The mystery of her early and mournful death is only known in heaven. She died from a dose of prussic acid, in her thirty-sixth year, which was also her bridal year.[1]

The infinitely sweet and touching poems of Mrs. Hemans were the outflow of a heart yearning for human affection and finding it not. Her domestic life also proved to be a marked failure. She separated from her husband after six years of married life, and never saw him again. Her genius was early developed; her poems were contributed to the London press at the age of fifteen.[2] She died at the age of forty-one, worn out by domestic unhappiness and ill health. She has herself said, "There is strength deep-bedded in our hearts, of which we reck but little till the shafts of heaven have pierced its frail dwelling. Must not earth be rent before her gems are found?" "It has been the fashion among youthful critics of late," says Epes Sargent, "to undervalue her productions; but not a few of these have a charm, a tenderness, and a spirit which must make them long dear to the hearts of the many." Her complete works, containing a tragedy entitled, "The Vespers of Palermo," are contained in six volumes. We may also

[1] Her husband, George Maclean, was Governor of Cape Coast Castle, and, as is well known, treated her with marked disrespect, even going so far as to introduce a favorite mistress into the castle. Some envious people circulated vile reports as to "L. E. L.," but no one of intelligence ever heeded them.

[2] "Her gladness was like a burst of sunlight," says one of her own sex who knew her well; "and if in her sadness she resembled the night, it was night wearing her stars. She was a Muse, a Grace, a variable child, a dependent woman, the Italy of human beings."

recall the sad, sad life of Charlotte Brontë, the poor
curate's daughter, whose orphaned childhood was so
miserable, and whose youth was drudgery as a school-
teacher at sixteen pounds a year. Under the pressure
of extreme ill health and a heart nearly broken with
sorrow, this daughter of genius produced "Jane
Eyre," a novel of such power, piquancy, and originality
as to take the reading world by storm. She was
finally married, but only to die in her bridal year.
The three daughters of Rev. Patrick Brontë were each
endowed with literary genius, which under happier circumstances might have developed into famous results.
Charlotte wrote, as we have said, "Jane Eyre;"
Emily wrote "Wuthering Heights," an almost equally
popular novel; and Anne wrote the "Tenant of
Wildfell Hall." The three unitedly published in 1846
"Poems by Currer, Ellis, and Acton Bell," the sisters' respective pseudonyms.[1] The father's income
was one hundred and seventy pounds a year, upon
which to support a family of twelve persons. He
was a man of more than ordinary culture and of
much poetic talent. A volume of his poems was published in 1811, entitled "Cottage Poems." He survived his whole family. Many critics have pronounced
"Villette," published by Charlotte a couple of years

---

[1] Charlotte married her father's curate, Mr. Nicholls. The
other two sisters died young and unmarried. "The bringing
out of our book of poems," writes Charlotte, "was hard work.
As was to be expected, neither we nor our poems were at all
wanted."

before her death, to be superior in construction and interest to "Jane Eyre."

It would seem that deep and thoughtful minds, like deep waters, must have a gloom in them, and that ideal life leads to turbulence of soul. Nathaniel Hawthorne, endowed by Nature with an acute and subtle intellect, always suffered more or less from a morbid sensibility. Even in his youth, like Burns, he was oppressed by fits of deep dejection, which gave his friends much anxiety. His order of genius was of the highest; of that there is no doubt. His style is simple, graceful, and forcible, with a power to awaken intense interest in the characters which he delineated. The "Scarlet Letter" is perhaps the best known and most popular of his several productions; and much of the same half-suppressed, feverish excitement is realized in its perusal as in a degree characterized Hawthorne himself. His most prominent trait as an author lay in his originality and power of analysis.[1]

Insanity is often the result of an overtasked sensitive brain wandering in the realms of fancy. Like a high-mettled horse, it sometimes throws the rider, — as in the instance of Cowper, Collins, and others already spoken of in these pages. Charles Fenno Hoffman, the ripe scholar, poet, and novelist, conceded

[1] Longfellow was a classmate of Hawthorne in college, and Franklin Pierce was his most intimate friend. When Pierce was chosen President, he at once appointed our author to the Consulship at Liverpool, which lucrative office he held for four years.

to be one of the best song-writers we have had in America, was bereft of reason and died the inmate of an insane asylum, where the last quarter of his life was passed. While yet a boy, Hoffman met with an accident so serious as to render necessary the amputation of one of his legs, and thenceforth he was obliged to go with a wooden one.

Béranger, like De Foe, was at one period the prime favorite of the Court, and presently was languishing within the dreary walls of the Bastile, where he wrote some of his most effective poems. Contemporary with Béranger was Alfred de Musset, a poet and littérateur of rare excellence, possessed of a flow of poetical genius characterized by passion, vivacity, and grace, notwithstanding that a morbid, misanthropic frame of mind consumed him in secret. His youthful liaison with George Sand is familiar to us all, and no doubt it left a weird influence upon his life. When De Musset received money he would squander it in the most reckless dissipation, then live on bread and onions until he earned another supply, to be lavished in the same manner. He was the intimate friend of the Duke of Orleans, Victor Hugo, and other notable men, but deliberately chose the debasing career of a drunkard, and died at the premature age of forty-seven, a victim to the demon of alcohol.

The grandmother of Alexandre Dumas the elder was an African negress. He enjoyed no educational advantages, until while yet a mere boy, actuated by a Bohemian spirit, which always influenced him more

or less, he wandered away from his native place
(Villers-Cotterets, France), and sought a stranger's
home in Paris. Many of the varied productions of
this prolific and sensual novelist bear testimony to
his African origin, in their savage voluptuousness and
barbaric taste. Dumas was one of the greatest plagiarists of modern times, so that it was said by his
critics that he introduced the sweating system into
literature. But no intelligent reader can deny that
he was a great genius,[1] — in evidence of which he
possessed the thousand and one conventional characteristics of the race. At one time he would resort
to all manner of expedients to dodge his creditors
and escape arrest for debt, at another scattering
gold with the most lavish and inconsiderate hand.
Unlike Lamartine, he failed entirely in politics, but
certainly was for years the most popular novelist in
France. Dumas was frequently in the receipt of
large sums in gold from the many popular books
which he wrote. When this money was received it
was placed in a pile upon the table of his sitting-
room, and if appealed to in behalf of a charity,
or asked for aid by an impecunious caller, he sent
the parties to *help themselves* as long as the pile of
napoleons lasted! Such reckless disregard of reasonable care for money seems almost incredible; but this

---

[1] Thackeray testifies to his hearty admiration of the elder
Dumas in these words: "I think of the prodigal banquets to
which this Lucullus of a man has invited me, with thanks and
wonder."

story is authenticated by his son, the present popular author and dramatist, Alexandre Dumas.

The life of Douglas Jerrold is still another example of the mutability of fortune; at first call-boy in a theatre, then a sailor, and finally a printer's apprentice, he became at last a famous dramatist, essayist, wit, and humorist. The anecdote of his first contribution to the press is perhaps not too familiar to repeat. He was a youthful compositor in a publishing office, where he ventured to drop anonymously into the editor's box a contribution consisting of a criticism on "Der Freischütz." He lay awake that night thinking of his venture, and the next morning was rendered half frantic with joy when his copy was handed to him to be put into type by his own hands. Appended to the copy the editor had written a note, asking the anonymous author for further contributions. Jerrold became a prominent member of the brilliant coterie which made "Punch," that daring wag, a great moral and political power. Many of his best sayings — flashes of wit like those of Wycherley, Congreve, and Sheridan — rarely found their way into print, being uttered in small social circles, or in the society of the London clubs, where he was rather feared for the keenness of his satire, as he was no respecter of persons. As a dramatist Jerrold is best known by those popular plays, "The Rent Day" and "Black-Eyed Susan,"[1] the latter being still considered the

[1] Jerrold was but twenty-five years of age when he wrote this the first of his dramas. It was a great success from the start, and

best nautical drama on the stage. Good-fellowship, as it is falsely called, was the bane of Jerrold's life; and though he realized a most liberal income, he died poor and grievously in debt. During the last years of his life he was editor of "Lloyd's Weekly Newspaper," from which he received one thousand pounds per annum, besides an income of a very handsome amount for other and various literary work.

Charles Dickens, whose early career was not without its severe discipline, and who was indisputably one of the greatest literary geniuses of modern times, certainly shortened his life by free living. He was extravagantly fond of the pleasures of the table, and a constant participant in convivial occasions.[1] Undoubtedly his domestic infelicity was largely attributable to a habit of overstimulating, besides which, brandy and continuous literary effort are incompatible with each other. His later works will not compare favorably with his earlier ones. "Our Mutual Friend" was not worthy of his reputation; and the half of "Edwin Drood" which was published was not of a character to make an intelligent reader desire more. At fifty-eight his brain was failing. Both Dickens and Thackeray were really sacrificed to the Moloch of conviviality. The latter was not only a remark-

---

had a run of three hundred consecutive nights, though the author received but seventy pounds for the copyright.

[1] Sydney Smith, when talking of the bad effect of late hours, said of a distinguished diner-out, that it should be written on his tomb, "He dined late," — to which Luttrell added, "And died early."

able novelist, but is entitled to distinct fame as a
poet. He was a man of noble impulses, and charitable to a fault. He inherited a small fortune, in
the expenditure of which he was very lavish, at one
time giving the impecunious Dr. Maginn five hundred
pounds, — an unfortunate brother author who appealed
to Thackeray when he was in a strait; and no needy
man was ever refused by the author of "Vanity Fair."

There are few objects which if held up against a
strong light, will not betray some defect. A perfect
emerald was perhaps never seen, and almost as rare
is a perfect diamond; the magnifying-glass is pretty
sure to detect some flaw in the gem, be it never so
small. So the microscope applied to genius is apt to
discover those imperfections of humanity from which
no mortal is entirely exempt. Washington said it
was lamentable that great characters are so seldom
without blot.[1] Edgar A. Poe, whose genius has so
lately received public recognition, was left an orphan
at a tender age, thus lacking the moral influence and
training which might have prevented the blight of his
after years. His father was a law-student, and his
mother an actress named Elizabeth Arnold. Heaven
had breathed into his soul the fire of a master-spirit,
but at the same time endowed him with a morbid sen-

---

[1] Some one told Father Taylor, the well-known seamen's
clergyman of Boston, that a certain individual who was under
discussion was a very good citizen, except for an amiable weakness. "But I have found," said the practical old preacher, "that
weakness of character is nearly the only defect which cannot be
remedied."

sitiveness which rendered his imagination weird and gloomy. He became the victim of strong drink, and was thereby marked for an early grave, dying, after an erratic career, in a public hospital. He was an editor, critic, and poet, wielding a most witty but bitterly sarcastic pen. When penniless and in absolute want, he wrote to a friend, with a supreme contempt of the very sinews of war for which he was suffering: "The Romans worshipped their standard, and the Roman standard happened to be an eagle. Our standard is only one tenth of an eagle, one dollar, but we make all even by adoring it with tenfold devotion." Even in boyhood Poe developed a wild, unruly disposition, being expelled from the University of Virginia, and afterwards from the West Point Academy. The writer of these pages knew Poe personally, and employed him as a regular contributor to a paper which the writer was editing. Poe's literary reputation rests mainly upon one remarkable poem, "The Raven." Mr. Lowell's portrait of the author of "The Raven" is both concise and true, — "three fifths of him genius and two fifths sheer fudge." He was unquestionably a man of genius, but wrong-headed from very childhood.

We must worship our literary heroes and heroines from afar: indeed, this will apply with force to all notables; intimacy is pretty sure to disenchant us. "The love or friendship of such people," says De Quincey, "rather contracts itself into the narrow circle of individuals. You, if you are brilliant like

themselves, they will hate ; you, if you are dull, they
will despise. Gaze, therefore, on the splendor of
such idols as a passing stranger.   Look for a moment
as one sharing in the idolatry, but pass on before the
splendor has been sullied by human frailty." Admiration is the offspring of ignorance ; even where
familiarity does not breed contempt, it blunts the
keenness of our homage, since to those that know
them best, authors quickly come down from their
pedestals and become only men and women.   One of
Byron's biographers lays it down as a rule to avoid
writers whose works amuse you; for when you see
them they will delight you no more, though Shelley,
he admits, was an exception.   Mr. Emerson thought
the conditions of literary success almost destructive
of the best social powers.   We are told by Lockhart
that Scott could not endure, in London or Edinburgh,
the little exclusive circles of literary society; he
craved the company of men of business and affairs.
" It is much better to read authors than to know
them," says Horace Walpole.   Speaking of young
Mr. Burke, he says (in 1761), that although a
remarkably sensible man, " he has not worn off his
authorship yet, and thinks there is nothing so charming as writers, and to be one.   He will know better
one of these days."   Even Byron hated authors who
were all author, — " fellows in foolscap uniform turned
up with ink."   Miss Mitford, in the ripeness of her
experience, wrote that authors " as a general rule are
the most disappointing people in the world;" much

preferring persons who loved letters to those who followed the profession of authorship. Sir Egerton Brydges, the prolific writer of sonnets, novels, essays, letters, etc., says: "I have observed that vulgar readers almost always lose their veneration for the writings of the genius with whom they have had personal intercourse."

We have spoken several times of the remuneration realized by authors for their literary productions, and perhaps a few more words upon this subject may be of interest to the general reader.

In the reigns of William III., Anne, and George I., literature, however excellent, could not find a sufficient market to fairly requite its authors. Intelligent, cultured men could not realize remunerative incomes by their pen; so the political chiefs of those days came forward and extended official patronage to them in a manner which was often princely and munificent. Thus Congreve, scarcely yet twenty-one years of age, was given a place under Government which made him independent for life. Rowe, poet and dramatist, author of "Tamerlane," was made under-secretary of state, and finally became poet-laureate, in 1714. Hughes, the poet and dramatist, also held a lucrative Government office; he was the author of the "Siege of Damascus," a drama, singular to say, which was played for the first time on the evening of his death. Ambrose Phillips, an author of similar character, was made judge of the prerogative court of Ireland. Locke, the English philosopher, philanthropist, and

voluminous writer, was the recipient of liberal Government patronage.   Newton, it will be remembered, was
made Master of the Royal Mint.   Stepney, the poet,
of whom Dr. Johnson said, " He is a very licentious
translator, and does not recompense the neglect of
his author by beauties of his own," was honored by
various appointments, as also was Matthew Prior, of
whom the same critic heartily approved.   Gay was
made Secretary of Legation at five-and-twenty, — he
whom we have seen come up to London and begin
life as a mercer's clerk.   Montague is another illustrious example of those geniuses who may be said to
have enjoyed at least a degree of sunshine as well as
of shadow.   His poem on the death of Charles II. led
to his various appointments and his earldom.   Steele
was made Commissioner of Stamps, and Swift came
very near being made a bishop.[1]   Addison was appointed Secretary of State, and Dr. Johnson was the
recipient of a pension.   The reader can easily add
instances to such as we have enumerated as those
most readily presenting themselves.   In our own day
excellence in literature is much more remunerative,
and in a legitimate business way.   Good books sell, and
authors receive fair royalties thereon ; but even among
us instances of official recognition for literary merit

---

[1] The prejudice excited in Queen Anne's mind by the Archbishop of York, on account of the alleged infidelity in the " Tale
of a Tub," is supposed to be the reason why Swift's aspirations
were not granted by his royal mistress.   His final unsatisfactory
appointment as Dean of St. Patrick was awarded to him instead
of the coveted bishopric.

are not wanting. We recall in this connection Bancroft the historian, as Minister to Germany; Lowell the scholar and poet, Minister to the Court of St. James. Hawthorne, Irving, Everett, Motley, Bayard Taylor, Howells, and others, have all been officially recognized in a similar manner.

CHAPTER VIII

EGOTISM in eminent characters is often amusing to us, but extremely undignified in them. It is almost always the betrayal of weakness, — the tongue of vanity. He who talks of himself, however humble the words, exposes a proud heart. Still, as Emerson says, "there are dull and bright, sacred and profane, coarse and fine egotists." Carlyle was an egotist of the first water, and so were many other famous authors. Demosthenes expressed his pleasure when even a fishwoman pointed him out in the streets of Athens. Margaret Fuller once wrote: "I have now met all the minds of this country worth meeting, and find none comparable to my own"! The admiration point is ours; the words evince most insufferable vanity. No wonder Emerson complained of her "mountainous me," or that Lowell called the whole of her being a "capital I." Even the gentle, undemonstrative Hawthorne was obliged to denounce her vanity; and yet Margaret was a woman full of kindly human instinct and of remarkable culture. Dickens was vain,[1] egotistical, and selfish, — traits which grew

---

[1] The author remembers him well on the occasion of his first appearance in this country as a lecturer and public reader. His

upon him as he advanced in years. Thackeray, in
his frank, open way, acknowledged his delight at
being recognized by street gamins as the author of
"Vanity Fair." Hans Andersen, like Dante, confi-
dently predicted his own future greatness. Kepler declared that "God has not sent in six thousand years
an observer like myself." Buffon's vanity was pro-
verbial and ridiculous; and yet the man was not
ridiculous according to Pope's idea, that "every man
has just so much vanity as he lacks understanding,"
for we all know that Buffon was a profound naturalist
and scholar. "I am the greatest historian that ever
lived," wrote Gibbon in his private diary; and Goethe
said, "All I have had to do, I have done in kingly
fashion." Albert Dürer, in reviewing his own work,
wrote, "It cannot be better done." Though he had
in his day many admirers, and has even some at the
present time, we confess that his pictures have no attraction for us. However, he has unquestionable merit
as an engraver, and was court painter to Charles V.
Ruskin's conceit peeps out everywhere in his writings.
Nothing could be more egotistical than Disraeli's
(Beaconsfield) novels. George Sand boastfully betrays
her own liaison with De Musset in her popular story of
"Elle et Lui." "I shall be read," says Southey, "by
posterity, if I am not read now, — read with Milton,
and Virgil, and Dante, when poets whose works are

style at that time (which was afterwards changed) was that of a
modern dude, wearing flash waistcoats, double watch-chains, gold
eye-glasses and rings.

now famous will only be known through a biographical dictionary." [1] Most of the eminent men among the ancients were superlatively conceited and vain. Plato quoted the oracle which pronounced him great ; Cæsar frequently commends himself, and so does Cicero. Pliny puts himself on record as one of this class when he wrote to Venator : "The longer your letter was, so much the more agreeable I thought it, especially as it turned entirely upon my works. I am not surprised you should find a pleasure in them, since I know you have the same affection for every composition of mine as you have for the author." "A modern instance" occurs to us here. When a certain distinguished lady asked Lord Brougham, the great English orator and author, who was the *best* debater in the House of Lords, his lordship modestly replied, "Lord Stanley is the *second* best, madam." That some people who despise flatterers do not hesitate to flatter themselves, is an axiom to the truth of which we must all subscribe.

In contradistinction to these, Whittier, the Quaker poet, wrote recently to a correspondent in that gentle, modest manner which is so characteristic of everything relating to him : "I have never thought of myself as a poet in the sense in which we use the word when we speak of the great poets. I have just said from time to time the things I had to say, and

---

[1] No father or mother thinks their own children ugly ; and this self-deceit is yet stronger with respect to the offspring of the mind. — *Cervantes.*

it has been a series of surprises to me that people
should pay so much attention to them, and remember
them so long." Voltaire betrayed his conceit when
he attempted to criticise Shakspeare. Balzac and
Victor Hugo were two egotists. " There are only
three writers of the French language," said Balzac,
— " Victor Hugo, Théophile Gautier, and myself."
Southey, Young, Pope, Dryden, and Wordsworth betrayed their vanity in an egregious manner. Goldsmith was conspicuously vain at times. Landor had
a supreme estimate of his own productions, and wrote
to Wordsworth, concerning his " Imaginary Conversations," as follows : " In two thousand years there
have not been five volumes in prose equal in their
contents to these." [1] Voltaire's remark upon Dante
served only to illustrate his own spleen and jealousy.
" His reputation," said the sarcastic Frenchman, " will
continually be growing greater, because there is now
nobody who reads him." As for Voltaire's tragedies,
De Tocqueville said he could not even read them
through, and he doubted if anybody else could.
Scott said he read the " Henriade " through, and
lived, but it was when he was a young man, and then

---

[1] No one can anticipate the suffrages of posterity. Every man
in judging of himself is his own contemporary. He may feel the
gale of popularity, but he cannot tell how long it will last. His opinion of himself wants distance, wants time, wants numbers, to set off
and confirm it. He must be indifferent to his own merits before he
can feel a confidence in them. Besides, every one must be sensible
of a thousand weaknesses and deficiencies in himself, whereas genius
only leaves behind it the monuments of its strength. — *Hazlitt.*

he read everything. Dr. Johnson once acknowledged
that he never read Milton through until he was obliged
to do so in compiling his dictionary. Southey said
he had read Spenser through about *thirty* times, and
that he could not read Pope once. It was perhaps
singular, but Southey, Coleridge, and Wordsworth
all failed to appreciate Virgil.

Hannah More tells us that on a certain occasion
when she was visiting the Garricks in 1776, David
read aloud to herself and Mrs. Garrick her (Hannah's) last poem. "After dinner Garrick read 'Sir
Eldred' with all his pathos and all his graces. I
think I was never so ashamed in my life; but he read
it so superbly that I cried like a child. Only think
what a ridiculous thing to cry at the reading of one's
own poetry." In another place she says: "Whether
my writings have promoted the spiritual welfare of
my readers, I know not; but they have enabled me
to do good by private charity and public beneficence.
I am almost ashamed to say that they have brought
me thirty thousand pounds." Burns was affected
almost to tears when he heard for the first time
George Lockhart, of Glasgow, sing his verses. "I'll
be hanged if I knew half their merit until now!" he
said. James Hogg, the "Ettrick Shepherd," wrote,
"I cannot express what my feelings were at first
hearing a song of mine sung by a beautiful young
lady in Ettrick to her harpsichord." One recalls in
this connection the legend told in Rome of Canova's
disguising himself and mingling with the crowd of

citizens that he might hear their comments upon a newly unveiled statue just completed by his own hands, and of the great satisfaction he bore away with him at their commendations. Thomas Hood could not suppress his pleasure at listening to the "Song of the Shirt"[1] as sung by the poor sorrowing work-people in the London streets, adapted to rude airs of their own composition. Béranger, the song-writer of France, acknowledged a similar delight in hearing his verses sung upon the Parisian boulevards by the common people. Francis Jacox speaks of the first visit of the old poet Ducis to his beloved master, Louis XVIII., when that monarch graciously recited to him some of his own verses. In an ecstasy of delight Ducis exclaimed: "I am more fortunate than Boileau or Racine; they recited their verses to Louis XIV., but my king recites my verses to me!"

Though people are said to be vainer of qualities which they fondly believe they have than of those which they do really possess, still we must allow to genius some latitude in the matter of conceit, since common people exhibit so much of that spirit on no capital at all. Dr. Holmes says of conceit, that "it is to character what salt is to the ocean, — it keeps it sweet and renders it endurable." Perhaps the acme of conceit is reached when Cicero says, "For all my

---

[1] The "Song of the Shirt" first appeared in "Punch," in 1844; and was Hood's favorite piece of all his published compositions, though the "Bridge of Sighs" was perhaps more popular with the public. Hood died in 1845, at the age of forty-seven.

toils and pains I have no recompense here; but hereafter, in heaven, among the immortal gods, I shall look
back on my beloved city, and find my reward in seeing
her made glorious by my career." Horace, referring
to his future fame, says, "I shall not wholly die."

Vanity, says Shakspeare, keeps persons in favor
with themselves who are out of favor with all others.
He was not himself without a portion of that conceit which he says "in weakest bodies strongest
works;" but there is this difference in his share of
vanity,—he had, indeed, a genius the gods themselves
might envy. He begins one of his sonnets,—

> "Not marble, nor the gilded monuments
> Of princes, shall outlive this powerful rhyme."

And again he says : —

> "Your monument shall be my gentle verse,
> Which eyes not yet created shall o'er-read,
> And tongues to be your being shall rehearse
> When all the breathers of this world are dead ;
> You still shall live — such virtue hath my pen —
> Where breath most breathes, even in the mouths of men."

Sydney Smith's definition occurs to us here, wherein
he defines vanity as "proceeding from the supposi-
tion of possessing something better than the rest of
the world possesses. Nobody is vain of possessing
two legs and two arms, because that is the precise
quantity of either sort of limb which everybody possesses." Fielding bluntly tells the truth when he
says, "There is scarcely any man, however much
he may despise the character of a flatterer, but will

condescend, in the meanest manner, to flatter himself." We have seen that even Diogenes was gratified by popular praise, not to say flattered thereby;
while the fact of his occupying so notable and peculiar an abode argued a degree of pride and vanity.
Did not Thoreau also affect humility in his rudely
built cabin on the borders of Walden Pond? Certainly the idea of Diogenes and his tub must have
occurred to so classic a scholar as the Concord hermit.
Southey's appeal to posterity to do him justice, in his
letter to his publisher, will be remembered: " My day
and popularity will come when I shall have said good-
night to the world." De Quincey remarks that posterity is very hard to get at; and Swift thought the
present age altogether too free in laying taxes on the
next. "Future ages shall talk of this; they shall be
famous to all posterity;" whereas their time and
thoughts, he believed, would be taken up with present
things, as ours are now. Carlyle thought Dr. Johnson's
carelessness as to future fame a very remarkable trait
in his character.

The vanity of authors is their shame, and ought
to be their secret. While it does not necessarily de-
tract from the merit of their excellent productions,
it prejudices all by belittling them in our estimation.
Oftentimes the career of these notables, as we have
seen, has been one of surmounted difficulties and
hardships endured for the sake of their chosen calling,
embittering their nature, perhaps, yet at the same time
tincturing them with an exultant spirit of success.

There are examples in abundance, however, of an opposite character — examples of true modesty and self-forgetfulness — among poets and authors generally. The poet Rogers, as well as Whittier, is a happy example of an equable life with a full share of reasonable blessings. Referring to his irreproachable career, Sheridan told Rogers it was easy for happy people to be good.

> " How noiseless falls the foot of time
> That only treads on flowers ! "

says William Robert Spencer. A modest estimate of self sits gracefully upon genius. Listen to Newton : " I do not know what I may appear to the world, but to myself I seem to have been only like a boy playing on the sea-shore, and diverting myself in now and then finding a smoother pebble or a prettier shell than ordinary, while the great ocean of truth lay all undiscovered before me." Scott was very little tainted with vanity ; indeed, he wrote in his diary that no one disliked or despised the " pap " of praise so heartily as he did. He said there was nothing he scorned more, except those persons who seem to praise one in order to be puffed in return. As a rule, he did not entertain a very high opinion of literary people, or, as we have seen, desire to associate with them. He said : " If I encounter men of the world, men of business, odd or striking characters of professional excellence in any department, I am in my element, for they cannot lionize me without my returning the compliment and learning something of them."

Some people think praise so pleasant and agreeable that they cannot have too much of it. Goldsmith said Garrick was a mere glutton of praise, who swallowed all he came across and mistook it for renown, — the fluffy of dunces. Not actors alone, but writers also, are endowed with a very ravenous appetite for the same sort of nutriment. There is a nest of vanity in almost every breast, and according to Burke it is omnivorous. Rochefoucauld declared that men had little to say when not prompted by vanity.

Another example of unbounded self-conceit occurs to us in the instance of the French poet and dramatist Scudéri, the protégé of Cardinal Richelieu. His genius was not to be doubted, but it was deeply shadowed by his vanity, as made manifest in the preface to his literary works, which abounds in gasconade pure and simple. Of his epic poem " Alaric " he says : " I have such a facility in writing verses, and also in my invention, that a poem of double its length would have cost me but little trouble. Although it contains only eleven thousand lines, I believe that longer epics do not exhibit more embellishment than mine." Poor, self-satisfied Scudéri! both he and his works are very nearly forgotten, though he was an honored member of the French Academy.[1]   John

---

[1] His sister, Mlle. de Scudéri, is better known to us in literature than himself. She was a distinguished member of the society which met at the Hôtel de Rambouillet, and which has been made so famous by Molière in his " Précieuses ridicules." She survived her brother some years.

Heyward, poet and jester, a court favorite in the days of Queen Mary, is another example of consummate vanity. He was among the earliest who wrote English plays. In a work which he produced, in 1556, called " The Spider and the Fly," a parable there are seventy-seven chapters, and at the beginning of each is a portrait of the author in various attitudes, either sitting or standing by a window hung with cobwebs. Dryden honestly declared that it was better for him to own his failing of vanity than for the world to do it for him; and adds : " For what other reason have I spent my life in so unprofitable a study ? Why am I grown old in seeking so unprofitable a reward as fame ? The same parts and application which have made me a poet might have raised me to any honors of the gown." Sometimes Goethe speaks with the true breath of humility, and sometimes quite the reverse. He says, " Had I earlier known how many excellent things have been in existence for hundreds and thousands of years, I should have written no line; I should have had enough else to do." And yet Goethe is not only the most illustrious name in German literature, but one of the greatest poets of any age or nation.

Eugene Sue,[1] who was born in luxury, and who

---

[1] Sue studied medicine at first, and was with the French army in Spain(1823) as military surgeon. After inheriting his father's fortune, he studied painting, but renounced that art finally to engage in literature. His romances were for a time as popular as those of Dumas, and in their character as immoral as those of Paul de Kock.

need never have written for support, would sit down
to write only in full dress, even wearing, as we have
seen, kid gloves, — an evidence of vanity which has
a precedent in Buffon, who when found engaged in
literary work was always curled, powdered, ruffled,
and perfumed. N. P. Willis was as dainty in his
dress as in his style of writing; and Emerson's remark
relative to Nature would well apply to him, when he
says, " She is never found in undress."   Ruskin, who
lives in a glass house as it regards the matter of self-
esteem, charges Goethe with self-complacency, and at
the same time adds that this quality marks a second-
rate character.   The reader will not be long in determining which of the two was the more amenable to
such criticism.   Before we dismiss Mr. Ruskin let us
quote a letter of his published not long since, and
written so late as 1881, addressed to Alexander Mitch-
ell.   " What in the devil's name," he writes, " have
you to do with either Mr. Disraeli or Mr. Gladstone?
You are a student at the university, and have no more
business with politics than you have with rat-catching.
Had you ever read ten words of mine with understanding, you would have known that I care no more for
Mr. Disraeli or Mr. Gladstone than for two old bagpipes with their drones going by steam; but that I
hate all Liberalism as I do Beelzebub, and that, with
Carlyle, I stand — we two alone now in England —
for God and the Queen ! "   So much for the vanity
and conceit of Mr. John Ruskin.

Pope never saw the inside of a university, or indeed

of a school worthy of the name. Two Romish priests attempted at different times to do something for him as personal tutors, but with little success. "This was all the teaching I had," he says, "and God knows it extended a very little way." And yet at the age of sixteen he thought himself, as he has recorded, "to be the greatest genius that ever was;" and we are afraid that this vanity and self-conceit never quite deserted him. Atterbury compared him to Homer in a nutshell. Dr. Johnson pronounces Pope's Iliad to be "the noblest version of poetry which the world has ever seen; and its publication must therefore be considered as one of the great events in the annals of learning." As soon as Pope was pecuniarily able he made himself a comfortable home, and brought his aged parents into it and made them happy. He calls his existence "a long disease;" but if he was "sent into this breathing world but half made up," Nature compensated him by the richness with which she endowed his brain. "In the streets he was an object of pity," says Tuckerman; "at his desk, a king." Though his life was embittered in a measure by his physical deformity and by ill-health, he was not lacking in the tenderness of heart which forms the key-note to all domestic happiness. "I never in my life knew," says Bolingbroke, "a man who had so tender a heart for his particular friends, or a more general friendship for mankind." As to his poetry there has always been a great diversity of opinion, but we think it reached the height of art. It is therefore difficult to realize the egotism which could prompt the following couplet from his pen in the ripeness of his fame : —

> " I own I 'm proud, — I must be proud, to see
> Men not afraid of God afraid of me."

Colley Cibber was a sharp thorn in Pope's side ; he was a witty actor, as well as clever dramatist and mediocre poet. He was chosen poet-laureate in 1730. His most popular comedy was " Love's Last Shift, or the Fool in Fashion," though it divided the honors with the " Careless Husband," in which Cibber himself enacted the principal rôle. Dr. Johnson disliked him because, " though he was not a blockhead, he was pert, petulant, and presumptuous." On the stage he excelled in almost the whole range of light, fantastic, comic characters ; but in poetry, which he much affected, his lyrics were all so bad that his friends pretended he made them so on purpose, and fully justified Johnson's remark that they were " truly incomparable." He was the recipient of a pension of two hundred pounds from George I.

There is a vein of vanity in most of us : few authors or artists are without a share ; and, singular to say, it most frequently arises from trivial matters in which there would seem to be the least cause for pride. William Mitford, the author of the " History of Greece," a scholarly and admirable piece of literary work, was most proud of his election to a captaincy in the Southampton militia. To be sure, his literary work challenged some severe criticism ; De

Quincey said of it, "It is as nearly perfect in its injustice as human infirmity will allow." Carlyle certainly magnified his own calling when he wrote: "O thou who art able to write a book, which once in the two centuries or oftener there is a man gifted to do, envy not him whom they name conqueror or city-builder, and inexpressibly pity him whom they name conqueror or city-burner." Great as he was in authorship, Macaulay in one of his letters remarks, "I never read again the most popular passages of my own works without painfully feeling how far my execution has fallen short of the standard which is in my mind." He is undoubtedly one of the noblest characters in English literature, and his mortal remains very properly rest in the Poets' Corner of Westminster Abbey, — a favorite resort of the great historian during his life. As an example of modest merit we recall the name of Robert Boyle, the Irish chemist and linguist, the great experimental philosopher of the seventeenth century, — he whom some wit called "the father of chemistry and the brother of the Earl of Cork." He translated the Gospels into the Malay language, and published the translation at his own expense; he was besides a thorough Hebrew and Greek scholar. His many published works are all profound and useful. He was chosen President of the Royal Soceity, but refused the honor, from an humble estimate of his own merit, and for the same reason declined a peerage which was tendered to him. We owe to him, according to Boerhaave, "the secrets of fire, air, water, animals, plants, and fossils." Boyle cared nothing for fame.

In realizing that genius is apt among its other foibles to be over self-conscious, we should be careful not to confound conceit with vanity, to which it is so nearly allied. The latter makes one sensitive to the opinions of others, while the former renders us self-satisfied. Few have possessed either genius or personal beauty without being conscious of it; though Hazlitt declares that no great man ever thought himself great, — an assertion which the reader will hardly be prepared to indorse. A famous American philosopher was persuaded that vanity was often the source of good to the possessor, and that among other comforts of life, one might consistently thank God for his vanity. Still, when evinced in social intercourse nothing is more derogatory to dignity; one becomes not only his own, but everybody's fool. "Vanity is so anchored in the heart of man," says Pascal, "that a soldier, sutler, cook, and street porter vapor and wish to have their admirers; and philosophers even wish the same."

Concerning localities rendered of special interest by association, Leigh Hunt said: "I can no more pass through Westminster without thinking of Milton, or the Borough without thinking of Chaucer and Shakspeare, or Gray's Inn without calling Bacon to mind, or Bloomsbury Square without Steele and Akenside, than I can prefer bricks and mortar to wit and poetry, or not see a beauty upon it beyond architecture, in the splendor of the recollection. I once had duties to perform which kept me out late at night, and severely taxed my health and spirits. My path lay through a neighborhood in which Dryden lived; and though nothing could be more commonplace, and I used to be tired to the heart and soul of me, I never hesitated to go a little out of the way, purely that I might pass through Gold Street, to give myself the shadow of a pleasant thought." Gibbon was twenty-three years in preparing the material for and in writing his " Decline and Fall of the Roman Empire;" that is to say, he began it in 1764, and did not finish it until 1787. He says as he " sat musing amidst the ruins of the capital, while the barefooted friars were singing vespers in the temple of Jupiter, the idea of writing the decline and fall of the city first occurred to his mind." The writer of these pages has visited the garden and summer-house at Lausanne, overlooking Lake Leman, where Gibbon completed his work, and where he laid down his pen in triumph almost exactly a century since.

James Watt has localized a spot of interest in connection with himself at Glasgow, where first flashed upon him the idea which resulted in the improvement of the steam-engine. Leibnitz recalls the grove near Leipsic where in his youth he first began to meditate and create. So Burns had his favorite walk at Dumfries, secluded, and commanding a view of the distant hills, where he composed, as was his wont, in the open air. He says in a letter to Mr. Thomson, August,

1793, "Autumn is my propitious season. I make more
verses in it than all the year else." Luther tells us
of the spot, and the very tree, under which he argued
with Dr. Staupitz as to whether it was his true
vocation to preach. Beethoven wrote to Frau von
Streicher, at Baden: "When you visit the ancient
ruins, do not forget that Beethoven has often lingered
there; when you stray through the silent pine forest,
do not forget that Beethoven often wrote poems there,
or, as it is termed, 'composed.'" How readily we
pardon the conceit that peeps out from the words of
the great magician of harmony! Hawthorne writes
in his note-book: "If ever I should have a biographer,
he ought to make great mention of this chamber in
my memoirs; because here my mind and character
were formed, and here I sat a long, long time, waiting for the world to know me, and sometimes wondering why it did not know me sooner, or whether it
would ever know me at all, — at least until I were
in my grave." Scott tells us of the precise spot where
at the age of thirteen he first read Percy's "Reliques
of Ancient English Poetry," beneath a huge platanus
tree, forgetting his dinner in the absorbing interest
of the book, whose influence upon the mind of the
youth may easily be traced in the future poet and
romancer. Cowper, who was not blessed with a particularly good memory with regard to what he was
accustomed to read, yet possessed a tenacious one for
localities, and therefore used in summer to select
certain spots out of doors by pond or hedges where

to read his favorite books and chapters. The recalling of these spots brought back, he said, the remembrance of the subjects and chapters read beside them. This was certainly an original and remarkable mode of memorizing ideas. William Ellery Channing localizes the clump of willows, a favorite retreat, where the view of the dignity of human nature first broke upon him, and of which he was ever after such a tenacious advocate. He often resorted hither, and speaks of the place with grateful solemnity. It overlooked the meadows and river west of Boston, with a background formed by the Brookline hills.[1] Washington Irving used to point out to visitors the spot, commanding the Hudson River, where he first read the " Lady of the Lake," with a wild-cherry tree over his head. In his old age he writes to a friend: "Come and see me, and I will give you a book and a tree."

As an example of the perseverance of genius under discouraging circumstances, we recall the trying experience of our own great naturalist Audubon, who had stored in a pine box a thousand and more of his drawings for his great work on " The Birds of America," while he pursued his studies. On opening the box, after the lapse of a few months, he found his carefully made illustrations destroyed and converted into a nest for rats. The work of years was irreparably gone

---

[1] He possessed a diminutive figure, with a pale, attenuated face, eyes of spiritual brightness, an expansive and calm brow, and his movements were characterized by a nervous alacrity. Until he reached the years of middle life he was embarrassed by restricted means and necessary habits of self-denial.

to nought. After a brief period of bitter disappointment, he says: "I took up my gun, my note-book, and my pencil, and went forth to the woods as gayly as if nothing had happened. I felt pleased that I might now make better drawings than before; and, ere a period not exceeding three years had elapsed, my portfolio was again filled."[1] The destruction of his first thousand drawings was a blessing in disguise, both to science and to its modest disciple, since it confirmed him in the resolve which culminated in producing what Cuvier denominated "the most magnificent monument art had ever erected to ornithology." The destruction of Sir Isaac Newton's papers by his favorite dog, embracing the careful calculations of years of study, will occur to the reader in this connection, as well as the loss of Carlyle's first manuscript copy of the "French Revolution," burned by a maid-of-all-work to kindle the fire. Having no draft or copy of the same, he was compelled to reproduce it as nearly as possible from memory. There is positive pleasure in the original production of a piece of literary work; but the reproduction under such circumstances must have been agonizing.

---

[1] With gun in hand, and note-book and drawing material by his side, Audubon explored the coast, lakes, and rivers from Labrador and Canada to the Gulf of Mexico. As early as 1810 he explored alone the primeval forests of North America, impelled more by a love of Nature than a desire to make himself famous. His original and finely hand-colored illustrated work sold in folio at a thousand dollars a volume, and is now rare and valuable.

The history of literature is full of instances wherein its votaries have by patient perseverance finally achieved the much-desired fame which has inspired them to endure deprivation and labor. We affirm this, though at the same time recalling Douglas Jerrold's words, — " How much of what is thought by idle people fame is really sought for as the representative of so many legs of mutton! We may make Fame an angelic creature on the tombs of poets, but how often do bards invoke her as a bouncing landlady!" Pope made his way from obscurity, overcoming by sheer perseverance obstacles that genius hardly ever before encountered. He was not only deformed, as we have said, but he was diseased, "unable to take his own stockings off — a woman nurse with him always." So far as we know it, there was not much to love, or even respect, in his personal character; but we must all admire the wonderful perseverance and genius that enabled him to write what he did. His translation of the Iliad alone was sufficient to give him lasting fame; and it did give him plenty of money, as he received a little over five thousand three hundred pounds from it. How Goldsmith would have scattered that generous sum of money, and how securely Pope hoarded it!

Gifford showed wonderful perseverance and resolve in the right direction, learning to write and to work out mathematical sums on scraps of leather with an awl, for the want of better facilities. This was at his native place, Ashburton in Devonshire, where he sat all day for five years upon a cobbler's bench, earning just enough to support life. But he conquered in the brave struggle with adverse fortune. " The nerve that never relaxes, the eye that never blenches, the thought that never wanders, — these are the masters of victory," says Burke. Gifford finally came to the editorial chair of the " Quarterly Review," where he remained for fifteen years, proving one of the severest critics of his day, as we have had occasion to observe, and regarding authors, according to Southey, as Izaak Walton did worms, slugs, and frogs. " Whatever may have been his talents," says Mr. Whipple, " they were exquisitely unfitted for his position; his literary judgment being contemptible where any sense of beauty was required."

As an example of calm, determined resolve and patience to accomplish an honorable end, we know of nothing more remarkable in connection with authorship or literature than that of Sir Walter Scott's deliberately sitting down to pay off a debt of one hundred and twenty-eight thousand pounds with his pen. Scott considered it a debt of honor, though it was not of his own contracting. Amid the pains and pressure of increasing age he worked on to fulfil this honorable purpose, until in seven years he had paid all but about twenty thousand pounds of this enormous load of debt, when the overwrought brain and body gave out, and he was laid to sleep forever. The great "Wizard of the North" says modestly : " It is with the deepest regret that I recollect in my

manhood the opportunities of learning[1] which I neglected in my youth; through every part of my literary
career I have felt pinched and hampered by my own
ignorance, and I would at this moment give half the
reputation I have had the good fortune to acquire, if
by so doing I could rest the remaining part upon a
sound foundation of learning and science."

[1] Like Milton, Swift, and other great geniuses, Scott was, as
Swift says of himself at school, "very justly celebrated for his
stupidity." But one is inclined to think that it was largely owing
to a want of talent in his master rather than in the pupil. It
will be remembered that it was the illustrious Samuel Parr, when
an undermaster at Harrow School, who first discovered the latent
talent and genius of Sheridan, and who by judicious cultivation
brought it forth and developed it.

CHAPTER IX.

THERE seems always to have been a natural attraction in literature which draws from other and less captivating professions. Bryant, Longfellow, and Washington Irving started early in life with the purpose of studying law; so did Bailey the poet, and Prescott the historian, — though each and all abandoned that profession for literature. Beaconsfield served an apprenticeship in an attorney's office in London. Burke, Lockhart, John Wilson, Shirley Brooks, Corneille, Layard, and Buffon began in life as solicitors, but soon drifted into literature. Byron's first poetical efforts were failures; so were those of Bulwer-Lytton and Beaconsfield, both in literature and oratory. "I have begun several times many things, and have succeeded in them at last," said the latter when he was hissed down in the House of Commons. "I shall sit down now, but the time will come when you will hear me." He toiled patiently, until the House laughed with him instead of at him.[1] Sheridan broke down completely on the occasion of his first effort at public

---

[1] In five or six years subsequent to that failure of his maiden speech, Disraeli, as he was then known, became leader of the Opposition in the House, and Chancellor of the Exchequer soon after, rising rapidly, until in 1868 he became Premier of England.

speaking, but declared that it was in him and should come out. Bulwer-Lytton worked his way upwards by slow degrees, and acquired his later facility only by the greatest assiduity and patient application. He wrote at first very slowly and with great difficulty; but he resolved to overcome his slowness of thought, and he succeeded. He was very systematic in his literary work, and rarely wrote more than three hours each day; that is, from ten o'clock in the morning until one. When regularly engaged, the product of a day in latter years amounted to twenty pages of printed matter, such as appear in the regular editions of his novels. Jean Paul Richter's first efforts as a writer were failures; but he possessed genius and the great element of success, — namely, patience. He fought long and hard to attain a position in literature, supporting himself by small contributions to the press, not all of which were accepted or paid for. " I will succeed in making an honorable living by my pen," he said, " or I will starve in the attempt." His triumph was near at hand.[1]

It is the overcoming of difficulties by heroic perseverance that in no small degree serves to secure and to fix success. " Every noble work is at first impos-

---

[1] Richter was a Bavarian, and of very humble birth. During his youthful career he was reduced to extreme indigence. He became a tutor in a private family, and afterwards taught school, all the while striving with his pen both for fame and money, until at last he " compelled " public appreciation. He is one of the few geniuses of that period who were happy in their domestic relations. He died at Baireuth in 1825.

sible," says Carlyle. " Even in social life it is per-
sistency," says Whipple, " which attracts confidence,
more than talents and accomplishments."

Thus it will be seen that the greatest geniuses have
not commanded success at the outset, but have finally
achieved it by deserving it. Voltaire was one of the
most brilliant and popular of dramatists; but when
" Mariamne " was brought out, it was played but once.
The question of its merit was settled oddly enough.
The farce which was given after Voltaire's production
was entitled " Mourning." " For the deceased play, I
suppose," said one of the critics, in the pit; and this
decided the fate of the piece. Again, when the
" Semiramis " of Voltaire was acted for the first time,
it was far from receiving all the praise which its
author anticipated for it. As he was coming from
the theatre, he overtook Piron, a less celebrated but
brother dramatist, and asked him his opinion of the
piece. "I think," said Piron, "you would be very
glad if I had written it!"

Dr. Samuel Parr, whom Macaulay pronounced to be
the greatest scholar of his age, was a very hard-work-
ing literary genius, sensitive more especially to the
tender emotions, so that he would weep like a woman
when listening to any affecting story. He was very
erratic and imaginative, having a special horror of
the east wind, which he believed had both a moral
and physical power over him. Sheridan knew this
very well, and kept the Doctor a prisoner in the house
for a whole fortnight by fixing the weathercock in

that direction. The Doctor was not without his share
of conceit, founded upon the possession of acknowledged talent and ability. He once said in a miscellaneous assembly, pertinent to the subject before the
company : " England has produced three great classi-
cal scholars : the first was Bentley, the second was
Porson, and the third modesty forbids *me* to mention."

In glancing through the records of the past no name
upon the roll of fame strikes the eye of appreciation
more pleasantly than that of Sir Philip Sidney, whose
life has been called poetry put in action. He lived
amid contemporary applause, and his memory is the
admiration of all. The bravest of soldiers, he was
also the gentlest of sons, equally illustrious for moral
qualities and for intellectual genius, controlled by
" that chastity of honor which felt a stain like a
wound." No incident in history is more familiar
than that of this exhausted warrior resigning the cup
of water to a fainting soldier, whose need, he said,
was greater than his own. Sidney was one of the
brightest ornaments of Queen Elizabeth's court.
Lord Brooke, who was his intimate friend, says of
him : " Though I lived with him and knew him from
a child, yet I never knew him other than a man with
such steadiness of mind, lovely and familiar gravity,
as carried grace and reverence above greater years.
His talk was ever of knowledge, and his very play
tended to enrich the mind." His death occurred at
the age of thirty-two, from a wound in battle, the
result of his self-abnegation. He was in full armor,

but seeing the marshal of the camp unprotected, he took off his armor and gave it to him, thus exposing himself to the mortal wound which he received. Fuller says, "He was slain before Zutphen, in a small skirmish which we may sadly term a great battle, considering our heavy loss therein."

Victor Hugo was banished from France for his opposition to the *coup d'état.* He was ever true to his convictions without counting the cost. " If there is anything grander than Victor Hugo's genius," said Louis Blanc, " it is the use which he has made of it." He affords us an instance of the highest fame and the favor of fortune culminating in ripe old age. When Hugo was but a rising man, he was still looked upon by the elder littérateurs with considerable jealousy. At the time when he was first an aspirant for the honors of the French Academy, and called on M. Royer-Collard to solicit his vote, the sturdy veteran professed entire ignorance of his name. " I am the author of ' Notre Dame de Paris,' ' Marion Delorme,' ' Les Derniers Jours d'un Condamné,' etc." " I never heard of them," said Collard. " Will you do me the honor of accepting a copy of my works ? " said Victor Hugo, with perfect urbanity. " I never read new books," was the cutting reply.[1] But the time came

---

[1] Royer-Collard was an eminent philosopher and statesman, the founder of a school called the " Doctrinaire," of which Cousin was a disciple. He was President of the Chamber of Deputies in 1828. His father's family name was Royer, to which he joined the name of his wife, Mademoiselle Collard.

presently when not to know the author of " Les Misérables " was to argue one's self unknown. When he had reached the age of sixty-three he wrote on a bit of sketching paper accompanying a scene he wished to delineate in the " Toilers of the Sea : " " On the face of this cardboard I have sketched my own destiny, — a steamboat tossed by the tempest in the midst of the monstrous ocean; almost disabled, assaulted by foaming waves, and having nothing left but a bit of smoke which people call glory, which the wind sweeps away, and which constitutes its strength."

Improvidence has ever been a distinctive and a common feature in the lives of men of genius. Sir Thomas Lawrence, the celebrated English portrait-painter, was an illustrious example. Of his natural genius there was ample evidence even in childhood, when at the age of six years he produced in crayon in a very few moments accurate likenesses of eminent persons. At the age of twenty-three he succeeded Sir Joshua Reynolds as first painter to the king. He received a hundred guineas each for his portraits, — head and bust, — and one thousand if full-length, which was a large price for those days ; and yet he was always embarrassed for money, and died deeply in debt while president of the Royal Academy.

Thomas Moore was very improvident; and though he realized over thirty thousand pounds from his literary productions, yet his family were obliged **to** live in the most economical manner, often experiencing serious deprivation of the ordinary comforts of life. "His excellent wife," says Rogers, " contrived to maintain the whole family upon a guinea a week; and he, when in London, thought nothing of throwing away that sum weekly on hackney-coaches and gloves." In order to escape the payment of his just debts, Moore was finally obliged to go to Paris, where, Rogers tells us, he frittered away a thousand pounds a year.[1]

Lamartine and the elder Dumas are notable examples of gross improvidence, — the first being reduced almost to beggary before his death, and supported solely by the liberal contributions of his admirers, while the latter was much of his life either squandering gold profusely or dodging his honest creditors.

Richard Savage, the unfortunate poet and dramatist, passed his life divided between beggary and extravagance. His undoubted genius and ability as an author attracted the hearty friendship of Johnson and Steele, both of whom made earnest efforts to save him from himself; but dissolute habits had taken too firm a hold of him. It is also honorable to Pope that he was his steady and consistent friend almost to the close of his life. Savage's ill-conceived poem of "The Bastard" was intended to expose the cruelty

---

[1] Hazlitt was a just but merciless critic. It was he who designated Moore's productions " the poetry of the toilet-table, of the saloon, and of the fashionable world, — not the poetry of nature, of the heart, or of human life;" and the force of the criticism lay in the fact of its truth.

of his mother, who was responsible in the main for the wreck of his life. He finally died a prisoner for debt in Bristol jail. Undoubtedly Dr. Johnson was right when he said that the miseries which Savage underwent were sometimes the consequence of his faults, and his faults were often the effect of his misfortunes.

The period of which we are writing has been vividly described by Macaulay, from whom we quote : —

"All that is squalid and miserable might now be summed up in the word Poet. That word denoted a creature dressed like a scarecrow, familiar with compters and sponging-houses, and perfectly competent to decide on the comparative merits of the Common Side in the King's Bench prison and of Mount Scoundrel in the Fleet. Even the poorest pitied him ; and they well might pity him. For if their condition was equally abject, their aspirings were not equally high, nor their sense of insult equally acute. To lodge in a garret up four pair of stairs, to dine in a cellar among footmen out of place, to translate ten hours a day for the wages of a ditcher, to be hunted by bailiffs from one haunt of beggary and pestilence to another, — from Grub Street to St. George's Field, and from St. George's Field to the alleys behind St. Martin's church, — to sleep on a bulk in June and amidst the ashes of a glass-house in December, to die in a hospital and to be buried in a parish vault, was the fate of more than one writer who, if he had lived thirty years earlier, would have been admitted to the sittings of the Kitcat or the Scriblerus club, would have sat in Parliament, and would have been intrusted with embassies to the High Allies ; who, if he had lived in our time, would have found encouragement scarcely less munificent in Albemarle Street or in Paternoster Row.

" As every climate has its peculiar diseases, so every walk
of life has its peculiar temptations. The literary character
assuredly has always had its share of faults, vanity, jealousy,
morbid sensibility. To these faults were now superadded
the faults which are commonly found in men whose livelihood is precarious, and whose principles are exposed to the
trial of severe distress. All the vices of the gambler and
of the beggar were blended with those of the author. The
prizes in the wretched lottery of book-making were scarcely
less ruinous than the blanks. If good fortune came, it came
in such a manner that it was almost certain to be abused.
After a month of starvation and despair, a full third night
or a well-received dedication filled the pocket of the lean,
ragged, unwashed poet with guineas. He hastened to enjoy those luxuries with the images of which his mind had
been haunted while he was sleeping amidst the cinders and
eating potatoes at the Irish ordinary in Shoe Lane. A
week of taverns soon qualified him for another year of
night-cellars. Such was the life of Savage, of Boyse, and
of a crowd of others. Sometimes blazing in gold-lace hats
and waistcoats; sometimes lying in bed because their coats
had gone to pieces, or wearing paper cravats because their
linen was in pawn; sometimes drinking champagne and
Tokay with Betty Careless ; sometimes standing at the
window of an eating-house in Porridge island, to snuff up
the scent of what they could not afford to taste, — they
knew luxury; they knew beggary; but they never knew
comfort. These men were irreclaimable. They looked on
a regular and frugal life with the same aversion which
an old gypsy or a Mohawk hunter feels for a stationary
abode, and for the restraints and securities of civilized
communities."

Notwithstanding Douglas Jerrold received a thousand pounds per annum from " Lloyd's Weekly News-

paper" alone, besides a respectable income from " Punch " and other literary labor, he never had a guinea in his pocket; every penny was forestalled, and he left his family in extreme penury.

Goldsmith, as we have seen, was the most improvident of men, and died owing two thousand pounds; which led Dr. Johnson to say, " Was ever poet so trusted before ? " It was at this time that Boswell, who was always a little jealous of Goldsmith's intimacy with Johnson, made some disparaging remarks about the dead poet; whereupon Johnson promptly replied, " Dr. Goldsmith was wild, sir, but he is so no more ! " " Cover the good man who has been vanquished," says Thackeray, — " cover his face and pass on ! " Some families seem to inherit impecuniosity; Goldsmith came thus rightfully, so to speak, by his weakness in this respect.[1]

Sheridan, according to Byron, wrote the best comedy, the " School for Scandal;" the best opera, the " Duenna;" the best farce, the " Critic;" and delivered the most famous oration of modern times. With genius and talents which entitled him to the highest station, he yet sank into difficulties, mostly through inexcusable improvidence, outraging every principle of justice and of truth, finally dying in

---

[1] Goldsmith himself tells us : " My father, the younger son of a good family, was possessed of a small living in the Church. His education was above his fortune, and his generosity greater than his education. Poor as he was, he had his flatterers ; for every dinner he gave them they returned him an equivalent in praise, and this was all he wanted."

neglect. The reader will be apt to recall the anecdote illustrative of Sheridan's impecuniosity. As he was hacking his face one day with a dull razor, he turned to his son and said, "Tom, if you open any more oysters with my razor, I'll cut you off with a shilling." "Very well, father," was the reply; "but where is the shilling to come from?" Sheridan thought if he had stuck to the law he might have done as well as his friend Erskine; "but," he added, "I had no time for such studies; Mrs. Sheridan and myself were often obliged to keep writing for our daily leg or shoulder of mutton, otherwise we should have had no dinner; yes, it was a *joint* concern."

All authorities combine in pronouncing the great speech of Sheridan on the impeachment of Warren Hastings to be one of the grandest oratorical efforts known to us. But the persuasive power of eloquence was never better illustrated than in the instance of Mirabeau when he pleaded his own case. His liaison with the Marchioness de Mounier surpasses, in fact, all stories of romance. Mirabeau induced her to run away with him, for which she was seized and thrown into a convent, while he escaped to Switzerland.[1] He was brought to trial, was convicted of contumacy, and sentenced to lose his head. The lady escaped and once more joined him; together they passed into

---

[1] It happened that a certain lady became charmed with Mirabeau by reading his writings, and wrote him rather a tender letter, asking him to describe himself to her. He did so by return of post as follows: "Figure to yourself a tiger that has had the small-pox." History has not handed down the sequel.

Holland, where they were a second time arrested, she being again immured in a convent and he confined in the Castle of Vincennes, where he remained for more than three years. After his liberation he obtained a new trial, pleaded his own case, and by the impassioned power of his all-commanding eloquence he terrified the court and the prosecutor, melted the audience to tears, obtained a prompt reversal of his sentence, and even threw the whole cost of the suit upon the prosecution.[1]

When the stupid, ill-bred Judge Robinson insulted Curran by reflecting upon his poverty while he was arguing a case before him, saying to him that he " suspected his law library was rather contracted," Curran answered the servile office-holder in words of aptest eloquence and cutting irony. "It is true, my lord," said Curran, with dignified respect, " that I am poor, and the circumstance has somewhat curtailed my library ; my books are not numerous, but they are select, and I hope they have been perused with proper disposition. I have prepared myself for this high profession rather by the study of a few good works than by the composition of a great many bad ones. I am not ashamed of my poverty, but I should be ashamed of my wealth could I have stooped to acquire it by servility and corruption. If I rise not to rank, I shall at least be

---

[1] Mirabeau and the Marchioness had agreed on mutual destruction, by exchanging poisoned locks of hair, if he failed to be acquitted.

honest; and should I ever cease to be so, many an example shows me that ill-gained reputation, by making me the more conspicuous, would only make me the more universally and the more notoriously contemptible!"[1]

Speaking of eloquence, Hazlitt describes how he walked ten miles to hear Coleridge the poet preach, and declared that he could not have been more delighted if he had heard the music of the spheres. The names of Fox, Pitt, Grattan, Patrick Henry, Daniel Webster, Wendell Phillips, and Rufus Choate, with many others, crowd upon the mind as we dwell upon the theme of eloquence in oratory. There is eloquence of the pen as well as of the tongue; Socrates of old, celebrated for his noble oratorical compositions, was of so timid a disposition that he rarely ventured to speak in public. He compared himself to a whetstone, which will not cut, but which readily enables other things to do so; for his productions served as models to other orators.

We have myriads of examples showing us that accident has often determined the bent and development of genius. Accident may not, however, create genius; it is innate, or it is not at all. Cowley tells us that when quite young he chanced upon a copy of

---

[1] To make the appropriateness of this retort clear, it should be known that Judge Robinson was the author of many stupid, slavish, and scurrilous political pamphlets; and by his servility to the ruling powers he had been raised to the eminence which he thus shamefully disgraced.

the "Faerie Queene,"[1] nearly the only book at hand,
and becoming interested he read it carefully and
often, until enchanted thereby he became irrevocably
a poet. The apple that fell on Newton's head with
a force apparently out of all proportion to its size,
led him to ponder upon the fact, until he deduced the
great law of gravitation and laid the foundation of
his philosophy. It was Shakspeare's youthful roguery
which drove him from his trade of wool-carding and
necessitated his leaving Stratford. A company of
strolling actors became his first new associates, and
he took up with their business for a while; but dis-
satisfied with his own success as an actor he turned
to writing plays, and thus arose the greatest dramatist the world has produced. Molière, who was of
very low birth, being often taken as a lad to the
theatre by his grandfather, was thus led to study the
usages of the stage, and came to be the greatest
dramatic author of France. "Tartuffe," which he
wrote a hundred and twenty years ago, still holds
the stage, as well as many others of his inimitable
productions. He was the Shakspeare of France.
Hallam says that Shakspeare had the greater genius,

---

[1] The effect the poem had upon the Earl of Southampton when
he first read it will be remembered. Spenser took it to this noble
patron of poets as soon as it was finished, and sent it up to him.
The earl read a few pages and said to a servant, "Take the writer
twenty pounds." Reading on, he presently cried in rapture,
"Carry that man twenty pounds more." Still he read on; but
at length he shouted, "Go turn that fellow out of the house, for
if I read further I shall be ruined!"

but Molière has perhaps written the better comedies. Corneille fell in love, and was thus incited to pour out his feelings in verse, developing rapidly into a poet and dramatist. He was intended for the law; but love tripped up his heels and made him a poet.

The chance perusal of De Foe's " Essay on Projects," Dr. Franklin tells us, influenced the principal events and course of his life; so the reading of the " Lives of the Saints " caused Ignatius Loyola to form the purpose of creating a new religious order, — which purpose eventuated in the powerful society of the Jesuits. Benjamin West says, " A kiss from my mother made me a painter."[1] La Fontaine read by chance a volume of Malherbe's poems, — he who was called " the poet of princes and the prince of poets," — whereby he became so impressed, that ever after his mind sought expression through the same medium. Rousseau's eccentric genius was first aroused by an advertisement offering a prize for the best essay on a certain theme, which brought out his " Declamation against the Arts and Sciences " (winning the prize thereby), and determined his future career. The husband and father of the woman who nursed Michael Angelo were stone-

---

[1] When a boy, West secretly pursued his first attempts at art, absenting himself from school to do so. Being one day surprised at his work in the garret of the house by his mother, he expected to be seriously reproved; but Mrs. West saw incipient genius in her son's work at the age of ten; so she kissed and congratulated him, promising to intercede with his father in his behalf that he would forgive him for his truancy.

16

masons, and the chisel thus became the first and most common plaything put into the child's hands; hence his earliest efforts were made to apply the hammer and chisel to marble, and the seed was planted which blossomed into art. It was the accidental observation of steam, lifting by its expansive power the heavy iron cover of a boiling pot, that suggested to the mind of James Watt thoughts which led to the invention of the steam-engine. The " Pickwick Papers," Dickens's earliest and best literary work, owes its origin to the publisher of a magazine upon which he was doing job-work desiring him to write a serial story to fit some comic pictures which were in the publisher's possession. The genius was in Dickens, but it slept.

The sight of Virgil's tomb, just above the Grotto of Posilippo, at Naples, determined Giovanni's literary vocation for life. So Gibbon was struck with the idea of writing his " Rise and Fall of the Roman Empire," as he sat dreaming amid the ruins of the Forum.[1] When Scott was a mere boy he chanced upon a copy of Percy's " Reliques of Ancient Poetry," which he read with eagerness again and again. As soon as he

---

[1] It was not without difficulty that Gibbon could obtain a publisher for his famous History. After it had been declined by several houses, it was finally undertaken by Thomas Cadell, " on easy terms," as the author expresses it. It was thought best to publish only five hundred copies at first ; this edition being soon exhausted, edition after edition followed in rapid succession, until, as Gibbon says, " my book was on every table and on almost every toilet."

could get the necessary sum of money, he purchased
a copy ; and thus the taste for poetry was early instilled
into his soul and found after expression in his charming poems.   Scott's first literary effort was the translation of " Götz von Berlichengen," to which Carlyle
ascribes large influence on the great novelist's future
career.   He says this translation was "the prime cause
of ' Marmion' and the ' Lady of the Lake,' with all
that has followed from the same creative hand.   Truly
a grain of seed that had lighted in the right soil.   For
if not firmer and fairer, it has grown to be taller and
broader than any other tree ; and all nations of the
earth are still yearly gathering of its fruit."

While in England, not long since, the writer of these
pages was told an anecdote relating to Mrs. Siddons
which was new to him, and which illustrates how often
accident has directed the future bent of genius.   When
quite a young lady, Sarah Siddons saw in some private
gallery an antique statue of great excellence, which
had a most electrifying effect upon her.   It suggested
to her at once the most effective position and manner in
which to express intensity of feeling.   The arms were
close down at the sides, and the hands nervously
clenched, while the head was erect, the chest expanded,
and the face half in profile.   " I cannot express how
indelibly the pose took effect upon my imagination,"
said the great actress many years afterwards, " or the
force of the lesson taught me by the marble."   If
memory serves us correctly, we recall an old engrav-
ing of Mrs. Siddons in the character of Lady Macbeth,

which would be nearly a reproduction of the pose described.[1]

Accident developed one of the greatest vocalists the world has ever known. Jenny Lind was at the beginning of her life a poor neglected little girl, homely and uncouth, living in a single room of a tumble-down house in a narrow street at Stockholm. When the humble woman who had her in charge went out to her daily labor, she was accustomed to lock Jenny in with her sole companion, a cat. One day the little girl, who was always singing to herself like a canary-bird, "because," as she said, "the song was in her and would come out," sat with her dumb companion at the window warbling her sweet childlike notes. She was overheard by a passing lady, who paused and listened, struck by the clearness and trill of the untutored notes. She made careful inquiries about the child and became the patroness of little Jenny, who was at once supplied with a music-teacher. She loved the art of song, and had the true genius for it. Jenny made rapid progress, surprising both patroness and teachers, and presently became the great Queen of Song.

---

[1] Sydney Smith said of Mrs. Siddons : " What a face she had! The gods do not bestow such a face as hers on the stage more than once in a century. I knew her very well, and she had the good taste to laugh at my jokes ; she was an excellent person, but she was not remarkable out of her profession, and never got out of tragedy even in common life. She used to *stab* the potatoes ; and said ' Boy, give me a knife ! ' as she would have said ' Give me a dagger ! '"

The world knows of Jenny Lind's splendid fortune, of her professional triumphs, and of her noble charities; but few, perhaps, have ever pictured her humble girlhood, cooped up in a cheerless room, with only her cat for a companion, in a dull quarter of the Swedish capital. The plain, awkward girl grew up under favorable culture to be a graceful, lovely woman. The courts of Europe treated her as a revered guest; she was covered with laurels and with jewels, but she was ever in disposition and character the same pure, simple Swedish girl. Adulation had no power to spoil this child of Nature and of art. The Swedish public cherish her name as that of their most favored daughter, and honor her for the noble educational institution which she has so liberally founded in her native Stockholm.

Christina Nilsson, another Scandinavian vocalist, was the daughter of an humble Swedish peasant, born in so lowly a cabin that it was difficult to conceive of the name of " home " being applied to it. While yet a child she was obliged to work with the rest of the family in the fields and on the mountain-side. Her sweet voice was first heard at the fairs and peasant weddings, where her simple Scandinavian melodies delighted the assembled crowds. At one of these public gatherings a man of taste and means heard the child's voice, and realized the hidden possibilities it indicated. He was a magistrate, and became her patron, taking her from her humble surroundings and supplying her with suitable teachers. She was carefully taught instrumental as well as vocal music, and became both an eminent pianist and singer, developing like her fair countrywoman, Jenny Lind, into a vocalist of grandest genius, and of such ability as the world affords but few examples.

Taglioni was also Scandinavian by birth, having been born at Stockholm, in 1804, of humble parentage, her father being a dancing-master. She had the genius of an artist, which she patiently developed through many dark hours of toil and deprivation, until she made herself acknowledged as queen of the ballet in the great cities of Europe. Her purity of character added a charm to her public performances, giving her a prestige never before enjoyed by any exponent of her art. She finally amassed a large fortune, and retiring from the stage married Count Gilbert de Voisins. Doubtless many of our readers have paused in their gondolas beneath the windows of her marble palace on the Grand Canal at Venice, to recall the story of the great danseuse, or have looked with pleasure upon her elegant villa on the Lake of Como.

CHAPTER X.

It is not the author's purpose to treat the names of painters, or indeed those of any other branch of art, especially by themselves. Were any single line to be selected, the peculiarities of its representatives would alone be sufficient to fill a volume. Under the general design of this gossip about genius, the pen is permitted to glide after its own fancy, treating only upon such individuals as readily suggest themselves, and who are illustrative of characteristics already introduced.

Upon beginning the chapter before us, we were thinking of John Opie, the distinguished English painter, born in Cornwall in 1761. When Opie was only ten years of age [1] he saw a person who was somewhat accomplished with the pencil draw a butterfly. The boy watched the process with marked interest, and as soon as the draughtsman had departed, produced upon a shingle a drawing equally good, which he showed to his mother. She, good woman, encouraged

[1] "I first discovered Opie," says Dr. Wolcott, "in a little hovel in the Parish of St. Agnes, Cornwall. He was the son of a poor sawyer. I was first led to notice him by some drawings which he had made." The good Doctor gave him material aid, took him to his house, and finally introduced him into London society.

him, as Mrs. West did her son on a similar occasion ; but the father, being a harsh, rude, low-bred man, was constantly punishing the boy for laziness, and for chalking figures, faces, and animals on every stray bit of board or flat surface at hand. The boy had genius, however ; what he required was opportunity. Good fortune sent Dr. Wolcott, better known as " Peter Pindar," that way. He saw the boy's dawning genius, and helped him with suitable material and some useful suggestions. It was not long before the lad got away from home, quietly aided by his good friend Wolcott, and soon earned money enough to clothe himself decently and to make a start in life. He finally married Amelia, daughter of James Alderson, who afterwards became the well-known authoress Amelia Opie. The husband developed into a distinguished artist, whose historical pictures, "The Death of Rizzio" and "Jephthah's Vow," were stepping-stones to his election as President of the Royal Academy. Does not this truthful sketch from life, of a poor woodsawyer's son, read like romance ?

Genius will assert itself ; it seems useless to strive against it. The secret suggestions of the soul are true, lead us whither they will. Salvator Rosa was the son of a poor architect who made ineffectual efforts to thwart his son's predilection for art, but all in vain. The young man, finding that he could not hope for any assistance from his father, strove all the harder to earn a livelihood by painting, but nearly starved before he reached his majority. About this time the patrons of art in Rome offered a grand prize for the best painting to be submitted at an exhibition to be held in the Eternal City. The young Neapolitan saw his chance, and painted a picture into which he infused all the glowing spirit of the art which burned within him. If it failed, he resolved that no one should know aught of its authorship. It was forwarded anonymously, and received the recognition of being hung in the most favorable position. That picture took the grand prize, the unknown artist being lauded as above Titian. Nought was to be heard for it but praise. This decided the fate of Rosa. He left his humble home near Naples and settled in Rome, where he secured the friendship and intimacy of the greatest men of the day.

Numerous and grand were the pictures sent forth from Rosa's hand ; orders pressed upon him faster than he could fill them, and thus he stepped at once into the highest contemporary fame and fortune.[1] "Salvator possessed real genius," says Ruskin, " but was crushed by misery in his youth." He was not only a painter, but also a poet and a musician ; nearly all cultured Italians are the latter. At the grand Carnival of the year 1639 there appeared upon the Corso

---

[1] He fought under Masaniello, and after the final defeat at Naples he escaped to Florence, where he was befriended by the Grand Duke, who was a liberal patron of art. His masterpiece is considered to be the " Conspiracy of Catiline," though he excelled in wild mountain scenery rather than in the grouping of human figures.

and in the squares of Rome an actor of fantastic dress,
who was marked like all the other revellers on such
occasions, but whose name was given as one Formica,
of Southern Italy. He attracted both public and private attention by his brilliant wit, his eloquence, and
especially by his songs, as he accompanied himself on
the lute. He was the hero of the Carnival of that
season. By and by the appointed hour arrived when
all the revellers unmasked, and lo! the stranger
proved to be Salvator Rosa.

Among painters, Rubens is one of the greatest and
most familiar names, though Ruskin disparages him
by saying that "he is a healthy, worthy, kind-hearted,
courtly-phrased animal, without any clearly percepti-
ble traces of a soul, except when he paints children."
Rubens became an artist from love of art, and his
career was one in which there was far more of sunshine than usually falls to the lot of genius. He throve
greatly in a business point of view as well as in art,
and became a man of wealth in his native city of
Antwerp, where he built a comfortable house and
adorned it inside with pencil and brush — the whole,
as he estimated it, worth about a thousand pounds ster-
ling. Presently there came to Antwerp the Duke of
Buckingham, who coveted the artist's house. A nego-
tiation was opened, and Rubens sold it to the Duke
for twelve times what it cost, or say in our currency
sixty thousand dollars.

Rubens must have possessed wonderful industry, as
we judge by the fact that a hundred of his paintings may

be found in the Munich Gallery alone, not to mention those contained in other European collections. Undoubtedly his "Descent from the Cross," now in the Antwerp Cathedral, is his grandest work. Our artist was by no means without his vein of vanity, as evinced by the family picture which he painted, and in which he gives himself due prominence. This picture is placed just above his tomb, back of the altar, in the Church of St. Jacques, at Antwerp. The presumptuousness is increased by the fact that the combined portraits of his first and second wife, his daughter, with his father, grandfather, and himself, are intended to represent a Holy Family, and the painting is typical of that idea. The whole is incongruous and in bad taste. Vandyke, Teniers, and Denis Calvart, the instructor of Guido Reni, were all natives of Antwerp. The city owes its attraction to travellers almost solely to the fact that here are so many masterpieces of painting.

William Hogarth was a great and original genius, who wrote comedies pictorially, satirized vice, and depicted all phases of life more in detail than is possible with the pen. He was early apprenticed to a silversmith; but the natural bent of his genius was too apparent and promising not to be encouraged by the study of art. In the dramatic and satirical departments of design he has never been excelled. It has been objected that his pictures are vulgar; but when we remember the period in which they appeared, and also the fact that they undoubtedly convey useful lessons of morality, we shall find ample excuse if not commendation for the artist. In 1753 he published his "Analysis of Beauty," in which he maintains that a waving line is essential to beauty. Hogarth composed comedies just as much as did Molière. It was a singular characteristic of this able designer and artist that he could not successfully illustrate another's work; he is known utterly to have failed in the attempt, though never in the successful illustration of his own ideas. Hogarth was also a historian, inasmuch as every picture he produced represented the manners and customs of the period. The interior scenes give us the exact style of the furniture and minutest domestic surroundings; while out of doors we have all the various modes of conveyance in use, and a faithful picture of the street architecture. Hogarth died in 1764.

James Spencer, who was a personal friend of Hogarth, began life as a London footman; but the genius of an artist was born in him, and it gradually forced its way to the front. At odd moments he practised drawing and even painting with oils, whenever and wherever he could seize upon a brief chance. It happened that a professional portrait-painter was engaged to make a portrait of the head of the family where Spencer had long acted as footman. When the likeness was finished, he heard his master express some just dissatisfaction at its want of resemblance to the original. Spencer very humbly asked permission of his master to copy the painting and

see if he could not get a good likeness. After expressing some astonishment at the request, his master
assented. In a much briefer period than the first
artist occupied, and without a single sitting on the
part of his employer, Spencer astonished the family
by producing not only a remarkable likeness, but an
entirely satisfactory painting. With such a start the
footman became a professional portrait-painter, and
accumulated the means ere long to set up a fine
London establishment.

In an earlier part of this volume we gave numerous
instances of genius being at its best in early youth,
when, as Burke says, "the senses are unworn and
tender, and the whole frame is awake in every part."
Of this early development we know of no more striking instance in art than that of Sir Thomas Lawrence,
who at the age of ten years surpassed most of the
London portrait-painters both in his certain likenesses and in the general effect of his portraits. He
was a remarkable genius, and for a considerable period
was the talk of all London.[1] Added to his ability as
an artist, young Lawrence was remarkably handsome.
Prince Hoare saw something so angelic in his face
that he desired to paint him in the character of

---

[1] Haydon, the historical painter, had power but not popularity.
Sir Arthur Shea, a man who rose to the height of his profession
as regarded popularity, was Haydon's special aversion. "He is,"
Haydon once began, "the most impotent painter in — " His
listeners supposed he would add "the world." That did not
satisfy Haydon's antipathy, and his conclusion was, — " in the
solar system!"

Christ. In about seven minutes Lawrence scarcely ever failed of producing in crayon an excellent likeness of any person present, and in a manner expressive of both grace and freedom. He succeeded Sir Joshua Reynolds, in due time, as first painter to the king, was knighted in 1815, and five years later became President of the Royal Academy.

To realize under what shadows many an artist has lived, worked, and died, yet who is known to us of the highest genius, we have only to recall some familiar names. Correggio was of very humble birth: and though one of the most original of all the brilliant masters of the sixteenth century, he enjoyed little contemporary fame. His works to-day are held at as high a valuation as those of Raphael, Titian, or Murillo.[1] His modesty was characteristic; his pretension, nothing. His pictures speak for him, and exhibit the softness, tenderness, and harmony of his nature. Nearly all his work was done at his native city of Correggio and at Parma; nor is he believed ever to have visited Rome. It was he who, after gazing on one of Raphael's finest productions, exclaimed, "I also am a painter!"

Correggio was chosen by the canons of the cathedral at Parma to paint for them the "Assumption of

---

[1] Many of our readers will remember a remarkable picture by Correggio in the Dresden Gallery, representing a "Penitent Magdalen," the ineffable and almost divine beauty of which no one can fail to appreciate. One of the Saxon kings paid six thousand louis-d'ors ($30,000) for this painting, which is only about eighteen inches square. Twice that sum would not purchase it to-day.

the Virgin." It was a subject well fitted to his style, and his conception and execution of the painting were beyond criticism. It may be seen, mellowed by age, in the Parma Cathedral to-day. When the work was done, the priests meanly haggled and found fault with it, in order to reduce the price, which had been previously agreed upon. Finally, they only paid the artist half the promised sum, stealing the balance to supply their secret luxuries. To add insult to their meanness, the priests paid the artist the price in copper coin. He could not refuse the money, for his poverty-stricken family awaited his return with it to supply their pressing needs. Correggio took the heavy burden on his shoulders and bore it two leagues and more, under a broiling Italian sun, to reach his home. On arriving there he was completely exhausted, and drank freely of the water his children brought to him ; then, disheartened at his ill-fortune and broken down by fatigue, he went sadly to his rude bed, to awake on the following morning in a burning fever and delirious. In two days Correggio was no more.

The development of the genius which slept in the soul of Canova when a lad was brought about by a happy accident. A superb banquet was preparing in the palace of the Falieri family at Venice. The tables were already arranged, when it was discovered that a crowning ornament of some sort was required to complete the general effect of the banqueting board. Canova's grandfather, who brought him up, was a

stone-cutter, often hewing out stone ornaments for
the architects; and as he lived close at hand, he was
hastily consulted by the steward of the Falieris.
Canova chanced to go with his grandfather to view
the tables, and overheard the consultation. His quick
eye and ready genius at once suggested a suitable design for the apex of the principal dishes. " Give me
a plate of cold butter," said the boy; and seating himself at a side table he rapidly moulded a lion of proper
proportions, and so true to nature in its pose and
detail as to astonish all present. It was put in place,
and proved to be the most striking ornamental article there. When the guests were seated and discovered it, they exclaimed aloud with admiration,
and demanded to see at once the person who could
perform such a miracle impromptu. Canova was
brought before them, and his boyish person only
heightened their wonder. From that hour he had
in the head of this opulent family a kind, appreciative, and liberal patron. He was placed under
tuition with the best sculptors of Venice and Rome,
to study the art of which he finally became a grand
master.[1]

The story of Spagnoletto is a romantic one, and not
without a vivid moral. Of such humble birth was he,

---

[1] Canova executed a statue of Washington, which ornaments
the State House in Boston, and is known to have produced during
his life fifty statues and as many busts, besides numerous groups
in marble. He died in 1822, having the reputation of being the
greatest sculptor of his age.

that nothing is said of it by himself or his friends. He suffered the very extreme of poverty; but feeling a deep love for art, and a consciousness within him that he was born to be a painter, he pursued this purpose through besetting difficulties for years. He still felt within him a power of genius superior to all and every disadvantage which he encountered. He was Spanish by birth, but made his way on foot to Rome, where he worked for his daily bread at anything which offered, and for many months was employed as a street porter, but at the same time followed the study of art in his humble way. One day a cardinal passing in his carriage saw in the streets a ragged person painting a board affixed to an ordinary house of Rome. The young man's wretchedness attracted his attention. It was Spagnoletto earning wherewith to purchase a loaf of bread. The cardinal questioned him, took him home to his palace and gave him every luxury he desired, as well as the means to pursue his beloved art. For a brief time all was well, and the art student made great progress; but, alas! the nature which could withstand the frowns of fortune wilted beneath her smiles, and pleasure thoroughly seduced the youth by her tempting wiles. He became a slave to the senses, neglected art entirely, and was fast going to ruin. One night Spagnoletto had a dream; it was the midnight visit of his better angel, and she prevailed. He awoke the next morning determined to leave the cardinal's palace with all its luxuries behind him, to resume his former condition

17

and industry. He worked his way to Naples, and by degrees rose steadily in art until he cast off his rags and was independent. He furnished so perfect a painting of Saint Bartholomew stripped to the muscles, that it became a valued study for anatomists, and from that day his fame was assured. His pictures were eagerly sought for, and to-day they adorn the best European galleries.[1] As Salvator Rosa, the Italian artist, delighted most in depicting wild, rugged mountain scenery and battles, so Spagnoletto, the Spanish painter, was most at home with martyrdoms, executions, and tragic scenes generally. He died at Naples in 1656.

Genius is confined to no line of art, to no special profession; we find its exponents in the legislative hall, in the pulpit, and on the stage. Garrick was undoubtedly one of the greatest geniuses of the English stage; he was not only an actor, but a successful dramatic author. He married a Viennese danseuse, and so far as the world knows was happy in his domestic relations. He was equally at home in tragedy and comedy, possessing in a most marvellous degree the art of imitating the physiognomy of others and the manner of expressing their various emotions. It is said of him that he could imitate anything, bird

---

[1] Spagnoletto was finally appointed court painter in Spain, and some of his best paintings still adorn the Madrid Gallery. His "Adoration of the Shepherds" is familiar to us all, and remains unsurpassed in power of conception and execution. In the Madrid Museo is another of his masterpieces, a "Mater Dolorosa."

or beast, both in voice and manner. On the occasion
of a grand dinner-party in London, at a certain lord's,
Garrick was a guest; in the course of the entertainment he was suddenly missed, and at last was discovered in the garden belonging to the house, where a
young negro boy was rolling on the ground convulsed
with screams of laughter to see Garrick mimicking a
turkey-cock that was strutting about in the enclosure.
The actor had his coat-tail stuck out behind, and was in
a seeming flutter of feathered rage and pride.[1] Garrick
declared that he would cheerfully give a hundred
guineas if he could say " Oh ! " as Whitfield did. A
noble friend wished him to be a candidate for Parliament. " No, my lord," said the actor, sincerely ; " I
would rather play the part of great men on the stage,
than the part of fool in Parliament."[2] He accumulated a large fortune, stated at over a hundred and fifty
thousand pounds. He died in 1779, and was buried
with such pomp as is awarded only to those who are
considered national characters. His ashes rest beside
the tomb of Shakspeare in Westminster Abbey.

[1] "Mr. Murphy, sir, you knew Mr. Garrick ? " asked Rogers
the poet of that individual. " Yes, sir, I did, and no man better."
"Well, sir, what did you think of his acting ? " After a pause :
" Well, sir, *off* the stage he was a mean, sneaking little fellow.
But *on* the stage " — throwing up his hands and eyes — " oh,
my great God ! "

[2] In the broad grounds of Abington Abbey, in Northampton-
shire, stands Garrick's mulberry-tree, with this inscription upon
copper attached to one of the limbs: " This tree was planted by
David Garrick, Esq., at the request of Ann Thursby, as a growing
testimony of their friendship, 1778."

Moore mentions having seen that excellent comic genius John Liston behind the scenes in a towering rage about some trifle, while he was dressed and " made up " for the part of Rigdum Funidos, — a contrast which must have been as ludicrous as when Washington Irving met Grimaldi in a furious rage behind the curtain, with the regular stage grin painted on his cheeks. Liston began his profession in tragic parts and developed his wonderful comic powers by chance, being suddenly called upon one evening to fill the low comedian's place on account of the illness of the actor cast for the part. He made a hit at once, such as he had not dreamed of, and it was seen by every one that he was naturally a comic actor. On the occasion referred to, by the exercise of his extraordinary facial powers he caused the spectators and actors, until the curtain fell on the closing scene, to roar with laughter, though but very little of the text had been audible to them. True genius loses itself in the character and the subject. Betterton, when he performed Hamlet, by reason of the violent and sudden emotion of amazement and horror at the presence of his father's spectre, absolutely turned as white as his neckcloth, although his natural cast of countenance was very florid, while his whole body seemed affected by an uncontrollable tremor. Had his father's apparition indeed risen before him, he could not have been seized with more real agonies. When a well-known actor of that period, named Booth, first took the part of the ghost, Betterton acted Hamlet; on which occasion his extraordinary look struck Booth with such horror that for a moment he remained silent, having forgotten his part.[1]

Samuel Foote, the witty English comedian, was one of the vainest of geniuses. "For loud, obstreperous, broad-faced mirth," said Dr. Johnson, "I know not his equal." Foote sought the stage to earn thereby a living after squandering his fortune at gaming and other vices. When visiting in the country, his vanity led him to boast of his horsemanship, an accomplishment of which he knew little or nothing; and when invited by Lord Mexborough to join the hunt, he could not decently decline. The consequence was that at the first burst he was thrown and broke his leg in two places, so that amputation was necessary. However, he managed to play nearly as well with a cork leg. To some one who made a reflection upon his "game" leg, Foote replied promptly: "Make no allusion to my weakest part. Did I ever attack your head ?" Garrick, observing that Foote had placed a plaster bust of him in his entry, remarked, "You are not afraid, I see, to trust me near your gold and bank-notes." "No," retorted the humorist, "you have no hands !" Foote was considered by his contemporaries the greatest master of comic humor after Molière. One day Foote, Garrick, and Dr. Johnson went together to Bedlam, — a hospital in London for the insane. Johnson, who

---

[1] Pope was younger than Betterton, but they were very warm personal friends, and it is thought that the poet aided the actor in the adaptations which he published from Chaucer, and for which he received hearty if not merited commendation.

was much affected at the sight of so much human misery, got into a corner by himself to meditate, and in the progress of his mood he threw himself into so many strange attitudes, and drew his face into such odd shapes, that Foote whispered mysteriously to Garrick to ask *how they should contrive to get him out!*

Of the moral character of Nell Gwynn, who was a favorite London actress and a mistress of Charles II., the less said the better; and yet she was not entirely void of good impulses, for it is well known that she persuaded the king to establish and endow Chelsea Hospital. But of Bracegirdle, the beautiful actress who captivated all hearts, and whom Congreve was thought nearly to worship, not a word reflecting upon her moral character could be truthfully uttered. At a London coffee-house one evening there chanced to be gathered a score or more of her admirers, including the Dukes of Devonshire and Dorset, besides other members of the peerage. Bracegirdle's name had been mentioned; when Lord Halifax said: "You all of you praise the virtue of this lady; why not reward her for not selling it? There are two hundred guineas *pour encourager les autres.*" A thousand guineas were raised on the spot, which the noblemen took to Bracegirdle, going into her presence in a body. As it was a testimony intended in honor of her virtue, she accepted it. No doubt a large portion of this handsome tribute found its way very quickly into the hands of her needy pensioners; for she was no more estimable in her profession than noble in her charities.

The best dramatists wrote for her; and two of them, Rowe and Congreve, when they gave her a lover in a play seemed palpably to plead their own passions and to make their individual court to her in fictitious characters.

Having spoken of Nell Gwynn and Bracegirdle, another English actress, Margaret Woffington, comes forcibly to mind; and though we do not propose to treat especially the profession of the drama, the incidental mention of some of its members in this gossip is not out of place. Her father was an Irish bricklayer in Dublin, where Peg Woffington, as she was best known, was a great public favorite long before she came to London to find an equally agreeable home. Her versatility of genius may be judged of from the fact of her personating Lady Macbeth and Sir Harry Wildare with equal excellence. The latter character was a favorite one with Garrick, but he gave up the part altogether after witnessing her excellence in its assumption.[1] She also was distinguished for her benevolence and open-handed charity. The manager of Covent Garden Theatre could always be sure of a full house when he announced her in the character of the gay, dissipated, good-humored rake, Sir Harry Wildare. Margaret built and endowed two almshouses at Teddington, Middlesex, and lies buried

---

[1] Garrick was for a long time at her feet, and indeed was at one time engaged to be married to her, but the nuptials were not consummated. It was generally believed that the engagement was broken from disinclination on her part.

in the principal church of the district. In the height of her popularity she declared that she preferred the society of men to that of women; the latter, she said, "talk of nothing but silks and scandal." Her end was singularly dramatic. She was playing the character of Rosalind with more than usual éclat, when she was struck with paralysis, and died soon after in the prime of life.[1]

We have spoken of accident as often determining the development and directing the course of genius. Edward Shuter was one of the most popular comedians on the London stage in 1776, but he began life as a pot-boy at a public-house in the neighborhood of Covent Garden. A gentleman came to the house one evening, and after refreshing himself he sent the boy Shuter to call him a hackney-coach. On reaching home he found that he had dropped his pocket-book; and suspecting that he had lost it in the coach, he went the next morning to the tavern to make inquiry. He asked Shuter if he knew the number of the hack. The poor boy could not read or write, and was totally unskilled in numerals; but he knew the signs by which his master scored the quarts and pints of porter that were drunk, and to the gentleman's inquiry as to the number of the coach which the boy had called

---

[1] During the vacation season Miss Woffington went to Bath, and on her return was telling Quin how much she had been pleased by the excursion. "And pray, madam," he inquired, "what made you go to Bath?" "Mere wantonness," she replied. "And pray, madam, did it cure you?"

for him Shuter said it was " two pots and a pint "
(771). This was unintelligible to the gentleman, but
was explained by the landlord. The coachman was
summoned, and the pocket-book recovered. This
acuteness of the boy interested the gentleman, and he
became his patron, sent him to school, and gave him
a start in the line of his choice, which was the theatrical profession. Such is the story in brief of one of
the famous London comedians.

How many of our readers remember the one recorded scene when Queen Elizabeth condescended to
coquet with Shakspeare? The great bard was performing the part of a king; Elizabeth's box was con-
tiguous to the stage, and she purposely dropped her
handkerchief from the box upon the boards, at the
very feet of Shakspeare, having a mind thus to try
whether her poet would stoop from his high estate of
assumed majesty. " Take up *our* sister's handkerchief," was his prompt and dignified order to one of
the actors in his train.

It will doubtless be found interesting to see recorded
in juxtaposition the words and the manner of death
of some of the great geniuses whom history mentions.
When Alonzo Cano, the famous Spanish artist, was
dying, the attendant priest presented before him an
ivory crucifix; Cano turned away and refused to look
at it because the sculpture was so bad, calling for a
· plain cross, which he embraced, and died. Chaucer
breathed his last while composing a ballad. When

the priest came whom Alfieri had been prevailed
upon to see, he requested him to call the next day.
"Death, I trust, will tarry four-and-twenty hours,"
he said, but died in the interim. Petrarch was found
dead in his library, leaning on a book. "I could wish
this tragic scene were over," said Quin the actor,
"but I hope to go through it with becoming dignity."
Pitt, the great statesman, died alone, in a solitary
house on Wimbledon Common. Rousseau, when dying, asked to be carried to the window of the apartment overlooking his garden, that he might look his
last on Nature.

When Malherbe the lyric poet was dying, he repri-
manded his nurse for making use of a solecism in her
language, and bade the priest stop his trite, cant talk
about heaven, saying, " Your wretched style only
makes me out of conceit with it." Bide, the English
monk and author, on the night of his death continued
to dictate to his amanuensis. He asked his scribe
how many chapters yet remained to complete the
work, and was told there was one. " Take your pen,"
he commanded, and went on with the work. By
and by the scribe said, " It is finished," just as his
master breathed his last. Roscommon, when expiring, quoted from his own translation of the " Dies
Iræ." " All my possessions for a moment of time ! "
were the dying words of Queen Elizabeth. The last
words of Cardinal Beaufort were, " What! is there
no bribing death ? " The last words uttered by Byron
were, " I must sleep now." In his last moments

Crébillon, who had composed two acts of his tragedy of "Catiline," regretted that he had not been spared to complete it.

Colorden on the day of his death was visited by his friend Barthe, who requested his opinion of the comedy of the "Selfish Man," which he came to read at his bedside. "You may add an excellent trait to the character of your principal personage," said Colorden. "Say that he obliged an old friend, on the eve of his death, to hear him read a five-act comedy!" "Let me die to the sound of delicious music," were the last words of Mirabeau. Herder died writing an ode to the Deity, his pen on the last line. Heller died feeling his own pulse; and when he found it almost gone, turning his eyes to his brother physician, said, "My friend, the artery ceases to beat!" "Tell Collingwood to bring the fleet to anchor," said Nelson, and expired. The last words of Charles I. were uttered on the scaffold, — "I fear not death! Death is not terrible to me!"

Curran's ruling passion was strong in death. Near the close of his earthly hours his physician at his morning call said he "seemed to cough with more difficulty." "That's surprising," said the almost exhausted invalid, "as I have been practising all night." "There is not a drop of blood on my hands," said the expiring Frederick V. of Denmark. "Let not poor Nellie starve" (Nell Gwynn, his mistress), were the last words of Charles II. "I have loved righteousness and hated iniquity, therefore do I die in

exile," said Pope Gregory VII. with his expiring
breath. Anne Boleyn turned to the executioner on
the scaffold, and pointing to her neck, said pathetically, "It is small, very small indeed!" The last
words of Maria Theresa were, "I do not sleep; I wish
to meet my death awake." Madam Roland exclaimed,
"O liberty! liberty! how many crimes are committed
in thy name!"

It was in perfect accord with his character when
Chancellor Thurlow said at the closing moment of
his life, "I'm shot if I don't believe I'm dying!"
"World without end, Amen!" said Bunyan as he
breathed his last. "Guilty, but recommended to the
mercy of the court," whispered Lord Hermand. "For
the last time I commit soul, body, and spirit into His
hands," said John Knox in dying. "Trust in God,"
said President Edwards, "and you need not fear."
These were his last words. "If I had strength
enough to hold a pen," said William Hunter, the distinguished anatomist, "I would write how easy and
delightful it is to die." The dying words of Louis
XIV. were, "I thought that dying had been more
difficult." Arthur Murphy the dramatist quoted in
his last breath Pope's lines, —

> "Taught by reason, half by mere decay,
> To welcome death and calmly pass away."

When asked if he heard the prayers which were
offered in his presence, the Duke of Marlborough replied, "Yes, and I join in them." He never spoke

again. "O Lord, open the King of England's eyes," said the martyr Tyndale as he died at the stake. When those noble English reformers, Latimer and Ridley, were being burned at the stake, "Be of good cheer, brother," cried Ridley, "for our God will either assuage the fury of this flame or enable us to abide it." Latimer replied: "Be of good comfort, brother, for we shall this day light such a candle in England as by God's grace shall never be put out." Lady Jane Grey's last words upon the scaffold were: "Lord, into thy hands I commend my spirit." "Many things are growing plain and clear to me," whispered Schiller, and died with these words on his lips.

Anna Lætitia Barbauld, the English authoress, wrote with great poetic feeling and moral beauty. Her husband became a lunatic, and she suffered much. It was her beautiful self-sacrifice that gave the best charm to her character. She wrote, among many other works, a popular life of the novelist Richardson, and some political pamphlets of great force and excellence. Her series of books for children would alone have given her lasting reputation. There occurs to us in these closing pages the stanza which she wrote in her old age, probably in her eighty-second year, not long before her death, — lines which Rogers and Wordsworth so much and so justly admired. The former says in his "Table Talk" that while sitting with Madame D'Arblay a few weeks before her death, he asked her if she remembered

these lines of Mrs. Barbauld's. " Remember them ! "
answered the famous authoress, " I repeat them to
myself every night before I go to sleep."

> " Life ! we 've been long together
> Through pleasant and through cloudy weather ;
>   'T is hard to part when friends are dear ;
>   Perhaps 't will cost a sigh, a tear ;
>   Then steal away, give little warning,
>   Choose thine own time ;
> Say not ' Good-night,' but in some brighter clime
>   Bid me ' Good morning.' "

CHAPTER XI.

GENIUS has its hours of sunshine as well as of shadow, and when it finds expression in wit and humor it is undoubtedly most popular. The Emperor Titus thought he had lost a day if he had passed it without laughing. Coleridge tells us men of humor are in some degree men of genius; wits are rarely so, although a man of genius may, among other gifts, possess wit. As in pathos and tenderness "one touch of nature makes the whole world kin," so is it in true wit and humor with the appreciative. Obtuseness will be unsympathetic under any circumstances. "It is not in the power of every one to taste humor," says Sterne, "however much he may wish it; it is the gift of God! and a true feeler always brings half the entertainment with him." Bruyere has somewhere said very finely that "wit is the god of moments, but genius is the god of ages." Some men of genius have found their most natural exponent to be the pen; others indulge in practical humor. Sheridan [1] belonged to

[1] From the volatility of his mind and conduct, it would be a misuse of language to say that he had good principles or bad principles. He had no principles at all. His life was a life of expedients and appearances, in which he developed a shrewdness and capacity made up of talent and mystification, of ability and trickery, which were found equal to almost all emergencies. — *Whipple.*

this latter class; he was full of fun and frolic, ever on the alert for an opportunity to exercise his humor. When on a certain occasion he had been driving about the town for three or four hours in a hackney-coach, he chanced to see his friend Richardson, whom he hailed, and invited into the vehicle. When they were seated together he at once introduced a subject upon which he and Richardson always differed, and a controversy naturally ensued. At last, affecting to be mortified at Richardson's argument, Sheridan said abruptly, " You are really too bad ; I cannot bear to listen to such things : I will not stay in the coach with you." And accordingly he opened the door and sprang out, Richardson hallooing triumphantly, "Ah, you 're beat, you 're beat ! " Nor was it until the heat of the victory had a little cooled that he realized he was left in the lurch to pay for Sheridan's three hours' coaching.[1]

Sheridan, profligate and unprincipled as he was, still was capable of fine expression of sentiment and true poetic fire. In a poem called " Clio's Protest ; or, the Picture Varnished," we find the following really beautiful lines : —

[1] Sheridan probably had not a penny in his pocket. He never did have for more than a few minutes at a time ; yet this was the man of whose famous speech in the House of Commons Burke said : " It was the most astonishing effort of eloquence, argument, and wit united, of which there was any record or tradition." And of which Fox said, " All that he had ever heard, all that he had ever read, when compared with it, dwindled into nothing, and vanished like vapor before the sun."

> " Marked you her cheek of rosy hue ?
> Marked you her eye of sparkling blue ?
> That eye in liquid circles moving ;
> That cheek abashed at man's approving ;
> The one Love's arrows darting round ;
> The other blushing at the wound :
> Did she not speak, did she not move,
> Now Pallas, now the Queen of Love ? "

The poets have frequently made satire an auxiliary of their wit; and when the proportions are properly adhered to, a favorable result is produced. Satire, like many subtle poisons used as a medicine, may be safely taken in small quantities, while an overdose is liable to be fatal. In Chaucer's[1] Canterbury Pilgrims he draws his portraits to the life. While he exposes the weakness of human nature, he does not do so in surliness; a pleasant smile wreathes his lips all the while. There is slyness, but no bitterness in his satire. He would not chastise, he would only reform his fellow-men. As illustrating exactly the opposite spirit, we may instance Pope, Dryden, and Byron, who, descending from their high estate, often prostituted their genius to attacks upon personal enemies or rivals, with keenest weapons, while their opponents had no means of defence. The " Dunciad " is a monument of satiric wit, or genius belittled.

[1] " A perpetual fountain of good sense," Dryden calls him ; " and of good humor, too, and wholesome thought," adds Lowell. He was scholar, courtier, soldier, ambassador, one who had known poverty as a housemate, and who had been the companion of princes.

Swift, who wrote "cords" of worthless rhymes, squibs, songs, and verses, which live as much by their vulgar smartness as for the slight portion of true wit which tinctures them, says: "Satire is a sort of glass wherein beholders generally discover everybody's face but their own; which is the chief reason for that kind of reception it meets with in the world, and that so few are offended with it." Hawthorne gave the Dean a merited thrust when he said, "the person or thing on which his satire fell shrivelled up as if the Devil had spit on it." The *double entendre* to be found in nearly all of Swift's effusions, epigrams, and verses, comes with ill grace from a dignitary of the Church. He was always ready with an epigram on all occasions. One "lives in our memory" which he addressed to Mrs. Houghton of Bormount, who took occasion one day to praise her husband in Swift's presence: —

> " You always are making a god of your spouse ;
> But this neither reason nor conscience allows :
> Perhaps you will say 't is in gratitude due,
> And you adore him because he adores you.
> Your argument 's weak, and so you will find ;
> For you, by this rule, must adore all mankind."

The wit and humor of Shakspeare endear him to our hearts; and what a rich harvest does the gleaner obtain from his pages! Take "Love's Labor's Lost," for instance, a play produced in his youth, so full of quips and quiddity as to live in the memory by whole scenes. There is no lack of scathing sarcasm in the

play, but it leaves no bitter taste in the mouth, like
the "doses" of Swift or the more unscrupulous productions of Pope in the same line.   Ben Jonson,[1]
who ranked so high as a dramatist, has been pronounced to be, next to Shakspeare, the greatest wit
and humorist of his time.   His expression was through
the pen, not by the tongue : no man was more taciturn in society.   Much of Jonson's matter was better
adapted to his time than to ours ; words which seem
to us so coarse and vulgar passed unchallenged in
the period which gave them birth.

Here are five lines from Jonson, with which he
closes a play directed against plagiarists and libellers
generally.   He sums up thus : —

> "Blush, folly, blush! here's none that fears
> The wagging of an ass's ears,
> Although a wolfish case he wears.
> Detraction is but baseness' varlet,
> And apes are apes, though clothed in scarlet."

It is said that Jonson was a "sombre" man.   We
have seen that it is by no means always sunshine
with those who brighten others' spirits by their pen.
The great luminary is not always above the horizon.

---

[1] Jonson died on the 6th of August, 1637, at the age of sixty-
three.   He survived both wife and children.   He was buried in
Westminster Abbey.   A common slab laid over his grave bears
the inscription, "O Rare Ben Johnson!" — not Jonson, as it is
always printed.   Jonson was a heavy drinker, and it has been said
that every line of his poetry cost him a cup of sack.   Canary was
his favorite drink ; of which he partook so immoderately that his
friends called him familiarly the Canary Bird.

A friend remarked to the wife of one of our wittiest poets, " What an atmosphere of mirth you must live in, to share a home with one who writes always so sportively and wittily ! " The answer was a most significant shake of the head.

We spoke of Dryden as a satirist; perhaps no writer ever went further in the line of bitterness and personality. His portrait of the Duke of Buckingham will occur to the reader in this connection : —

> " A man so various that he seemed to be
> Not one, but all mankind's epitome ;
> Stiff in opinions, always in the wrong,
> Was everything by starts, and nothing long ;
> But, in the course of one revolving moon,
> Was chymist, fiddler, statesman, and buffoon."

When a boy at school in Westminster, Dryden more than once showed the budding promise of the genius that was in him. When put with other classmates to write a composition on the miracle of the conversion of water into wine, he remained idle and truant, as usual, up to the last moment, when he had only time to produce one line in Latin and two in English ; but they were of such excellence as to presage his future greatness as a poet, and elicit hearty praise from his tutor. They were as follows : —

> *Videt et erubit lympha pudica Deum !*
> " The modest water, awed by power divine,
> Beheld its God, and blushed itself to wine."

Dryden's complete works form the largest amount of poetical composition from the pen of one writer, in the English language; and yet he published scarcely anything until he was nearly thirty years of age. From that period he was actively engaged in authorship for forty years, and gave us some of the finest touches of his genius in his second spring of life. Addison wrote of Dryden at this period the following lines : —

> " But see where artful Dryden next appears,
> Grown old in rhyme, but charming e'en in years ;
> Great Dryden next, whose tuneful Muse affords
> The sweetest numbers and the fittest words.
> Whether in comic sounds or tragic airs
> She forms her voice, she moves our smiles or tears ;
> If satire or heroic strains she writes,
> Her hero pleases and her satire bites ;
> From her no harsh, unartful numbers fall,
> She wears all dresses, and she charms in all."

Richard Porson, the profound scholar, linguist, and wit, reared many monuments of classic learning, which have however crumbled away, leaving his name familiar to us only as a writer of *jeux d'esprit;* but these are admirable. He was full of the sunshine of wit; and though sarcastic and personal, as the nature of his *bon-mots* compelled, he had no bitterness in his reflections, and uttered them with a good-natured laugh. Wonderful stories are told of his powers of memory. He could repeat several consecutive pages of a book after reading them once. It was he who wrote a hundred epigrams in one night on the subject of Pitt's drinking habit, one of which occurs to us : —

"When Billy found he scarce could stand,
  ' Help, help ! ' he cried, and stretched his hand,
    To faithful Harry calling.
  Quoth he, ' My friend, I 'm sorry for 't,
  'T is not my practice to support
    A minister that 's falling.' "

The " faithful Harry " was Dundas, Viscount Melville.

The reply of Pitt to Walpole, March 6, 1741, is one of the finest, most polished, and biting retorts on record: " The atrocious crime of being a young man, which the honorable gentleman has, with such spirit and decency, charged upon me, I shall neither attempt to palliate nor deny, but content myself with wishing that I may be one of those whose follies may cease with their youth, and not of that number who are ignorant in spite of experience."

Dr. Gilles, the historian of Greece, and Dr. Porson used often to meet and discuss matters of mutual interest relating to the classics. These interviews were certain to lead to very earnest arguments; Porson was much the better scholar of the two. Dr. Gilles was one day speaking to him of the Greek tragedies and of the Odes of Pindar. " We know nothing," said Gilles, emphatically, " of the Greek metres." Porson answered : " If, Doctor, you will put your observation in the singular number, I believe it will be quite correct." In repartee he was remarkable. " Dr. Porson," said a gentleman with whom he had been disputing, — " Dr. Porson, my opinion of you is most contemptible." " Sir," responded the Doctor promptly, " I never knew an opinion of yours that was not contemptible." Porson was a natural wit, so to speak. Being once at a dinner-party where the conversation turned upon Captain Cook and his celebrated voyages, an ignorant person in order to contribute something towards the conversation asked, "Pray, was Cook killed on his first voyage?" "I believe he was," answered Porson, "though he did not mind it much, but immediately entered upon a second."

The sharpest repartee is both witty and satirical. James II., when Duke of York, made a visit to Milton, prompted by curiosity. In the course of his conversation the Duke said to the poet that he thought his blindness was a judgment of Heaven on him because he had written against Charles I., the Duke's father; whereupon the immortal poet replied: "If your Highness thinks that misfortunes are indexes of the wrath of Heaven, what must you think of your father's tragical end? I have lost my eyes — he lost his head."

Few men equalled Coleridge in the matter of prompt readiness of retort, and few have so misused the lavish gifts of Providence.[1] On a certain occasion he was riding along a Durham turnpike road, in his awkward fashion, — for he was no horseman, — when a wag,

---

[1] Coleridge says sadly in his "Literary Life," "I have laid too many eggs in the hot sands of this wilderness the world, with ostrich carelessness and ostrich oblivion. The greater part, indeed, have been trodden under foot and are forgotten. But yet no small number have crept forth into life, some to furnish feathers for the caps of others, and still more to plume the shafts in the quiver of my enemies, — of them that, unprovoked, have lain in wait against my soul."

noticing his peculiarity, approached him. Quite mistaking his man, he thought the rider a good subject for a little sport, and so accosted him : " I say, young man, did you meet a *tailor* on the road ?" "Yes," replied Coleridge, " I did, and he told me if I went a little further I should meet a *goose !* " The assailant was struck dumb, while the traveller jogged leisurely on.

Lord Bolingbroke, the ardent friend of Pope, was often bitterly satirical, and notably quick at retort. Being at Aix-la-Chapelle during the treaty of peace at that place, he was asked impertinently by a Frenchman whether he came there in any public character. "No, sir," replied Bolingbroke, very deliberately ; " I come like a French minister, with no character at all." Bolingbroke's talents were more brilliant than solid, but the style of his literary work is admirable. It is generally believed that he wrote the " Essay on Man " in prose, and that Pope put it into verse, with such additions as would naturally occur in such an adaptation.

Painters, like poets, are equal at times to producing the keenest epigrams. Salvator Rosa's opinion of Michael Angelo's " Last Judgment " is an instance of this. The brother artist wrote not unkindly as follows : —

> " My Michael Angelo, I do not jest ;
> Thy pencil a great judgment has expressed ;
> But in that judgment thou, alas ! hast shown
> But very little judgment of thine own !"

We have already spoken of Molière[1] in these pages, though only too briefly when his just fame is considered. England has her Shakspeare, Spain her Cervantes, Germany her Goethe, and France her Molière. We have seen how triumphantly his powerful genius made its way amid adverse circumstances, until it enabled him, as Disraeli says, "to give his country a Plautus in farce, a Terence in composition, and a Menander in his moral truths." In short, Molière showed that the most successful reformer of the manners and morals of the people is a great comic poet. Did not Cervantes "laugh Spain's chivalry away"? It is a curious fact, worthy of note, that Molière, who was so great a comic writer, and such an admirable comedian upon the stage, should have been socially one of the most serious of men and of a melancholic temperament. It was a considerable time before his genius struck out in the right direction and became self-reliant. At the beginning of his dramatic authorship he "borrowed bravely" from the Italian, as Shakspeare did; and Spanish legends were also adapted by his facile pen to dramatic purposes, himself enacting chosen comedy parts of his own plays.

This course, however, did not satisfy the genius of Molière; he felt that he was capable of greater origi-

---

[1] So disgusted was the paternal upholsterer, Pocquelin, at his son's choice of the stage for a profession, that he virtually disowned him. Molière was an assumed name, to save the family honor; but how rapidly that name became famous.

nality and of more truly artistic work. After much communing with himself he sought a new and more legitimate field of inspiration and employed fresher material. Having now the entrée to the Hôtel de Rambouillet, he began to study with critical eye the court life about him, soon producing his "Précieuses Ridicules," which was a biting satire upon the follies of the day, though delicately screened. The author skilfully parried in the prologue any application to his court associates, by averring that the satire was aimed at their imitators in the provinces. The *ruse* was sufficient, and the play was performed without offence; but its significance was nevertheless realized, and had its reformative influence without producing too great a shock. It was almost his first grand and original effort, and from thenceforth his career was a triumphal march. He is said to have exclaimed, "I need no longer study Plautus and Terence, nor poach on the fragments of Menander, I have only to study the world about me." Subsequently the brilliant success of his "Tartuffe," his "Misanthrope," and his "Bourgeois Gentilhomme" confirmed him in his conviction. Although society felt itself arraigned, it was also humbled and powerless. The author had become too great a power to be suppressed.

Molière's domestic life, like that of only too many men of genius, and especially of authors, was a wreck.[1]

---

[1] Molière was fascinated by his young wife; her lighter follies charmed him. He was a husband who was always a lover. The

It may be doubted if such persons ought to marry at
all. Rousseau is another instance of domestic infelicity; and so are Milton, Dryden, Addison, Steele;
indeed, the list could be indefinitely extended. A
young painter of great promise once told Sir Joshua
Reynolds that he had taken a wife. "Married!" responded the great master; "then you are ruined as
an artist." Michael Angelo's answer when he was
asked why he never married will be remembered:
"I have espoused my art, and that occasions me sufficient domestic cares; my works shall be my children."
The marriage of men of genius forms a theme of no
little interest in the history of literature. It is here-
in that genius has oftenest found its sunshine or its
shadow. Even Emerson has said, "Is not marriage
an open question, when it is alleged from the beginning of the world that such as are in the institution
wish to get out, and such as are out wish to get in?"
Rousseau married a kitchen-girl, and Raphael allied
himself for the last eleven years of his life with a
common girl of Rome, whom he first saw washing
her feet in the Tiber. Judging from her portrait,
which he painted, and which still hangs in the Bar-
berini Gallery, she was by no means beautiful, though
the ensemble of head, face, and neck strikes the eye

actor on the stage was the very man he personated. Mademoiselle Molière, as she was called by the public, was the Lucile in
" Le Bourgeois Gentilhomme." With what a fervor the poet feels
her neglect! with what eagerness he defends her from the ani-
madversions of the friend who would have dissolved the spell!—
Disraeli.

as forming a very attractive whole. Margarita belonged to the lower classes of the Eternal City, and when Raphael died she went back to her former obscurity. There must have been many noble qualities in this young Roman girl, to have held the consistent devotion of so great an artist for an entire decade. She must have possessed some inspiring influence over him other than forming his mere physical model. Sympathetic she undoubtedly was, or else no such union could have lasted; and one feels that he must have imparted to her a portion of the glowing aspirations which fired his own genius.

Goethe married to legitimize his offspring; Niebuhr, to please a mistress; Churchill, because he was dispirited and lonely; Napoleon, to obtain influence; Wilkes, to oblige a friend; Lamartine, in gratitude for a fortune which was offered to him, and which he rapidly squandered; Wycherly married his servant to spite his relations. And so we might fill pages with brief mention of the influences which have led men of note to assume matrimonial relations. Balzac's marriage forms a curious example. He met by chance, when travelling, a youthful married lady, who told him, without knowing who he was, how much she admired Balzac's writings. "I never travel without a volume of his," she added, producing a copy. Greatly flattered, the author made himself known to the lady, who was a princess by birth, and who became his constant correspondent until the death of her husband, when she gave him her hand and fortune. They were married, and settled to domestic life in a château on the Rhine.

But we have wandered away from Molière before quite concluding the consideration of himself and his works. One of his most popular productions, "L'Impromptu de Versailles," has often been borrowed from; indeed, the general idea has been appropriated bodily both on the English and American stage. In this piece Molière appears in his own person and in the midst of his whole theatrical company, apparently taken quite aback because there is no suitable piece prepared for the occasion. The characters are the actors as though congregated in the Green Room, with whom the manager is consulting, now reprimanding and now advising. In the course of his remarks he throws out hints of plots designed for plays, criticises his own productions, gives amusing sketches of character, and in short presents a humorous, realistic, and unique scene which formed as a whole a very complete comedy, and which proved a grand success. Louis XIV. was his friend and patron; being himself particularly fond of theatrical performances, he often made shrewd suggestions, which the actor and dramatist took good care faithfully to adopt. Indeed, it was said that this then unique idea of the Green Room brought before the curtain was from his Majesty's own brain, though greatly improved upon by Molière. Some of the plots hinted at by the manager before his company in this play were afterwards amplified and perfected so as to become popular dramas, not only by Molière, but by other dramatists. This is notably the case with Beaumarchais' " Barber of Seville," which is but the elaboration of one of these incipient plots. However, Molière was himself so liberal a borrower, like Montesquieu, Racine, and Corneille, he could well afford to lend to others. Bruyère embodies whole passages from Publius Syrus in his printed works; and La Fontaine borrowed his style and much of his matter from Mazot and Rabelais. Though we have referred to this subject before, we will add that Voltaire looked upon everything as imitation; saying that the instruction which we gather from books is like fire: we fetch it from our neighbor's, kindle it at home, and communicate it to others, till it becomes the property of all.

CHAPTER XII.

EVERY thoughtful person must often have realized how close is the natural sympathy between artists in literature and artists of the pencil and brush ; between painters and poets. Belori informs us of a curious volume in manuscript by the hand of Rubens, which contained among other topics descriptions of the passions and actions of men, drawn from the poets and delineated by the artist's own graphic pencil. Here were represented battles, shipwrecks, landscapes, and various casualties of life, copied and illustrated from Virgil and other classic poets, showing clearly whence Rubens often got his inspiration and ideas of detail. The painter and the poet are the Siamese-twins of genius. The finest picture ever produced is but poetry realized, though each art has its distinct province. The same may be said as to sculpture and poetry. It has long been a mooted question whether the Laocoön in sculpture preceded or was borrowed from the idea expressed in poetry. Lessing believed that the sculptor borrowed from the poet. All the sister arts [1] — music, sculpture, poetry, and painting —

[1] Campbell the poet and Turner the artist were dining together on a certain occasion with a large party. The poet was called

are most intimately allied. When great composers, like Mozart, were contemplating a grand expression of their genius, they endeavored to inspire themselves with lofty ideas by reading the poets; while masters in literature and oratory have sought for a similar purpose the elevating and soothing influence of music.

Orators have not infrequently depended upon more material stimulus, as we have seen in the instances of Pitt and Sheridan. The biographer of More tells us that when Sir Thomas was sent by Henry VIII. on an embassy to the Emperor of Germany, before he delivered his important remarks he ordered one of his servants to fill him a goblet of wine, which he drank off at once, and in a few moments repeated it, still demanding another. This his faithful servant, knowing his master's temperate habits, feared to furnish, and even at first declined to do so, lest he should expose him thereby before the Emperor. Still, upon a reiterated order, he brought the wine, which was rapidly swallowed by Sir Thomas, who then made his address to the sovereign in Latin, like one inspired, and to the intense admiration of all the auditors, the Emperor himself complimenting him upon his eloquence. More was a strange medley of character. Devout in his religious convictions, he was yet as

upon for a toast, and by way of a joke on the great professor of the "sister art" gave, "The Painters and Glaziers." After the laughter had subsided, the artist was of course summoned to propose a toast also. He rose, and with admirable tact and ready wit responded to the author of "Pleasures of Memory" by giving "The Paper-stainers."

light-hearted as a child, — at times wise as Solomon
in his discourse, and anon descending almost to
buffoonery ; a truly good man at heart, and yet often
espousing the worst of causes. Though a pronounced
reformer, he predicted that the Reformation would
result in universal vice. He is represented to have
had a supreme contempt for money and a true generosity of spirit. With the most solemn convictions
of the realities of death, he yet died upon the scaffold
with a joke upon his lips.

That imaginative English artist Barry, the great
historical painter, advised his pupils as follows : " Go
home from the Academy, light your lamps, and exercise
yourselves in the creative part of your art, with Homer,
with Livy, and all the great characters ancient and
modern, for your companions and counsellors." Barry
has left behind him works upon art which should not be
read except with care, unbiassed judgment, and honest
appreciation. His own eccentricities, all arising from
a passion for art, led his contemporaries to criticise the
man and ignore his work. He was wildly enthusiastic
in all things relating to art, but yet sometimes exhibited the coarseness of his early associations. He
was born at Cork, from whence his father sailed as a
foremast hand aboard a coasting vessel, and designed
his son for the same humble occupation ; but the lad
had other and higher aspirations, until finally he attracted the notice of people able to advise and help
him. Humbly born and self-educated as he was, he
presented some of the highest aspects of genius. By

19

the generosity of Edmund Burke he was sent to Rome, where he studied art for three or four years under favorable circumstances. On his return to England he took high rank, and was engaged by the Academy as a professor. At times in his lectures before the students he would burst into such vehement enthusiasm as to electrify his listeners, and they in turn would rise to their feet and shout applauses long and deep, entirely heedless of the great turmoil which they created. Then Barry would exclaim: "Go it, go it, boys; they did so at Athens!"

Literature and art should be wedded together. The careful reader and the keen observer gather up a mental harvest and store it for use. What many conceive to be genius is often but reproduction. Hosts of ideas have passed through the crucible of the author's mind and have been refined by the process, coming forth individualized by the stamp of his personality. He is none the less an originator, a creator; originality is after all but condensed and refined observation.

There is a great deal of nonsense written and credited by the world at large as to the inspiration of authorship. Some of the very best poetic turns of thought are the children of purest accident. Sir Joshua Reynolds, calling upon Goldsmith one day, opened his door without knocking, and found him engaged in the double occupation of authorship and teaching a pet dog to sit upon his haunches, now casting a glance at his writing-table, and now shaking his finger at the dog to make him retain his upright position. The last lines upon the paper were still wet, — as Sir Joshua [1] said when he afterwards told the story, — and formed a part of the description of Italy : —

> "By sports like these are all their cares beguiled :
> The sports of children satisfy the child."

Goldsmith, with his usual good humor, joined in the laugh caused by his whimsical employment, and acknowledged to the great painter that his boyish sport with the dog suggested the lines.

Goldsmith was always the wayward and erratic being whom we have represented in these pages. His habit on retiring at night was to read in bed until overcome by somnolence ; and he was so little inclined to sleep, that his candle was kept burning until the last moment. His mode of extinguishing it finally, when it was out of immediate reach, was characteristic of his indolence and carelessness : he threw his slipper at it, which consequently was found in the morning covered with grease beside the overturned candlestick.

If, as we have attempted to show, authors exhibit oftentimes a spirit of vanity, it must be admitted that readers as frequently exhibit evidence of captiousness.

---

[1] Sir Joshua Reynolds was inclined to tell stories about Goldsmith's negligence in his habits, his want of neatness in dress, his unkempt appearance at all times, and his absolute want of cleanliness. No doubt the reflection was merited by the careless author ; but the famous artist was himself such a gross consumer of snuff that his shirt-bosom, collars, and vest were never in a respectable condition.

Those who sit down to peruse a book without a good
and wholesome appetite for reading are very much
in the same condition as one who approaches a table
loaded with food, without a sense of hunger. In
neither case can one be a proper judge of what is before him ; mental or physical pabulum requires for just
appreciation a wholesome appetite. Unjust criticism
often grows out of an attempt to force the appetite,
the censor coming to his task in a wrong humor.
The author is usually severely judged ; he is solus, his
critics are many : if he satisfies one class of readers
he is sure to dissatisfy another. Swift's definition of
criticism, in his " Tale of a Tub," is pertinent. " A
true critic," he says, " in the perusal of a book, is like
a dog at a feast, whose thoughts and stomach are
wholly set upon what the guests fling away, and consequently is apt to snarl most when there are the
fewest bones."

Edgar A. Poe's sarcasm upon the " North American
Review," in the matter of criticism, will long be remembered. It was generally considered at the time
not only a keen but a just retort. Our erratic genius
writes : " I cannot say that I ever fairly comprehended
the force of the term ' insult,' until I was given to
understand, one day, by a member of the ' North
American Review ' clique, that this journal was not
only willing but anxious to render me that justice
which had been already accorded me by the ' Revue
Française,' and the ' Revue des Deux Mondes,' but
was restrained from doing so by my ' invincible spirit

of antagonism.' I wish the 'North American Review' to express no opinion of me whatever, — for I have none of it. In the mean time, as I see no motto on its titlepage, let me recommend it one from 'Sterne's Letter from France.' Here it is: 'As we rode along the valley, we saw a herd of asses on the top of one of the mountains: how they viewed and *reviewed* us!'" No one can deny that Poe possessed remarkable genius; but his best friends could not approve either his temper or his habits.

Balzac complained of lack of appreciation; though, as has just been shown, he captivated one of his readers to such a degree as to bring him a wife and a fortune. "A period," he says, " shall have cost us the labor of a day; we shall have distilled into an essay the essence of our mind; it may be a finished piece of art, and they think they are indulgent when they pronounce it to contain some pretty things, and that the style is not bad!" Montaigne said that he found his readers too learned or too ignorant, and that he could please only a middle class who possessed just knowledge enough to understand him. To read well and to a consistent purpose is as much of an art as to write well. It was said of Dr. Johnson by Mrs. Knowles that "he knows how to read better than any other one; he gets at the substance of a book directly; he tears out the heart of it."

A literary friend of the writer has long adopted an effective aid to memory in connection with reading. After perusing a book he writes down the date, the place, and under what circumstances it was read, and in a few concise lines gives the impression it has left upon his mind. This he does not design as a criticism; it is intended for himself only. At a future day he can take up the volume, since perusing which he may have read a hundred in a similar manner, and by turning to his brief comment at the close, the power of association enables him to recall the subject of the volume and virtually to remember the contents. He assures us that the circumstances under which he became familiar with the book, if fairly remembered, recall even its detail. For our own part, we have trusted solely to a retentive memory, and the choice of such lines of reading as inclination has suggested. The books which we consult lovingly will long remain with us, requiring very little effort to impress their contents upon the brain.

How suggestive is this theme of books and the reading of them! Whipple eulogizes them thus appropriately: " Books, — light-houses erected in the great sea of time; books, — the precious depositories of the thoughts and creations of genius; books, — by whose sorcery time past becomes time present, and the whole pageantry of the world's history moves in solemn procession before our eyes. These were to visit the fireside of the humble, and lavish the treasures of the intellect upon the poor. Could we have Plato and Shakspeare and Milton in our dwellings, in the full vigor of their imaginations, in the full freshness of their hearts, few scholars would be affluent enough to afford them physical support; but the living images of their minds are within the reach of all. From their pages their mighty souls look out upon us in all their grandeur and beauty, undimmed by the faults and follies of earthly existence, consecrated by time."

Poets have been more addicted to building castles upon paper than residences upon the more substantial earth. Though the old axiom of "genius and a garret" has passed away, both as a saying and in the experiences of real life, still it had its pertinency in the early days of literature and art. Ariosto, who was addicted to castle-building with the pen, was asked why he was so modestly lodged when he prepared a permanent home for himself. He replied that palaces are easier built with words than with stones. But the poet, nevertheless, had a snug and pretty abode at Ferrara, Italy, a few leagues from Bologna, which is still extant. Leigh Hunt says: "Poets love nests from which they can take their flights, not worlds of wood and stone to strut in." The younger Pliny was more of a substantial architect, whose villa, devoted to literary leisure, was magnificent, surrounded by gardens and parks. Tycho Brahe, the great Danish astronomer, built a grand castle and observatory combined on an island of the Baltic, opposite Copenhagen, which he named the " Castle of the Heavens."

Many of our readers have doubtless visited the house which Shakspeare built for himself in his native town on Red-Lion Street. In passing through its plain apartments one receives with infinite faith the stereotyped revelations of the local cicerone. Buffon was content to locate himself for his literary work and study in an old half-deserted tower, and Gibbon, as we have seen, to write his great work in the summer-house of a Lausanne garden. Chaucer lived and wrote in a grand palace, because he was connected with royalty; but he never dilated upon such surroundings,— his fancy ran to outdoor nature, to the flowers and the trees. Milton[1] sought an humble "garden house" to live in; that is, a small house in the environs of the city, with a pleasant little garden attached. Addison wrote his "Campaign" "up two pair of back stairs in the Haymarket." Johnson tells us that much of his literary work was produced from a garret in Exeter Street. Paul Jovius,[2] the Italian author, who wrote three hundred concise eulogies of statesmen, warriors, and literary men of the fourteenth century, built himself an elegant château on the Lake of Como, beside the ruins of the villa of Pliny, and declared that when he sat down to write he was inspired by the associations of the place. In his garden he raised a marble

---

[1] Milton was a London boy in his eighth year when Shakspeare died (1616); he was seventeen years old when Fletcher died (in 1625); and twenty-nine when Ben Jonson died (in 1637).

[2] Paul Jovius was from an ancient Italian family. He wrote altogether in Latin. Clement VII. made him a bishop, and he enjoyed the favor of Charles V. and Francis I., which enabled him to amass great wealth. He died at Florence in 1552.

statue to Nature, and his halls contained others of
Apollo and the Muses.

The traveller visits with eager interest Rubens'
house in his native city of Antwerp, a veritable
museum within, but plain and unpretentious without.
Rubens is to the Belgian capital what Thorwaldsen
is to Copenhagen. Spenser lived in an Irish castle
(Kilcolman Castle), which was burned over his head by
a mob; and, sad to say, his child was burned with it.
In his verses Spenser was always depicting "lowly
cots," and it was on that plane that his taste rested.
Moore's vine-clad cottage at Sloperton is familiar to
all. In the environs of Florence we still see the cottage home where Landor lived and wrote, and in the
city itself the house of Michael Angelo, — plain and
unadorned externally, but with a few of the great
artist's household gods duly preserved in the several
apartments. The historic home of the poet Longfellow, in Cambridge, has become a Mecca to lovers
of poetry and genius; while Tennyson's embowered
cottage at the Isle of Wight is equally attractive to
travellers from afar.

Pope[1] had a modest nest at Twickenham, and
Wordsworth at Rydal Mount, the beauties of both being
more dependent upon the surrounding scenery than
upon any architectural attraction. Pope declared all

[1] "Pope died in 1744," says Lowell, "at the height of his
renown, the acknowledged monarch of letters, as supreme as
Voltaire when the excitement and exposure of his coronation-
ceremonies at Paris hastened his end, a generation later."

gardens to be landscape-paintings, and he loved them.
Scott made himself a palatial home at Abbotsford,
which was quite an exception to that of his brother
poets. Dr. Holmes's unpretentious town house in
the Trimountain city overlooks the broad Charles,
and affords him a glorious view of the setting sun.
Emerson's Concord home was and is the picture of
rural simplicity. Hawthorne's biographer makes us
familiar with his red cottage at Lenox. Bryant made
himself an embowered summer cottage at Roslyn,
New York State. Lowell has a fine but plain residence overlooking the beautiful grounds of Mount
Auburn. Nothing could be more simple and lovely
than Whittier's Danvers home. None of these poets
have built castles of stone, whatever they may have
done under poetical license.

"I never had any other desire so strong, and so like
to covetousness," says the poet Cowley, "as that I
might be master at least of a small house and a large
garden, with very moderate conveniences joined to
them, and there dedicate the remainder of my life
only to the culture of them and study of Nature, and
then, with no desire beyond my wall, —

> '—— Whole and entire to lie,
> In no unactive ease, and no unglorious poverty.'"

Cowley at last got what he so ardently desired, but it
was not until he was too old and broken in health to
find that active enjoyment which he had so fondly anticipated. He died in the forty-ninth year of his age.

We spoke of the contrast which was manifest between the private and public life of Molière. These paradoxes are strange, but by no means uncommon in the character of men of genius. It will be remembered that Grimaldi, the cleverest and most mirth-provoking clown of his day in England, was often under medical treatment on account of his serious attacks of melancholy. It seems almost incredible that men of such profound judgment in most matters, as were Dr. Johnson and Addison, should have been so inexcusably weak as to entertain a belief in ghosts, — an eccentricity which neither of them denied. Byron,[1] who as a rule was noted for his shrewd common-sense, was so superstitious that he would not help a person at table to salt, nor permit himself to be served with it by another's hand. There were other equally absurd "omens" which he strenuously regarded. Cowper, who was a devoutly religious man, deliberately attempted to hang himself, — an act entirely at variance with his serious convictions. So also Hugh Miller, one of the most wholesome writers upon the true principles of life, wrested his own life from his Maker's hands.

Pope, who was such a bravado with his pen, boldly

---

[1] No other man presented within himself such a bundle of contradictions. "He seems an embodied antithesis," says Whipple, — "a mass of contradictions, a collection of opposite frailties and powers. Such was the versatility of his mind and morals, that it is hardly possible to discern the connection between the giddy goodness and the brilliant wickedness which he delighted to exhibit." In all his relations he was consistently inconsistent.

denouncing an army of scholars and wits in his "Dunciad," was personally an arrant coward, who could not summon sufficient self-possession to make a statement before a dozen of his personal friends. The paradox which existed between Goldsmith's pen and tongue passed into an axiom : with the one he was all eloquence and grace ; with the other, as foolish as a parrot. Douglas Jerrold, whose fort was as clearly that of wit and humor as it is the sun's province to shine, was ever wishing to write a profound essay on natural philosophy. Newton, highest authority in algebra, could not make the proper change for a guinea without assistance, and while he was master of the Mint was hourly put to shame by the superior practical arithmetic of the humblest clerks under him. Another peculiarity of Newton was that he fancied himself a poet ; but who ever saw a verse of his composition ? Judged by all accepted rules, Charles Lamb experienced ills sufficient to have driven him to commit suicide ; whereas the truth shows that with " his sly, shy, elusive, ethereal humor " he was ordinarily the most genial and contented of beings.

Curious beyond expression are the many-sided phases of genius, and indeed of all humanity. Let us therefore have a care how we judge our fellow-men, since what they truly are within themselves we cannot know, and may only infer by what they seem to be relatively to ourselves. Undoubtedly the germs of virtue and of vice are born within the soul of every human being ; their development is contingent

upon how slight a cause! Nor in our readiness to
censure should we forget in whose image we are all
created, — "a little lower than the angels, a little
higher than the brutes." It is the nature of man, like
the harp, to give forth beautiful or discordant sounds
according to the delicacy and skill with which it is
touched. We find what we come to find, — what, indeed, we bring with us. Richard Baxter, the prolific
author upon theology, at the close of a long life said:
" I now see more good and more evil in all men than
heretofore I did. I see that good men are not so good
as I once thought they were ; and I find that few are
so bad as either malicious enemies or censorious pro-
fessors do imagine."

INDEX.

University Press : John Wilson & Son, Cambridge.